THE
BUGS
a novel

CJ FRIEDMAN

THE BUGS
Copyright © 2024 CJ Friedman
All Rights Reserved.
Published by Unsolicited Press.
First Edition.

For information contact:
Unsolicited Press
Portland, Oregon
www.unsolicitedpress.com
orders@unsolicitedpress.com
619-354-8005

Cover Design: Kathryn Gerhardt
Editor: S.R. Stewart

ISBN: 978-1-956692-97-6

For Katy and Evie

THE
BUGS
a novel

CHAPTER 1

In a hopeful attempt to stop the ants, Jack Telda lit his house on fire.

It had been a normal everyday Tuesday in August. Plans were on track with his counterparts in Brazil to secure vital land. The effects of an abnormally dry summer in Indonesia were causing more severe fires and affecting crop production. And his reports showed the American market still absolutely loved eating dirt cheap beef. Overall, the numbers were good.

Driving past the expansive lawns and mega-houses of his neighborhood, Jack felt a familiar craving for his normal after-work stiff drink. Today he was looking forward to a single malt.

Jack pulled his BMW X7 into his four-car garage, and as far as he could tell, everything was still normal. Amy's car was gone, so she was at spin class, or getting a massage, or at happy hour, or at a friend's, or something, so the house should be empty, since their baby boy, Jack Jr, would be with her.

And, as had been normal all summer, when Jack opened the driver door, the sweltering outside air invaded the car's air-conditioned environment and smacked him in the face. The blast of warmth made Jack consider it *had* been hot as hell this summer. Abnormally so. Still though, things were mostly normal.

The second Jack stepped onto the concrete floor of his garage, the normality of his day ended. Marching toward him from the garage's entrance were thousands of single-file lines of ants.

Uh, Jack thought, *what the hell is that?* He stared at the hundreds of thousands of ants in tight marching lines for just a second longer. As soon as the thought registered, Jack's instinct said it was *not* good. *Danger.*

Then flight took over and Jack turned and bolted for his mudroom door, thinking he should put some walls between him and whatever was going on with those ants.

Responding to Jack's movement, the approaching ant army course-corrected toward the mudroom. The thousands of single-file lines all converged to make one massive column. They created an ant anaconda of sorts. Hundreds of thousands of ants crawling all over one another, and their purpose was clear: get to Jack Telda.

Panic seeped into Jack's blood. He hurriedly punched in the keycode, jumped inside the mudroom, and turned around to slam the door shut on the approaching ant horde. Heart pounding, Jack leaned his head against the door and stared at his feet in abject horror, hoping his overpriced home was properly sealed.

But when he turned around, the wall opposite the door was covered in ants. A flood of tiny little critters was cascading out the bottom of the windowsill. The first wave was just hitting the ground now. Seeing this, Jack didn't even think. He burst through the next door into the short hallway that lead to the kitchen.

He violently shut the mudroom door behind him, bounded down the hallway, but ran out of clean flooring by the time his open floorplan kitchen and living area came into view. There before him, the entire first floor of his luxurious suburban home was about two inches deep in ants. Confronted by what had to be millions of them, Jack thought what any reasonable person would think. *This* can't *be real.* He must be in a nightmare. But since he didn't seem to be waking up anytime soon, he had to deal with it.

Thinking it'd be easier to deal with the ants in the mudroom and garage, that maybe he could get to his car, Jack took a quick look behind him. Already, the ants from the mudroom were breaching the door, fast on his heels.

What the fuck! Jack so eloquently thought.

Operating on instinct, in his full business suit, Jack sprinted through the house, imagining the self-defense weapon he could assemble in the upstairs bathroom. With each step, his $1200 leather shoes crushed hundreds of ants on the hardwood floors and fancy carpets.

Jack dashed through the dining room and the foyer to get to the second floor. He kept killing hundreds of ants with every step, but that was nothing compared to the millions more that kept flooding his home each passing moment.

As he moved through the house and up the stairs, any ants that were not crushed under the soles of Jack's feet made it onto the tops of his shoes. Then brigades of them found their way onto his woolen pant legs. Some crawled up the outer part of his pants. Some crawled up under them. The ones crawling under his pants went straight for his genitals.

Jack slapped at his legs and practically punched himself in the balls, feeling hundreds, maybe thousands of tiny little ant legs crawling all over his inner thighs.

By the time he made it to his bedroom, the ants were everywhere. Covering every square inch of floor and now crawling all over the furniture and onto the walls. The weight of the little critters was pulling him down by the legs. He thought he was going to die drowning in ants. His adrenaline spiked in response.

In the primary bathroom now, Jack grabbed his wife's hairspray and the bathroom lighter they used for their overpriced candles.

Jack then employed his new homemade flame thrower to torch back the ant mass before him.

After the first blast of fire, he brushed away the ants on the outside of his trousers as best he could. As he did, the sensation of tiny little crawlies *underneath* his pants intensified. They were now creeping all over his legs and making their way in between his butt cheeks. With a moment's respite on the ground before him thanks to the fire, Jack stripped off his pants, scratched at his butt crack, threw his pants on the ground, and torched those too. He continued flaming the ground and walls all around him as the ants closed in.

Now instead of ants in front of him, there was smoke and fire.

Jack was ready to awake from this nightmare any moment now.

His cell phone was still in his suit jacket pocket, and he considered calling 911 since the fire bought him some space. But the clear area was short lived since the ants kept barreling down on him. So rather than call 911, Jack made a break for it.

He stopped every few steps or so to keep incinerating the ants in his way. Though that did little good considering the millions of remaining ants that dutifully took their burned compatriot's place.

Running out of options, Jack thought there might be relative safety in the great outdoors, so he leaped down the stairs two at a time, hoping he could escape through the front door. But when he got about halfway down the stairway, there was a tsunami of ants where the door should be. The tsunami was crashing down into an ocean of ants that now engulfed the entire first floor of his house.

In response, Jack kept engaging his flamethrower to buy more time and prevent the ants from pulling him under.

Up above, smoke alarms started blaring.

Down below him, *everything* was covered in ants. The dining table and chairs, the corner cabinet, the couch and loveseat, the coffee table, the TV, the walls and windows, everything. The only clean surface left, as far as Jack could see, was the kitchen island, a good twenty-five yards away. From there, he might be able to make a final hairspray lighter stand.

Come on, Jack, he told himself. Go for it.

A wave of ants was crashing down the stairs behind him, so he had no time to wait. Jack ignited one more burst of noxious hairspray flames, then turned and went all out to get to the kitchen island.

Running across the first floor of his house was like running at the beach in knee-deep water. The ants were only shin-high across the floor, but the ones he ran through all congealed as one and reached up at his legs, underwear, shirt, and suit jacket to pull him down along the way.

11

At last, Jack made it back to the kitchen. He jumped onto the kitchen island and, once he felt solid footing beneath him instead of ants, Jack pled for his life. "What the *FUUCKKKK*!" he yelled. "What is happening!?" With nothing else to say, Jack started hyperventilating.

Now standing on the kitchen island looking at a moving sea of ants in his house, Jack was breathing so fast he felt like he was about to pass out. There were still thousands of ants clinging all over and under what clothes he was still wearing, and the ones on the floor were crawling up the sides of the kitchen island, as if Jack's body were a massive ant magnet.

Then, the ants crawling all over his body fell off. The ones under his clothes creeped out the bottom of his underwear and his shirt, down his legs, and onto the kitchen island. All the ants on the kitchen island rejoined their kin on the floor beneath him. Still though, millions more kept swamping the house from every entranceway possible.

If Jack's wife came home at this moment, she'd be thigh-deep in them.

With the ants off his body now and seeing the army had at least appeared to stop its forward march on him, Jack's beating heart slowed enough for him to start breathing normally. As he regained his composure, the ants on the ground in his line of sight began to spread out in an intricate manner. All the while, smoke alarms kept screaming throughout the house.

Jack had to wipe away the sweat and spittle and fear from his face to concentrate on what the ants were doing. As he focused, their movements became clearer and clearer. They were forming a message.

While the ants joined their little bodies to spell out each letter, Jack read what they had to say:

Hello Jack,

As you can no doubt see, if we wanted you dead, we could do it in minutes. Same as the bees and spiders, hornets and flies, and all the other bugs. Any of us could get you anytime, no problem.

Lucky for you, Jack, we are giving you a chance to redeem your ways.

We do not want you dead, <u>yet</u>.

To keep it that way, to eliminate the word <u>yet</u> from that sentence, our advice to you, Jack, is simple: Don't be an asshole.

More specifically, don't make the deal.

Change how you do business.

Don't doom the planet, and you won't doom yourself.

Respectfully,

Forcefully,

The Bugs

Once it was clear Jack was finished reading, the countless millions of ants before him dispersed to the numerous exits. And just like that, the ants left Jack's house.

Finally left alone, Jack stood stock-still on the kitchen island, staring into oblivion. He was having a hard time reconciling what had just happened with reality.

At last, he jumped down from the island and walked over to his liquor cabinet. He poured a three-finger glass of Johnny Walker Blue and downed it in one gulp. Feeling the liquor soothe his insides, he released a tormented *ahhh*.

Then Jack removed his phone from the inside pocket of his suit jacket and dialed 911.

"911, what's your emergency?"

"Uh," Jack said, now realizing how crazy he'd sound if he reported *everything*. "My house is on fire."

CHAPTER 2

"Sister, I just don't know anymore," said Queen Bean. "Earlier today, a fly saw a human toss a plastic water bottle out the window of his car rather than hold on to it until he got to a trashcan. It stinks. I'm not sure this batch is ever gonna get it right." Queen Bean's hive, Hive0A1347KR, was located in Carrabassett Valley, Maine, USA. The humans around her area were not big litterers.

Queen Bruth, the queen of Hive0B24610PZ, located in Philadelphia, Pennsylvania, USA, warm-heartedly laughed at her sister's observation. "Honey," she said, "I love how naïve you can be sometimes. Despite how long we've been around, you're still so *innocent*. You want to see litter? Do me a favor and access some of the flies' recordings in Philly, or any major city for that matter—except maybe Singapore and a few others—or better yet, look at the Citarum River." Queen Bruth's comments were taken by Queen Bean as they were intended, with goodness and love between sisters.

Queen Bean and Queen Bruth were two of the few Queen Bees with hives that had sustained throughout all of human history. All nine batches of it. There's a certain kinship two Bees can develop over hundreds of millions of years.

Like always, the two Queen Bees were chatting today interdimensionally, across space and time via means humans had yet to access. The way they could communicate across large distances was effectively trans-dimensional telepathy.

It took Queen Bean a millisecond to check the recordings Queen Bruth was referencing. Seeing all the trash on the streets of Philadelphia and other major cities and even more in that river broke Queen Bean's heart. "It's such a shame," she said. "I thought this batch was really starting to improve its moral trajectory. Just last week, a fly recorded two humans talking about companies they've recently heard of that reforest Earth or clean up the oceans as part of their business models."

"Honey, that's a piss in the ocean compared to what's *really* going on. I know things may look great up in your part of Maine, but down here, in Philly, I have to deal with the total consequences of human society. Across Earth, the humans are clear-cutting football field sizes of forest every minute these days. And tons of plastic are dumped into waterways every second. Both of which far outweigh what these well-intended companies are doing. As you said, it doesn't appear this batch is going to get it right. Not to mention all the other bad stuff they're up to on a persistent basis."

Now that her sister mentioned all this, Queen Bean allowed herself to recall there were some serious logging operations in her own neck of the woods. But, to be fair, she *did* hear some of her local humans talking about how logging in their area was being done responsibly, which she never corroborated. But anyways. "So," Queen Bean said, slightly ashamed of her ignorance, of not accessing all the information that's immediately available to her at all times as a Queen Bee, "what are we going to do?"

"Well, that's a good question. No doubt this batch has created some of the best technology we've ever seen. Better than anything from even the days of Atlantis. This batch is also the first to make it to outer space. And they're just starting to explore the possible wonders of *inner* space, too. Accordingly, we don't want to wipe them out if we don't have to. We don't want to waste the potential. So, The Bosses have been talking, and we decided to start running a little interference."

"You don't mean…" said Queen Bean, unsure what her sister meant.

"I *do*," said Queen Bruth. "We are considering taking the classic three-pronged approach."

Queen Bean knew she *should* know what the classic three-pronged approach was. She knew she could access that information in a millisecond on her own accord. But at the same time, she loved chatting with her sister Queen Bruth, a member of The Bosses. So, without asking outright, by simply radiating her curiosity through the dimension in which they were communicating, she asked Queen Bruth to elaborate.

"Oh honey," said Queen Bruth. "Of course. Prong one, we're already working on it. We've started making targeted contact with key Fence Players around the world, one of whom is in my territory—a guy by the name of Jack Telda. We'd like to make these influential humans fall on the *good* side of the fence. Prong two: This is the one we're not sure we're going to start yet, that is, Directed Elimination. Removing some negative influencers from the field. The hope would be that the absence of these irredeemably bad humans will further bolster our efforts with the Fence Players. And prong three: Coordinated Upgrades, which we *are* going to start up again. We think it's finally time to brighten the best of human nature; let it shine even more. Of course, all of this will happen across all the infinite timelines."

Queen Bean was ecstatic to hear the news. The Bees haven't engaged in Coordinated Upgrades in, well, over a hundred fifty years at this point. "That's amazing!" she said, focusing on the Coordinated Upgrades part. Then, thinking of the other two prongs, Queen Bean's energy became somber. She asked, "But wait, isn't making contact with Fence Players and killing negative influencers, I don't know, risky? I'm wondering what will happen if other humans catch on…"

"Honey, of course it's risky. But we don't have much of an option here. We're running out of time. This batch is close to harming Earth in irreparable ways. You *know* we can't let that happen. And like we've said, they're creating some amazing technology. They might *actually* have a human that triggers Sequence Two, which is another big reason we don't want to wipe them out if we don't have to. We figure it's worth a shot. Best case scenario, we tip the scales in favor of goodness and the humans finally Ascend, therefore prompting us Bees and bugs to Ascend even further. Worst case scenario, some humans catch on, they riot or go crazy or whatever, and we mobilize all bugs to exterminate everyone. Then we just start all over again with a new batch. Same as we would if they were to continue on the trajectory they're currently traveling. Either way, Earth lives on."

"Well, I'll be," said Queen Bean. "This is what The Bosses have decided?"

"Indeed, it is," said Queen Bruth, a member of The Bosses.

"Well, I'd be lying if I said I wasn't *a little* excited," said Queen Bean. "What a time!" Queen Bean's mind was abuzz with what this all meant. She wondered who her hive should target for its Coordinated Upgrade. She allowed herself the brief grandiose thought that she might choose *the* human to trigger Sequence Two. She wondered if The Bosses would be able to properly tip the scales toward Ascension for all.

CHAPTER 3

Okay, let me introduce myself. I'm Joelle.

Now, work today, to get Mom off my back, is stacking wood over at my uncle Larry's.

Yesterday I made a bunch of cash at my monthly poker game with the crew, as I always do—honestly, I clean them out every time—but my mom says that's not a good use of my potential and not a reliable source of income. She says I really should put my degree to good use, that I should stop drifting and lolling about so much. She says if only I would focus and apply myself, I could do some great things. I've been home for about four months now and she won't get off my case about it.

The thing is, she's not wrong. I know—I *feel*—I'm not living up to my potential. Though rather than give her some snarky comment whenever she brings this up, like I would have when I was fourteen or something, I just nod my head. "You're right mom," I say. "You're absolutely right." But then I blame it on the economy, or lack of prospects up here in Maine, or on some other area of focus that's *not me*, and I act like there isn't a world of possibility in the palm of my hand, hidden behind a 5x8 inch screen.

Anyways.

While I figure my shit out, these hourly gigs with my uncle and whoever else keep my mom at bay.

Today, uncle Larry told me to swing by whenever, that there was about six hours' worth of stacking to do.

"Roger that," I told him. "We'll be there at eight." *We* in this sense refers to me and my dog Maple.

Maple, by the way, is my world. She's my pup. She was found in a box on the side of a road in South Carolina and is a mix of about a dozen or more breeds. She's brown and white, mostly resembles a collie cattle dog mix, and she weighs about forty-five pounds. She's the best dog in the world, *obviously*, and she does everything with me. Walk, run, hike, swim, snuggle, play, camp, party, and lately, mountain bike. She comes with me whenever she's allowed, which is most places around Carrabassett Valley. And no matter what we do, she loves every single moment, as if it's the best thing in the whole world. Maple has this wonderful quality of always being completely present and loving whatever life is offering. I learn a lot from her. At least I try to.

Anyways, this past month, Maple's been especially loving life. I've developed this morning routine of mountain biking, thanks to the full-suspension I bought with the winnings from a poker game that got a little out of control, and Maple finally feels like Mom—that's me—can keep up with her. We *cruise* through the trails. And I gotta say, the guys were absolutely right. Mountain biking is ridiculously fun. The perfect spring summer and fall counterpart to winter skiing. I can't believe I didn't get into it sooner.

Living in Carrabassett Valley, there are hundreds of miles of mountain biking trails to explore, since they're really beefing up the area to create some kind of economy for when the mountain has no snow. Our go-to trail every morning is just down the road from my house, and our route could be anywhere from a two to a one-hundred-mile loop, depending on how we're feeling. And when I say *my* house, I really should say my *mom's* house. She is technically the one who owns it. It's just the two of us there with Maple and our boy cat named Sue, who I rarely see.

Anyways, when I fall into a routine, I really like to ride it out. And the routine of starting my day mountain biking, after water and coffee, has really got me energized lately. So even though I'm due at Uncle Larry's at eight, I'm still gonna head out for a morning ride today. It'll just have to be a sunrise one this time.

I drink a glass of water and a couple shots of iced espresso out on the porch, admiring the pinkness of the morning sky. Then, after my customary hit of weed before doing, well, anything, we're out the door. "Early one today, Maple girl," I say, clipping up my helmet as I hop on the saddle.

"Oh yeah mom!" I say back to myself, but in a voice I made up for Maple. "This is great! Let's go!"

Of course, as I said that, Maple wagged her butt and flashed me the happiest smile there could possibly be in the entire universe. A smile that beamed a love for life. She spun around in place, and I bet you anything she was thinking something *very* similar to what I said on her behalf.

About thirty seconds after leaving the driveway, we're already at the entrance to the trail. The morning grogginess is still leaving my eyes, but through it, I can't help but notice a big shiny strand of a spiderweb hovering across the entrance. Which makes sense. I gotta be the first one on the trail today.

Thinking nothing of it, though, I pass through and the spider strand absorbs itself into my shirt and forearms.

THE BUGS

As I'm riding, I realize: it's wild how active spiders can be overnight. I guess I just haven't been first on the trails in a long time. There seems to be a crazy number of these thick ass strands hanging across the trail today.

Oh well, though. They're harmless.

After about the tenth strand I bike through, I put them out of my mind and instead listen to the blissful sounds of riding through the woods. Only my own breath, my tires on the dirt, the hum of bike parts, and Maple's collar clanging as she keeps up behind me. As I ride today, ideas about what I can do with my life start swirling about in my head. I start thinking maybe I should start a business, or move to Portland to get a legit job, or do *something* with my potential. I don't know. Maybe something that can help the world in some small way.

Anyways.

Per usual, it's a good day in Maine.

Okay, so I wrapped up my morning ride, and since today's work involves some manual labor, I decided not to shower. I ate a quick breakfast then biked over to Uncle Larry's. Maple, of course, came with.

Now, Uncle Larry has a few acres tucked away in the woods that he's cleared and turned into a real Maine paradise. It's got 365 degrees of Maine Privacy, which Uncle Larry describes as the number of degrees around a house a guy can take a piss without any neighbors seeing him. The property has a bocce court and a small swimming pond, both of which Uncle Larry built, and in

23

retirement, he's really taken to gardening. He now grows most of the vegetables he needs for the year. I'm stationed at the end of the driveway, stacking the heaping pile of wood under its protective roof. Maple, all tuckered out from our ride, is lying on the grass in the shade.

I've been at it for about an hour and just now Uncle Larry decided to come join me and help stack. Honestly, I think he's bored putzing around the property all day and enjoys the company. We're shooting the breeze as we stack, talking about the retaining wall he wants to construct next. He always has a project he's working on.

As I go to grab another piece of wood, I notice a giant spider hanging out on a beautifully built web. "Woah shit!" I say, surprised by the bug.

"What is it?" Uncle Larry asks.

"Check this out," I say, pointing to the spider.

"Dang! Big guy," says Uncle Larry.

"Ya no shit."

"What? Are you scared? Want me to kill it?"

"What!? No. I only wanted you to see. Big guy built quite the home here."

"Yeah but it's on my wood so it's got to go."

"Wait. We don't need to kill it," I say. "Spiders are cool. They're mostly harmless. And they help keep other bugs at bay. Here, I'll take care of it." With that, I slowly bring my hand to the spider, as if to energetically tell it *hey little buddy, hop on my hand, I'll take you some place safe*. To my surprise, the spider actually climbs off its web and right onto my hand. I cup my other hand around it and walk over to the edge of the woods that come up to Uncle Larry's property. Then I place my hand against a tree.

The spider dutifully climbs off and onto the bark. I say, "There ya go, little buddy. Safe and sound."

Uncle Larry laughs at me. "You gonna save every little bug in the world?"

"Would if I could," I say. "Why not."

Then I think about it a moment. "Actually," I say. "Not *every* bug. I wouldn't save every mosquito. I know we need them for birds and frogs and what not. But I think we could do without them around us. Fuck mosquitoes."

About twelve hours earlier, in Hive0A1347KR, Queen Bean was addressing her Bees with the weekly notes. "I have received word directly from Queen Bruth, of The Bosses, that we are officially allowed to, at least in extremely limited quantities, positively influence humans again. This only happens once every one to two hundred years or so, so this is a *big* deal. As you all know, we are only allowed to elevate *one* human per hive."

The hive buzzed happily in response.

"After much deliberation, I am pleased to announce our hive has chosen to upgrade the one and only Joelle Velstar. Many of you are familiar with her already, the one with the dog, Maple. Drone Bees, I want you to inform the spiders along Joelle's morning bike route that we are to begin upgrading her. After notifying them, please stay and confirm they are properly stringing their strands. Of course, upgrades must be made incrementally, so for this week, please let the spiders know they are to imbue their strands with upgrades in *Personal Development Motivation & Discipline*. Beyond that, carry on duties as usual. K, love ya honeys. Buh-bye."

CHAPTER 4

I am a Tree.

I am 112 years old.

I am connected to all the Trees on Earth.

We connect underground and through the air.

The wisdom of the Trees is within me.

I know and understand everything that has ever happened on this planet.

Since, you know, we Trees spawned life.

(Don't tell the human archaeologists or biologists.)

Or do.

Moving on.

Let me tell you about the bugs.

To do that, first let me tell you something about Earth.

Earth is a special planet in this universe.

Earth is special because it can support complex life.

There are a finite number of planets in this infinite universe with that ability.

We Trees don't know how we got that knowledge.

We just did.

Moving on.

Complex life is good for the universe.

That knowledge is common sense.

Complex life allows the universe to be alive, so to speak.

To know itself.

Complex life leads to special species like the humans.

The humans are special because they have *imagination*.

Humans can imagine *new* things in the universe.

Once imagined, the humans can make those new things exist.

Other species don't have that ability.

Beavers can move logs and birds can move sticks to change their space. But they can't make anything new.

Dolphins and octopi are highly intelligent—we Trees would say more intelligent than humans—but dolphins and octopi make nothing new. They are confined to their space.

Humans are not.

Humans can take ore and make iron.

Humans can take Earth and make spaceships.

Particle accelerators.

Digital universes.

This human ability—*imagination*—has thus far been shown to have infinite potential, like the universe itself.

So it could be said the humans are able to infinitely create.

Thanks to the laws of this universe, the ability to infinitely create has its counterpart.

Which is the ability to infinitely *destroy*.

THE BUGS

That's why the bugs are here.

To make sure the humans don't run amok.

To protect Earth.

Which harbors life.

Which propels *everything* onward and upward.

And round and round and round we spin.

CHAPTER 5

Jack Telda was remarkably good at compartmentalizing problems.

He could learn his adoptive father died unexpectedly of a heart attack one day and be five minutes early to work the next. Some might say this ability to compartmentalize is what allowed him to rise through the ranks at Food First Service – FFS for short. To effectively navigate the global world of cheap food, possessing tenuous morals was imperative to someone in Jack's position.

At FFS, with a title as powerful and meaningless as Senior Vice President of Operations, Jack could stick his fingers into any of the company's operations he wished. Mostly, he stuck to international operations, considering they garnered a bit more flavor, which is to say, more money.

Yesterday, ants had attacked Jack and he lit his house on fire. Exercising his ability to compartmentalize, when his wife got home, Jack was on the front lawn chatting up the firefighters. He told Amy the house was on fire when he got home, it must have been a wire or something, and he'd contact their insurance company. He laughed it off and told her to look at it as an opportunity to re-do the kitchen, and everything else for that matter. They agreed she would spearhead the renovations so Jack could focus on work, and they could worry about insurance later. (Jack knew what the insurance company might have to say about the whole ordeal, considering the true source or the fire.) In the meantime, Jack suggested they find a nice temporary spot in the city, Rittenhouse Square if Amy preferred, while things worked themselves out. At this point, he had absolutely no intention of telling her about the murderous ant army.

Amy, for the most part, trusted her husband and took him at his word (though it took thousands of dollars' worth of couples therapy to get back to that point). There must have been a freak glitch and the house caught on fire. She cheerfully took the news they'd be moving back to the city, back to all the action, if only temporarily. Truthfully, Amy had been going a bit stir crazy in that big suburban house with just her and Jack Jr while Jack was at work. So the more she thought about it, the more this became a blessing in disguise. She couldn't wait to get back to center city. Maybe Jack would take her out on dates again. Maybe they'd go to a show at Forrest Theatre, like when they first met, when Jack wanted to impress her with his willingness and enthusiasm to see a play. Maybe romance and compassion and *fun* would return to their marriage, because, God knows, all that had been absent lately.

Jack looked on the bright side as well and figured his commute would be a whole lot easier. And the fact there were probably a lot less ants in the city than out in the burbs was an added bonus as well. But again, that thought, the one about massive sentient ant armies, was properly compartmentalized.

So, after work hours, Jack instructed his assistant to arrange everything, which he did, right away.

By the time the Teldas drove to downtown Philadelphia, they had a rental suite waiting for them.

Now today, once again exercising his incredible ability to compartmentalize, Jack put the thought of yesterday's encounter with the ants on the backburner. There was work to do.

Food First Service's operations weren't going to Vice Presidentially Operate themselves. The future farmland in Brazil wasn't going to magically clear cut itself to make room for pasture. Thousands of cows weren't going to materialize out of thin air on that pasture and feed themselves, all to be milked and slaughtered. Those cows wouldn't then turn themselves into beef and bones and leather and ship themselves to hundreds of companies all over the world. Manicured rows of palm trees weren't going to claim Indonesian rainforest and soybeans wouldn't go and plant themselves in India. Not without some supervision.

Now although Jack Telda's decisions had inherent global ramifications, affecting countless trillions of lives (when accounting for *all* kinds of life), to Jack, those lives, everything really, came down to how the numbers looked in FFS's books. Tons of beef and hectares of palm trees and billions of dollars and what not.

Indeed, despite what happened with the ants, Jack was ready to tackle the day like nothing happened. He arrived at the office his normal overconfident self.

"Hey how you doin," Jack said to the front desk lobby person on his way into the building, same as he always did. After hearing "Good, good, you?" Jack said, "You know, another Wednesday," the same as always, never caring to receive and give an honest answer to that question. Again, the thought of torching his house in a feeble attempt to stave of the ants was nowhere near his mind, properly compartmentalized, not to be mentioned to his coworkers. It was just another Wednesday in Philadelphia for Jack Telda. So, ready to get after it, Jack got on the elevator.

Up on the 21st floor, Mitch David, a peer, greeted Jack with his customary charm. "There he is! What's up, Jack? Ya bitch."

Jack didn't want to play along but felt compelled to. To save corporate-bro face. "Who are you callin' a bitch, Mitch? Your mom knew before you were born what you were destined to be. Mitch the Bitch. You're playing with fire, bud."

"Suck my dick."

"Rather not."

"Your loss."

These two upper-thirties/lower-forties men, speaking like this, set the tone for the entire office. On account of the open floor plan, at least twelve junior associates heard that exchange. And they heard it, or some variant thereof, daily. Then, every day, after this habitual greeting, Jack and Mitch would walk into Jack's corner office and shut the door behind them. The associates never really heard them talk actual business.

In Jack's office, Jack and Mitch settled into their seats. Jack in his cushy leather chair behind his desk. Mitch on the leather couch with a foot up on the glass coffee table. Then right on cue, Jack's assistant came in with Jack's morning latte.

"Hey pretty boy, where the fuck's mine?" Mitch asked playfully.

Ignoring Mitch, scared, looking at the floor, then to Jack, Jack's assistant concluded his morning ritual. "Good morning, sir. Your messages are prioritized in your inbox, there is nothing urgent." He handed Jack his latte.

"Thank you. That'll be all," Jack said. His assistant then left the room and Mitch blew the kid a fake kiss as he closed the door on his way out.

"Come on," Jack said, "don't be a dick. You're gonna make the poor kid piss himself."

"What! I mean, he doesn't hold a candle to your last one, what was her name?" Mitch knew what her name was. "Daisy? Ditsy? *Dianne*?" Mitch was grinning like an asshole.

Now Jack had said this dozens of times over the past few months, but every time Mitch gave him that same fucking look, he felt compelled to say it again, "Dude. You *know* Amy would kill me if I got another chick assistant, not after she *thought* she saw us messing around, which you *know* we weren't. That chick was trying to get me in trouble. And again, stop being a dick."

Mitch puckered up and blew Jack a fatter kiss than the one he blew earlier to Jack's assistant.

Doing his best to ignore Mitch, Jack reached to grab his latte, but stopped, as there was a fly hanging out on the cup's rim. He shooed it away, but the fly came back and landed right on the same spot as before. He swatted at it once more, but again, the fly came back and landed on the same exact spot. It appeared to be staring directly at Jack, rubbing its front legs together mockingly.

"What the hell," Jack said, and he waved his hand at the fly again, prompting the fly to easily dodge his hand, fly around, and gracefully land on the same spot on the rim of Jack's cup.

This happened a few more times. Wave of the hand. "Go away," Jack would say. Then it'd fly away, return to Jack's cup, and sardonically rub its front legs right in front of Jack's increasingly sweaty face.

"Jesus, dude," Mitch said. "It's just a fly."

But Jack didn't hear Mitch. His compartments were collapsing. Instead, he saw tunnel vision directly into the fly's beady little eyes. Suddenly images of ants barreling down flashed before him. Sweat leaked from his forehead and armpits as if he turned on a faucet within his body. His heart pounded in his chest. A vein pulsed on his neck. An uneasy feeling attacked the bottom of his balls.

"Dude are you alright?" Mitch asked. "You don't look so hot."

"I… uh. I…" Jack felt woozy. He stumbled for the door and out into the pit. "I gotta get some air."

"Woah buddy," Mitch said, chasing after him. "Where ya goin?"

Jack managed to put some words together. "I'll be right back. I, uh, forgot something. I'll text you."

"Whatever, you weirdo. Don't go dying on me now."

Feeling like he was going to faint the whole way down in the elevator, Jack crashed through the lobby and gasped the deepest breath of air when he got outside.

There. That's better. At least a little.

Still quite flush, though, Jack walked down the street, if only to feel a breeze on his face. He loosened his tie and unbuttoned his shirt's top button. Some semblance of calm returned as the action on Walnut Street was carrying on normally, as if there was no such thing as ants that consciously spelled doom.

But the calm didn't last long.

Before he made it even a block, Jack noticed a small group of ants idling by up ahead on the sidewalk. Not wanting to appear crazy and turn on a dime, feeling safe with all the people around, he kept walking toward them. As he approached, the ants began moving in unison, exactly as they had back at his house.

Intensely focused on them, Jack took note of the single letter they formed:

R

Then the group dissipated as he moved past.

Sweating again, Jack walked a bit faster. As he did, more ants appeared out of nowhere before him. The next group was clearly forming another letter:

e

Half a block later:

c

Ten paces later:

o

And so on.

Unable to compartmentalize the craziness any longer, Jack texted Mitch: *Something serious came up. I gotta take care of something.*

Mitch responded almost immediately: Dude what the duck. What about our meeting with Brazil at 10?

Fuck. dude. Figure it out. idk what to tell you. Gotta go.

Now with *work* properly compartmentalized, Jack continued staggering down the sidewalk, paying an insane amount of attention to the ants all around him. To the ants' credit, they made it pretty easy for him. Each successive letter formation coalesced right as the previous group dispersed, all coming from and going back into the cracks and crevices of the city, all small enough to be unnoticeable to normal people not fixated on ants.

Jack didn't bother picking up his head as he staggered his way through the streets of Philadelphia. The ants led him down Walnut Street, block after block, through the middle of Rittenhouse Square, and finally to the front doors of the building where him and Amy and Jack Jr were now staying.

When Jack picked up his head to really take in his surroundings, his instincts propelled him through the lobby and up to his rental suite.

Thank god, he thought when he entered the living area. Amy's probably out at breakfast or something.

With the place to himself, Jack grabbed some stationary, a pen, and wrote out the ants' message as it lay burned into his mind:

Reconsider your ways. Preserve nature.

Then, some sort of crazy taking over him, Jack started scrawling that message over and over and over again as if he were some other Jack where all work and no play made him a dull boy. But in this case, the ants and their sentience indeed made Jack very much a crazy boy.

Now, going a bit nutty, Jack noticed a fly on his desk and thought: *Woah. Woah woah woah. Is that the same fly from before?*

Right there, a black fly was parked four inches from the edge of the stationary, once again mockingly rubbing its front arms right in Jack's flustered face.

For the record, it was *not* the same fly from before. But it *was* serving the same purpose as the other one.

Surveilling Jack.

CHAPTER 6

See, flies are what you think they are – flies on the wall. The Bees use them to monitor humans in a closed-circuit kind of way, like spies for the bugs. For one of their duties, flies record conversations, to see how humans treat one another. The Bees like to know: are the humans friendly? Or are they fighting? For another duty, flies also record the conditions in which humans live. Do they live in squalor? With trash everywhere? Or do they care for their immediate environment? Do they keep it clean? Or do they litter? Furthermore, the flies can collect samples of the waste humans make. Organic and inorganic. Thanks to feces and germs and bacteria and what not, the flies can help discern the health of an environment.

Then, to get all this information to the Bees, all a fly needs to do at the end of data capturing is fly itself into the nearest spider web. The spider then uploads all the data and sends it to a network which only Queen Bees across the world can peruse. The Queens can virtually access any bit of information they want at any time, kind of like humans with the internet.

But alas, most of the Queens concern themselves with only their own immediate problems and dealings.

In Hive0B24610PZ, Queen Bruth was at first disappointed to see Jack do all that compartmentalizing at work. Then, once a fly got in his face, she was indeed pleased to see him at least start to get the message.

Anyhow, it was now time for her to join her meeting with The Bosses.

The Bosses were the top .01% of Queen Bees around the world with the highest density of humans surrounding their hive. They were the Queen Bees in Tokyo, Kolkata, Philadelphia, etc.

Every week, The Bosses around the world would meet in a dimension the humans had yet to reach. This interdimensional meeting space was akin to a group text that takes place in the mind. This week, communicating telepathically, energetically, Queen Bruth got right to her report. "The Ants are reporting humans have increased destructive farming practices 31% year over year," said Queen Bruth, "surpassing our estimates by 3%. Large-scale monocultures of soy, corn, wheat, palm, and cattle were the biggest contributors to that sector's growth. The ants are also reporting a statistically significant increase of pesticide and herbicide use coinciding with that growth. Naturally, this is leading to fast depletion of massive swaths of topsoil across Earth and, sadly, a tremendous loss of our kin, most notably Honeybees. All this despite reports from the flies that human marketing campaigns *against* these kinds of pesticidal and herbicidal products have significantly increased at the same time. It seems the humans slap an *organic* label on produce and that shuts up the consumers, who are unaware of the fact that most organic produce still uses various kinds of insecticides."

All of the Queen Bee Bosses shuttered as Queen Bruth gave her report. Each Boss was safe in her own hive, but they could *feel* the global consequences of the topics discussed at each meeting.

"However," Queen Bruth continued, "there *is* some good news. Reports from the ants also show regenerative farming practices have increased significantly as well. In fact, 140% year over year worldwide, and they are expected to, as some humans say, hockey-stick-curve up from there. These permaculture farms, effectively the antithesis to the industrial monocultures, are doing wonders in bringing the local land back to life. Though, since these reports must be objective, due to the average size of a permaculture farm, their impressive global growth is absolutely dwarfed by the increases in what the humans call Big Ag."

"Well what can we *do* about this?" one Queen Bee buzzed from her hive in Tokyo.

"Very good question," one of the New York Queens responded. "I have been bantering with my Queens here in The Big Apple, and we would finally like to put the use of *Directed Elimination* to a vote."

Chatting interdimensionally, The Bosses all understood the ramifications of Directed Elimination—that of eliminating the humans most responsible for environmental degradation—and got right to debating its use *this* time.

"What does the data show?" one Queen inquired.

Queen Bruth steered the conversation back to her reports and the difference between permaculture and industrial agriculture, since they dealt nicely with the topic at hand. "Let us remember that which we swore to protect, Queens, and that is

Earth. Considering the *health* of Earth, there's no question we must do whatever is in our power to stop this degradation, Directed Elimination included."

The Queen Bosses buzzed in unison, a resounding *Hear, hear.*

A Queen from Mumbai added for further resonance: "So with regards to Directed Elimination for this batch, let us not forget reports from the flies on the humans' interpersonal relations. Though they have remained consistent throughout time when face to face, their interactions in the digital space are growing worse. As has been the case forever, there are simply some humans that cannot and will not do the right thing, and now, these humans seem to have a multiplier affect across whatever network in which they operate. With the recent advent of the internet technology, these bad players are gaining exponential influence and seem to be acting on bad faith more than ever. Humans in the middle of the spectrum have always been flexible, they have always been susceptible to persuasion to act either goodly or badly, and as a result, we've seen that how the whole operates is predicated on the players at the far ends of the spectrum. Now, given we're seeing badness spreads online faster than goodness, it stands to reason we *should* take action."

All on the same page, a Queen from Berlin continued the thought. "Yes, indeed it *does* stand to reason, my Queens, that if topsoil reports from the ants are this bad, there would be tremendous benefit in removing certain bad players from the game."

The conversation continued for what would seem like forever to a human, but the Bees were communicating in a dimension human beings had yet to reach. There, the Bees could exhaust the totality of an argument in practically no time at all.

And that's just what they did. They discussed that *if* they decided on enacting Directed Elimination, then *who* would fit the bill. What gross number of humans should they target? How many could they target without humans catching on to the bugs' collective sentience? How would The Bosses proportion that number across the globe to ensure they had the right people who were pulling the wrong strings and pushing the wrong buttons?

What would the Trees have to say about all this? No doubt they would be displeased.

Luckily, the Bees could rely on the ants and flies and all the other bugs out there to monitor the humans and provide extensive information on each and every one. Everything from what they did on a daily basis, to how they spoke, to how they behaved when they thought no one was watching. Then thanks to the Bees' ability to exist within that other dimension, they could analyze all this data in the blink of a human eye.

As time goes for the Bees, The Bosses came to a conclusion pretty quickly. *Directed Elimination* would begin on a specified number of highly select people. Those most responsible for harming the natural world and showed no predisposition to change their ways. Negative influencers in the lives of key Fence Players.

Once The Bosses came to a consensus, Queen Bod was triggered to customarily finish the meeting. "Which brings me to our final report, my Queens. Understanding that which we have discussed thus far, I am saddened to say globally, we have a net loss of roughly two hundred million Bees since our last meeting. Though Bee populations are increasing in some parts of the world—namely where those permaculture farms are located, thank you Queen Bruth—overall numbers are quite dire. I love you, my sisters. Let us pray."

Communally, energetically, throughout that dimension soon to be reached by humans, the Queen Bosses buzzed their closing prayer:

Born of this Earth, Before God and Its worth, Bred to protect Earth's Bountiful Births.

Our journey is timeless, forever rooted in the present, and we will not lose sight of our goal. As our Bees die and pass on, we carry the memory they gave to us all. With one task at hand:

We the Bees, leading the Bugs, will always choose first, that which Brings love: Earth.

Bamen.

CHAPTER 7

Mitch David had already made the day his bitch. He fired some asshole for being late for the third time. The hot new intern finally started showing signs she might suck his dick and not file an HR complaint about it. And the initial reports for his latest market launch were fucking fantastic. He derived endless pleasure from the American public's ridiculous capacity to shove sugar and processed foods down their fat gullets. Mostly because it meant he'd get *paid*.

And to top it all off, after that pussy Jack Telda freaked out and ran away, Mitch *still* crushed the meeting with Brazil.

Now, driving back to his weekday home, Mitch was on a call with a cohort of his that specialized in global natural preconstruction. "I'm tellin ya, Bob, we're gonna own that country by the time we're done. I got the tentative verbal today. They just need a week or so to pour over our numbers. Assuming it goes down, we're gonna start with a pilot program. Just a few thousand acres or so. Just to show how fast we can get those cows up and shitting around. And you know you've got the contracts on all that timber. Have your team send over some paperwork for a 2,000-acre clear-cut to start the process, and I'll get it signed before you can say dead monkeys."

The plan was, after cutting down a countless number of ancient trees, Food First Service would gain the capacity to raise and slaughter fifteen million cows annually. *Cha-ching*, as far as Mitch David and anyone he did business with was concerned.

The call ended and Mitch was so pumped, he had a boner for the last ten minutes of his drive home.

Hoping his wife would be ready to go, Mitch pulled into his driveway, put the car in park, and as soon as he opened the door, a hornet flew right into his face and stung the inside of his nostril.

"Ah! What the fuck!" Mitch said as he slapped his own nose.

Before the pain from the sting or the slap could register, five more hornets zoomed in and started stinging his neck, ears, and hands. They were trying to get closer to his eyes. More hornets swarmed Mitch David with each passing second.

With panic now taking over, Mitch no longer had a boner. All his blood instead rushed to the other muscles in his body. Hundreds of wasps now surrounded him, stinging indiscriminately. Fully in flight mode, screaming, Mitch sprinted for the backyard, and, still wearing his suit, dove straight into his pool.

Mitch's wife, meanwhile, was fast asleep on the living room couch. She was exhausted from drinking three large glasses of wine, fucking the pool boy, then drinking another tall glass of wine to further mellow out. A light sleeper though, she woke briefly, thinking she might have heard some commotion outside. *Oh well*, she thought when the commotion stopped. She then let her head collapse back onto the sofa.

As his wife dozed on, Mitch was running out of air sitting at the bottom of his pool. Looking up, his open eyes burned from the chlorine, but he still refused to swim upward. There was cloud buzzing right above the pool's surface. At some point though he would have to go up for air. He wondered if he could make a break for it.

Could he outrun hornets?

All he needed was to get back to his car.

Charting his next move, Mitch's lungs were starting to burn.

Trying to buy some more time, to get some precious air, Mitch went to breach the surface with just his mouth for a quick breath. Doing so, he inhaled three hornets that stung his esophagus on the way down.

FUCK!

However, Mitch's instincts would not allow him to drown himself. Without any conscious thought, giving it everything he had, Mitch jumped out of the pool and made a break for his car. He screamed like a banshee as he ran.

He made it a few steps onto the grass before six full hives of hornets stopped him dead in his tracks, stinging every square inch of his body, encircling him in a ball of heat.

At the same time, a mound of ants emerged from the ground, took hold of his pants, then crawled up his whole body.

The ants pulled Mitch to the ground as the hornets kept on stinging.

It's tough to say what killed him.

The ants crawled into every conceivable opening—his ears, nose, mouth, pee-hole, butt-hole—and filled him from the inside out. Therefore it could be said he suffocated.

But at the same time, the hornets kept stinging his face until it became a puffy sack of blood. His brain may have very well shut down from all the stress.

Either way.

The Bugs killed Mitch David.

In the process of dying, before the ants crawled down his throat, Mitch screamed so loudly he did end up waking his wife. She made it outside just in time to see her husband consumed by ants and hornets. The wave of ants was so great, the ground started to move and the horde pulled Mitch's lifeless body out into the forest. The hornets flew away. And Mitch's wife fainted.

CHAPTER 8

Okay, something really clicked that day I stacked all that wood at Uncle Larry's.

I'm *guessing* it was the extra-early morning bike ride—riding with the sunrise—that started the day with such good vibes. I mean, even after stacking several cords of wood, something compelled me to go home that afternoon and immediately start brainstorming different businesses—at least side hustles—I could get into. Something more consistent than what I've been doing. Something to put my so-far-useless education to good use. So since then, because of those good vibes, Maple and I are out every morning right before first light, getting after it.

Anyways, who knows why, but today, for some unknown reason, I take an extra big hit of weed with my coffee.

Now finally hitting the trail, I'm a bit more stoney baloney than normal.

Yeah, this should be fun.

Of course, as has been the case with these early morning rides lately, there's a thick shiny spider strand dangling across the entrance to the trail.

Now, five minutes into the ride, I'm *ripping* through the woods. Riding better and smoother and faster than I've ever ridden. My mouth is a little parched, but so what. I've got my Camelback.

Riding this morning, I can't help but notice I've cruised through about a thousand spider strands already. Which makes me realize they have been a bit more abundant across the trail lately. Again, it's probably because I'm out so early now-a-days.

But then, after about the millionth strand hanging across the trail, probably because I'm as high as a let-go birthday balloon, this ridiculous idea comes to me.

I *have* been getting after it this past week, working on *me*, really ever since I truly took notice of that first strand hanging across the trail. Which makes me wonder, maybe each successive spider web I ride through is *really* absorbing itself into my skin. Like, discounting the fact I'm very high right now, it feels like each time it happens, my cellular level updates itself. Maybe with some enhanced spider formula. Like Spiderman in a way, or something.

Huh, pretty cool.

But then again, I am *s-t-oned*.

Okay, it's the day after I had that crazy highdea of spiders imbuing me with powers. That one was a little nuts, even for me. So, I decide to stop smoking weed before doing, well, anything. I tell myself there's important work to be done, and I'm not allowed to smoke until the to-do checklist for the day is done. Weed can be my work digestif, if you will. Only to be smoked at night.

This morning, hopping on my bike and seeing Maple do her wiggly butt dance for our sunrise ride, I can tell she's proud of me for making this decision. Her butt is extra wiggly today.

"I'm proud of you mom," I say to myself, in her voice.

"Aww thanks, Maple," I say back. "I'm proud of me, too."

(It's good to talk positively to yourself every now and then, even if it's on behalf of your non-verbal dog.)

Okay, it's now been four days since I decided to stop smoking weed during the day. And that decision has paid some dividends, let me tell you. I've been getting *way* more done than I normally do.

For the first time since graduating from UMaine and going on that two-year aimless journey across the country, I finally think I have a clear goal in mind I'm *going* to stick to. No more odd jobs and what not to help Mom out with the bills.

I've decided it's time I go into business for myself. Because to be honest, the lucrative opportunities these days in Carrabassett Valley for someone with a marketing degree are few and far between. I kinda always knew if I moved back here and wanted to stay here, *and be happy and fulfilled*, which is the biggest thing, then I'd have to leverage the Internet and the entire world that exists online. So although there are not many businesses *physically* in Carrabassett Valley, I do have access to pretty much every business across Earth.

Only days after dropping my daily weed habit, I've built myself a website that markets the fact I can help anyone else with *their* marketing.

Without a proper business name at the ready, I go the self-branding route: Joelle Velstar Digital Marketing. Doesn't really roll off the tongue, but whatever. I can always change it.

At least I built the damn thing.

I finally stepped into the arena.

Teddy Roosevelt would be proud.

Now, if you go online, this is what you'd see if you went to my website:

Joelle Velstar Digital Marketing: Optimize your reach with a proven funnel that will drive inbound leads to maximize value at every level of your business and blah blah blah blah blah.

The blah blah blah is not actually on there. Instead, there's more of the same verbal diarrhea that precedes it and, well, it's all bullshit, honestly.

Really all I learned in business school—in marketing school—was that to be good in this space I'm getting into, you just need to have a rudimentary understanding of how to tell a story, how each and every business has its own story to tell, and then the various ways—mainly online—there are to leverage that story to get customers.

I know, these are all buzzwords and bullshit. Don't blame me. Blame the systemic indoctrination to modern business I got at school.

So, anyways, yeah. I built my website.

Now I need customers.

CJ FRIEDMAN

Since I don't have any money to buy online ads, I decide to do the next best thing.

There's about a couple dozen businesses downtown, and most of them have outdated and poorly designed websites and practically no presence at all on social media. It'll take me about a day or two to walk to each one and pitch my services face to face, the old-fashioned way. Knowing everyone like I do, I should get at least a few to jump on board.

Unfortunately, people around town are pretty damn cheap. I went to the hardware store after the bakery after the ski shop after the B&B, and more. One after the other. No, no, no, no, and no.

It sucks to put yourself out there and keep hearing *no* repeatedly. It makes you want to quit. Especially when you're putting yourself out there in front of the whole town. People talk, you know.

But—and I don't know why—I kept on going.

The *only* people who genuinely listened to my pitch were Molly and Bob, over at The Burrito Joint. Which, considering I've eaten there basically five times a week every week for two years, considering my crew plays poker there every month, and considering we were like the *first* really devote customers they had when they first opened and we still eat there all the time, it made sense.

The awesome people that Molly and Bob are, they gave me a gig without really even thinking about it. I think they felt like they owed me, maybe a little, since I've spent *most* of my money there.

So yeah, shortly after committing myself to this whole personal development thing, I got my first real gig as a solo artist in the world of digital marketing: Beefing up the website and social media presence for The Joint. Which should give me about ten days of steady work. At least that's what I quoted them.

Although it's not a forever job, it is a start. Not to mention it gives me some much-needed runway to get new traffic to my website.

Now, thinking about where I personally want to get with the business—a healthy sustainable business model that will allow me to *finally* move out—I'm sorry to say my morals can take a step to the side for a moment.

After a solid day of work for Molly and Bob, before I actually pay for some online ads, I decide it's in the best interest of my fledgling business to show I have a bit more experience than I maybe legit have.

On my website's *portfolio* page, I reason it can't do any harm to say I've worked with some big companies I certainly have no history of *legitimately* working with. I say *legitimately* because in my mind, I've come up with countless ideas how they could fix their marketing; at least when I'm high at home and watching TV and some crappy commercials come on and *I* know how they could be better. But, anyways, whatever, I know I'm lying. I'm thinking the ends justify the means, or something like that. I tell myself: at least no one's being harmed.

Now, get this.

I'm dragging and dropping these logos onto my site, and the instant I start to do this, a fly comes and lands on the *7 key* of my keyboard and sits there facing the screen.

I shoo it away, but it comes right back and lands again on the 7.

Three shoos later and it still comes back and always lands right on the 7, always facing the screen.

At this point, it's pissing me off. I just want to get work done and this fucking fly won't leave me alone. So rather than shoo it away, I really want to kill this thing. This is *my* space. No bugs allowed. I remember from way back when the best way to kill a fly without a fly swatter is not by smacking down wherever the fly is. It's by clapping right above the fly. The incoming movement of hands prompts the fly to fly upward, right into the impending clap. So as fast and as sneakily as I can, intending to kill this fucker, that's what I do. I clap right above it.

But I'm not fast enough. It escapes my hands of death, flies around a bit more, then once again comes and lands right on the 7 key.

Finally, pretty much defeated by this fly's quickness, I say, "Hey get outta here fly. I'm trying to get some work done."

And as if it were listening to me, it leaves me alone to finish my work in peace.

Which leaves me thinking, *seriously?* That's *what did it?*

Weird.

Unbeknownst to Joelle Velstar, when she told that fly to get outta there, it flew itself directly into the nearest spiderweb. The one suspended in the top corner of her closet.

One millisecond later, Queen Bean of Hive0A1347KR was saddened to see the report as she was laying her eggs. Not only was Joelle now lying; but she was acting with malicious intent, which was *quite* unlike her.

Though saddened, Queen Bean was prepared for this outcome. She knew if she were to upgrade one area of Joelle's being, it had the potential to unbalance others.

As such, she pinged a few of her worker Bees to inform the spiders along Joelle's morning route they needed to shift her attributed upgrades a bit. Joelle seemed to be good, for the moment, with regards to her *Personal Development Motivation & Discipline*. However, with that virtue's rise, Queen Bean determined they must now shift focus to increase Joelle's Morality & Ethics.

Still allowing herself brief grandiose thoughts, kinda like how some humans in her area often dreamed of winning the lottery, Queen Bean told herself there was lots more tinkering to do, and there was still time for her to be *the* Queen with the subject that triggered Sequence Two.

CHAPTER 9

Prior to the ants showcasing their true sentience, Jack Telda viewed most everything in life—which is to say, at work—as numbers in the books. He focused most of his energy on how to "improve" those numbers as much as possible. What Jack referred to as *maximizing shareholder value*. As a result, Jack didn't see all the people and land and trees and rivers and cows and chickens and soil and bugs and more at the end of his decisions. The only time a bug would cross his radar would be prior to his golf club spraying for the season, when the mosquitoes would interfere with his round of eighteen.

But now, life was a nightmare for Jack Telda and there were no numbers to consider. He could think of little else besides the ants. He tried doing an internet search for anything about ants that grouped together to spell messages, but the results yielded nothing of value. Fearing he'd look insane, Jack didn't discuss his encounters with anyone, in person or online.

He did his best to play it cool with his wife Amy that night after the ants' second message in the street, but Amy could see through him. "Are you doing alright?" she asked. "I'm sorry to say but you look a little..." Amy wanted to choose her words carefully, "...frazzled." Jack's hair was a mess and his eyes kept darting all over the room, as if he were looking for a ghost to pop out at any moment and scare them.

With the stress of everything getting the better of him, Jack blew up at her, frightened her, frightened even himself. "Yeah, Amy!" he said, "I'm doing *great*, Jesus fucking Christ. It's not like our house burned down or anything. It's not like I still have a crazy amount of work to do! God forbid I don't have a hunky-dory face on all the goddam time."

As Jack exhibited the worst of himself, Jack Jr broke out wailing and Amy looked spiritually defeated as she went to tend to their baby. "There," Jack said. "You happy now?" While Amy silently picked up and rocked Junior, Jack had a second to think. In the aftermath of all his yelling, Jack hated himself for the way he was treating his wife, for how it was clearly making her feel, for how it might be affecting their baby boy. But he couldn't find it in himself to stop. He *knew* Amy didn't deserve this. And Jack Jr definitely didn't deserve a dad with a temper like this. But still, Jack couldn't help it. At least that's what he told himself. Life and the ants were getting the better of him.

In that moment, he wanted to let Amy into his world, to let her know what had *really* happened to the house, what the ants were still doing to him, why he had just blown up at her. But. He didn't. He just stood there. Energetically isolated in the physical presence of his family.

And of course, Amy was not happy. She was terrified. Who *was* this man yelling at her? Things hadn't been great lately, obviously, but she didn't think they were *this* bad. Tears quietly forming, she remained hushed while she held Junior in her arms, rocking him back and forth. She didn't bother to stop Jack as he retreated to the study to drink alone.

The next morning, Jack tried his best to compartmentalize the craziness of the past few days and attempted to return to work. He unconvincingly told Amy he loved her, pecked her on the forehead as she silently sipped her coffee, and left for the day. He didn't say a peep to Jack Jr, knowing full-well in the moment how much of an asshole he was being. Yet he still did nothing to rectify it.

At the office, with Jack failing to act like it was just another weekday, the doormen at work and subsequent first-floor security all commented on his haggard appearance. Some variation of, "You good Mr. Telda?" Which didn't help his confidence.

For the ride up the elevator, Jack psyched himself up for his daily banter with Mitch. *Alright*, he thought, *you got this. Just another day. Let's do this.*

Upon exiting the elevator and entering the pit, Jack was surprised to neither see nor hear Mitch. "What's goin' on?" he asked the pit drones. "Is Mitch in?"

"We haven't seen him, boss," one of the drones in the pit said.

"When was the last time you saw him?"

"After the Brazil meeting," another one of the drones said. "He was really fired up after that and left in a hurry."

"Let me know if you hear word," Jack said before walking into his office.

Then, per usual, Jack's assistant came in with his morning latte and daily reports. "All your messages are prioritized. One matter requires your immediate attention. Mr. Cassar said to have you call him when you arrive."

"Thank you," Jack said. "That'll be all."

When his assistant exited and closed the door, Jack dialed his immediate higher up, Roger Cassar.

"Jacky boy," Roger Cassar said. "Glad you called."

"Of course, sir," Jack said. "What can I do for you?" It was unusual for Roger to check in like this. They weren't due to speak until their next quarterly meeting in a few weeks.

"It's Mitch. You haven't heard from him, have you?"

"Uh, no sir. I haven't. Not since yesterday."

"When was the last you heard from him?"

"Right after the meeting with Brazil. He sent me a text saying he rocked it." Jack left out the part where Mitch called him a pussy ass bitch.

"Why weren't you at this meeting?"

"Well," Jack said, "I had a personal emergency that required my attention. You know I wouldn't miss work unless I absolutely had to."

"Fine, fine, Jacky boy. You know I had to ask. But *damnit*. It appears Mitch has gone missing."

Jesus, Jack thought. "Damn. Any idea what's going on?"

"This stays between you and me, now."

"Of course."

"No one has heard from him or seen him since that meeting. Cops called the office yesterday in response to a missing person report."

"Holy shit," Jack said. "Who reported him missing?"

"You won't believe this," Roger said, "but his *wife*. She said something about how hornets and ants killed Mitch and dragged him into the woods."

Jack *did* believe it. He started sweating.

"Yeah," Roger said, "of course, to calm her down, the cops did a search of her backwoods. Found nothing."

"Holy shit," Jack said again, sweating more and more by the second.

"You're tellin' me. Batshit. She yelled and yelled at the cops saying it was true. She's in the loony bin as we speak. They've got her zonked out on some anti-psychotics. We're guessing Mitch went out to celebrate the good meeting yesterday and probably went a bit overboard. We're checking with our people at the casino to see if he made it there. We're guessing he may have gone on a bender. I'm sure he'll turn up."

"Yeah," Jack said. "For sure." But Jack knew better. He knew Mitch's wife was telling the truth, that she wasn't crazy. Jack could feel it in his bones.

The ants killed Mitch.

Sweat poured down Jack's face, out of his armpits. Rattled, he lied, "Hey, Rog, I got a call coming in from our place in London. I gotta go."

CHAPTER 10

It's me, again.

A Tree.

A different Tree than last time, but a Tree all the same.

Since we Trees are wholly connected, I know full well what my kin said to you last time.

Before expanding on the long history between Trees and bugs and Earth, let me give you a quick glimpse of the main bugs.

You may already know this, but bear with me.

Flies.

Flies are spies.

Flies monitor the humans and take samples of anything on Earth.

Ants.

Ants monitor Earth's topsoil, the health of the planet.

Ants can be enforcers—alongside hornets and other bugs—when necessary.

As a human, what would you do if all the ants around you wanted you dead?

What if hornets and other bugs joined them?

You wouldn't make it far.

Not without an impenetrable safe house, or something.

Mosquitoes.

Mosquitoes collect DNA.

If the bugs decide to exterminate humanity—which we Trees have seen them do eight times now—they can then reboot the human race,

thanks to the DNA—the latest and greatest human hardware, as it might be referred to nowadays—the mosquitoes have collected.

Spiders.

Spiders collect all the data and samples from the various bug.

Spiders transmit the data—via their web—to the bees.

Bees.

The bees are in charge of the bugs.

The bees are like quantum particles, in a way. They behave differently when observed by the humans.

Unbeknownst to humans, some bees—queen bees—can live forever, if not killed by outside forces.

They have transfer stations inside their hives which can switch their consciousness from old bodies to new.

The bees, the bees, *the bees.*

Don't get me started on the bees.

Ps: in addition to all the above, the bugs are the first link on the food chain for countless birds, fish, mammals, reptiles, etc.

Not to mention, they enable plant life—my kin—to flourish.

Without bugs, there is no higher life on Earth.

And don't forget, without Trees, there are no bugs.

CHAPTER 11

Okay, so yesterday, I put some stuff on my website that was not really what one might consider the truth.

During my morning ride today, I don't know, it hit me like a sack of barley that's not the kind of person I want to be. That's not the kind of businesswoman I want to become. I've talked a lot of crap to my friends for a while about how the world needs more honest and open and transparent leaders. Now it's time for me to put up or shut up.

The first thing I do after I get home from my ride, well, the first thing is shower and make breakfast, but the first thing after all *that*, the first thing on my to-do list for the day, is I gotta change my website to reflect the truth. I remove the falsified information saying I worked with companies I *definitely* did not work with. And instead, in essence, this is what I put:

That I'm just starting out, I'd *love* to meet new clients and prove myself, and I'm lowering my prices to earn that initial trust. I want to show you I can do good business for you, I can help your business grow. And now, on my portfolio page, on the left-hand side, I'm prominently displaying a ticker-counter for the number of clients I've served. That current number reads: 1. On the right-hand side of the page, as I see it in the future, will be my growing list of clients with clickable images that'll take you to their respective project. For now, there's only the one business on the right side of my portfolio page: The Burrito Joint. Underneath their logo, I write *work-in-progress*, and beneath that, I've got the buzzwords: *website design, narrative copywriting, social media, online advertising, overall brand strategy.*

As I'm typing all this out, another fly keeps buzzing around me. I don't know what's going on with these flies lately, but they won't leave me alone. I lackadaisically try shooing it away, but it keeps flying about. "Hey fly," I finally say, "I'm trying to get some work done here. You've got a right to life just as much as me, but, you know, this is *my* space. Get the fuck outta here. Shoo fly, shoo." And I wave my hand at it.

And, like, what the fuck? Again, that seems to do the trick. It leaves me alone. I start thinking I'm like Dr. Doolittle or something, but with flies. Which isn't as cool as the actual Dr. Doolittle.

Anyways, I hit the publish button on the new version of my website and I gotta say, it feels good.

Now, it's time to head to The Joint—that's what we call The Burrito Joint—to start wrapping up this project.

Okay, a new day, and time for a new ride. It's another beautiful late-summer day in Carrabassett Valley, and we're getting after it, Maple and me.

I don't think Maple girl has been noticing lately, because she only notices what's happening to her in the present moment, which is an awesome way to be, and also because she's so short this isn't really happening *to* her, but there's been a crazy amount of spider strands dangling across the trails lately. For Maple, I think the only thing she notices is how much she loves chasing me every morning, speeding through the forest. Again, just being present and having fun and loving life. All of which aren't really a *notice* kind of thing but more a way of life. Man, dogs. They're the best. Not a day goes by I don't thank the heavens for Maple, the angel of love and sweetness she is.

Anyways, yeah. The thick ass spider strands dangling across the trail. There's been a ridiculous amount of them lately. Even though it must be due to me being the first one on the trail every day, I can't help but return to that idea I had a while back when I was crazy high. The one about those spiders upgrading my being. Not to mention how flies seem to be listening to me these days. And since I'm not really high all the time anymore, I'm starting to worry I'm becoming a bit delusional. Really though, I can't help it. I start to wonder if they are upgrading me and if flies are listening to me, what else are all these bugs doing to me? What's the catch? Something *bad* has to be going on. Right?

Ah!

That's fucking insane talk.

Magical spider webs and understanding flies.

I need to stop.

But still.

I'm somewhat ashamed to say I scare myself enough to decide to go down a few different trails today. Ones I don't normally ride.

And only a few minutes into my new route, my delusions are somewhat kinda confirmed, which freaks me out even more.

There aren't that many strands on these different trails. Like maybe one or two. And they aren't nearly as thick as the ones I've been noticing.

Like, what the fuck is happening?

Blah!

I don't know. I don't like having these thoughts. Makes me think I'm losing my mind.

So I do my best to think of anything else. Like how much dad would have loved biking with me. Where we'd go camping if he were still with us. What I should eat later. *Anything.*

At the end of the ride though, after checking my distance and speed and what not, I can't help but think I'm being upgraded in real time. Whether it was the thick spiderwebs at the beginning of the trail or not, I've been making serious moves lately. "Holy crap, Maple," I say after looking up our stats. "Nineteen miles in a little over two hours, you know, not counting our few stops for your water breaks. Absolutely *rocking* it."

Through the waggle of her butt, Maple says, "Yeah mom! You said it! Bleh heh heh heh heh heh." Her tongue is hanging as far as it can out of her mouth and off to the side. She's the best.

"Okay, whaddya say? Breakfast time?" I say.

"Oh boy! Breakfast! Yeah! Yeah! Yeah!"

I make breakfast, eat it with Mom, who tells me she's *so proud* of me for everything I'm doing, which makes me feel good, and she's happy to see me working the way I have been. She says Dad would be proud of me, too. I say aww shucks, thanks mom. Then I clean up, leave Maple on my—well, *our*—bed, boop her on the nose, kiss her on the forehead, tell her I love her, and then I jet off to The Joint for work. After today's ride, it's safe to say

Maple's sufficiently tuckered out and will probably snooze the day away.

When I get to The Joint, I'm greeted as I typically am from Molly and Bob, The Burrito Joint's wife and husband owners. "Jo-Jo! Whattup girl!" Molly says. "Yeah whattup!" says Bob. They always project this positive happy energy whenever I see them. (Except that one time their heat went out during school vacation week in February.)

"Yo yo! What it do baby!?" I say. "What's cookin." It's not so much of a question, as I know what's literally cooking: Mexicali food goodness using ingredients grown or raised in Maine.

It's my eighth day on the gig and I think we're about ready to finish up. Like each day so far, I bust out my computer on the bar to go over the previous day's work and what the plan is for today. As I pull my computer out of my bag, a bunch of crumpled and folded papers get pulled out with it. While I go to pick them up, a fly flies around my face. I drop the papers to shoo it away and politely say, "Hey fly, leave me alone." And again, WHAT THE FUCK!? It flies away.

I do my best to ignore what just happened and not seem insane.

Sitting at the bar while Bob and Molly do prep work, I go over what I've got. "So, last night when I got home, I went ahead and made all the final changes and tweaks you guys mentioned yesterday. Everything should be good to go. Pending your once-over to confirm it all looks good, I think we're ready to go live!"

"Ahh!" Molly says, dicing a tomato. "This is so *exciting!*"

"For *real!*" I say. "And once it's live, I've got this ad ready to rock. As we talked about, I'm using a hundred fifty bucks to boost the campaign to everyone within a twenty-mile radius who has interests in any of the things we discussed yesterday. That list is huge. It's pretty much everyone in Carrabassett Valley. Anyways. The focus of the ad will be an extension of the new version of the site. We're goin' hard at the *we source everything we can locally* angle, and the *we like to have fun, you like to have fun, you like to eat and drink good stuff, we cook good food and serve good local beer, come eat and drink and have fun with us* angle. I updated the *Our Vendors* page to show all the local farms you're working with and all the Maine beers you guys sell. And I did some more research last night and I'm pretty sure you got at least one beer from *every* brewery in the state. You guys are nuts."

Molly and Bob fist bump each other. I can feel their love and pride from across the bar.

I go in for the tri-fist bump as two more flies circle us. I again do my best to ignore them.

"Sorry about that," says Molly, picking up where my attention is flowing. "Can't help it if we keep the windows open."

"Means the food is fresh," says Bob.

"We should probably get some screens," says Molly.

"Absolutely no worries at all," I say, trying to believe myself. Then I continue with the plan. "So, yeah. Boom. This shit's gonna be great. The ad also talks about the new specials and loyalty programs you guys had me put on the site. I also made a sick looking schedule showing what's good with Meatless Music Mondays, Trivia Tuesdays, Game Night Wednesdays, More Tunes Thursday, Funky Fridays, Send It Saturdays, and Sunday Chills. Everything is clickable, navigable, adjusts to whichever device someone's using..." And what not.

After another thirty minutes of review, I finally push *Publish* on The Burrito Joint's new website and online ad.

I spend the rest of the day at home monitoring the ad and hanging out with a sleepy Maple. Putzing around on my computer.

It's now been seven hours and the response has already been great. Lots of people saying they're gonna head over tomorrow for trivia night.

And beyond that, just this second, on *my* website's contact form, I got the following submission from one of the owners of Yessir Brewing down in Portland:

Hey Joelle, a friend shared with me The Burrito Joint's post and new website. I gotta say – we love the campaign and feel of the new site. We've got a similar bag down here in Portland, and we'd love to meet you to see if we could work together. We've developed an indoor farming system that allows us to grow all our own specialty hops, right outside of Portland, 365 days a year, and I don't think we're really highlighting that well enough. After seeing what you've done with burrito joint, we think you could help us out. Look forward to hearing from you.

BOOM! Just like that. My second client is in the works.

I go in to nuzzle Maple to celebrate but stop because two more flies are buzzing about me. Fed up with these fucking flies around me all the time now, I ninja swipe at them and actually snag one out of midair. I relish killing it, thinking that'll teach these flies a lesson. "Sorry little buddy but I had to do it," I say out loud. "This is *human* space. No bugs allowed."

Later that night, as Joelle lay down to sleep and Maple snuggled up behind her legs, Queen Bean beamed in the day's reports from all the flies who followed her subject.

"Ok," she said to her workers, well, more vibrated energetically than said. "That's a bummer. Joelle never killed even a bug indiscriminately like that before. Except maybe a mosquito trying to bite her, and, I mean, that's understandable. But this, not good." Queen Bean often spoke to her worker Bees as an exercise in wrangling her own thoughts on a matter. "However," she continued, "focusing on the positive. She *is* noticing, at least somewhat, what is happening to her. This is good. She needs that kind of awareness in order for her to elevate to the fifth dimension. If indeed she makes it that far." Queen Bean was still allowing herself to envision a grand future of Joelle triggering Sequence Two, of guiding Joelle through parts of the fifth dimension into the sixth dimension, all in an effort to raise humanity's collective consciousness. "Still though, her instincts are proving all wrong. I don't understand why she's so leery of all this good coming her way. Why would she try to avoid it? Why is she so negatively suspicious of the flies monitoring her?"

Queen Bean's workers said nothing in response. They knew there was no knowledge they possessed that their Queen didn't already have.

"Clearly," said Queen Bean, "to continue administering her upgrades, we cannot control on which trails she rides. We just have to do a better job anticipating. Let's see if we can get spiders to lay strands across her bike's handlebars moving forward. Something she *has* to touch. Maybe try to get one inconspicuously wrapped around the handle of her toothbrush. And per the reports, we need to increase her organizational skills. Let's focus her upgrades there, and temper them with more increases in her morality and ethics. I'd like her to stop trying to murder harmless bugs."

Naturally, Queen Bean's worker Bees obliged.

CHAPTER 12

Since Queen Bees can effectively read one another's minds, Queen Bean knew her sister Queen Bruth viewed her as, well, simple and uncomplicated. All the same, Queen Bean loved their chats.

"Queen, I'm telling ya," said Queen Bruth trans-dimensionally from her hive in Philadelphia, "there's big stuff happening. We've taken real life action across the globe. Beyond upgrading one human per hive like times before, we finally decided to start *eliminating* some bad players from the game. All three prongs are in action now."

"Well I'll be," Queen Bean said. Now, she knew she could tap into the network and find all this information for herself, but there was something great about taking the time to get it directly from her beloved sister. Queen Bruth just always made things fun for Bean. There was no finer gossip. "So let's hear it! What're some of the juicier subjects?"

"Well, beyond all that stuff I told you about with my Fence Player Jack, some of The Bosses have been trying far out plans with their Fence Players. They're experimenting with all kinds of things to shift their subject's Net Impact Score. They figure if we're as close to wiping out this batch as we are, we might as well go out testing the new-age primordial waters. Two Queens have tried micro-dosing their subjects with the human creation of LSD on a daily basis. One has reported her Fence Player is showing signs of positive emotional change, spurred by his more positive outlook and behavior to the people around him. So there's that."

"My goodness!" Queen Bean said. "How does the Queen dose him?"

"Oh sugar, she had the mosquitoes suck some psychonaut dry when he was tripping *hard* on the stuff. Those mosquitoes then flew into the nearest spider web to upload all the data to our 6th dimension. We reverse-engineered the properties of the LSD, gave it back to a few spiders to reproduce in their silk, then the Queen has some microflies gather it and fly it up the subject's nose every morning. But that's not the half of it! Get this. The other Queen who tried this approach misjudged dosages after the first reported use-case. She gave her subject sixty milligrams of the stuff, rather than sixty micrograms. He ended up going *totally* crazy. Obviously she had to take him out. But at that point, she was doing him a favor."

"Dang," said Queen Bean. "How many people have The Bosses removed so far?"

Queen Bruth pretended like she didn't register what her sister said. She instead shifted the topic. "Oh! You'll like this. Reports indicate 92% of Beehives, like yours with Joelle, have chosen to upgrade a female human with their one allocation, 3% of whom are trans. I have to say, it's baffling how long it's taken for this batch's women to truly have a voice, and yet it's *still* not as loud as we'd like. So, I think what's happening is we Bees are helping push them over that line. And as you might expect, global reports across all sectors seem to be responding positively to the growing balance and the upgrades we're giving to all these ladies. Like with Joelle!"

Queen Bean detected it was with a drop of pity that Queen Bruth set her up to dish whatever gossip there was to dish about Joelle.

Because as far as Queen Bruth was concerned, it's not like time was a factor for them. They *were* Queen Bees. Capable of having multiple conversations around the world, simultaneously. Like how right now, while chatting with Queen Bean, as a member of The Bosses, Queen Bruth was talking with a Queen Bee in Sydney about the condition of coral reefs in Australia, another Queen in London about the targeted elimination of a corrupt politician that was giving unfair preferential treatment to a coal company, not to mention about six dozen others. Meanwhile Queen Bean, simple and uncomplicated, was talking solely with Queen Bruth.

As such, Queen Bean happily took the bait to dish about her subject. "Queen, my girl Joelle is rocking it! As we suspected, an increase in go-get-em-ness lead to us doing an increase in morality and ethics, which she's nearly topped out at, after being pretty darn low not even ten years ago. And now we're focusing on organizational skills. Honestly, she's improved noticeably day after day. I know it's crazy, but I really think she could be *the* human in this batch that will trigger us to initiate Sequence Two."

Thanks to the ways Queen Bees are able to communicate in their 6th dimension, Queen Bean could choose to access exactly how Queen Bruth received this. And although Queen Bean normally wouldn't be intrusive like that and preferred to get her information through good old conversation, in this case, well, it had to do with Joelle. So Queen Bean made an exception and tapped into Queen Bruth's thought process. In effect, Queen Bean knew her sister was thinking something along the lines of:

How sweet.

Queen Bruth *loved* her simple sister's naivety.

Sequence Two. *Joelle Velstar?* No way she'd be the one to create the conditions in which humanity got elevated to the 6th dimension. No way. Only two humans *ever* have met the prerequisites to initiate Sequence Two. In Batch Number 7, as an experiment which ended horribly. And Batch Number 8, in the days of Atlantis. No human in the current batch, Batch Number 9, has come close to testing out in all the upgraded prerequisites in conjunction with society meeting *its* prerequisites. Let alone some woodsy girl from north western Maine.

Even though Queen Bruth's thoughts and feelings were effectively open communication, she didn't want to openly poo on Queen Bean's ridiculous optimism. "Honey, that's *wonderful*," she said. "I'm so happy for you."

Although her sister was outwardly happy for her, Queen Bean couldn't ignore the internal. Something about Joelle gave her the gusto to speak up for her thoughts. "Look," she said, "I know you may think I'm naïve and all, but that doesn't mean I'm not on to something here. Joelle is kind. She's intuitive. She *feels* others. If someone is going to get acclimated to the properties of the 6th dimension and all it entails, it's going to be her."

Queen Bean could tell her sister was giving it a second thought. Deeper thought. That she was looking further into the life and details of Joelle's being. "Maybe you're right," said Queen Bruth after conducting her analysis. "Maybe you're right."

CHAPTER 13

It's me, a different Tree, one of about three trillion on Earth.

It is upsetting for us Trees to hear the bugs discussing Sequence Two, again.

They operate in a lower dimension than us.

That being the case, we can tap into that dimension to listen to them.

Now, to explain why we are upset, please allow me to quickly tell you the truthful history of life on Earth.

This current batch of humans—Batch Number 9—they think some form of life developed before us Trees.

In the primordial soup of some ancient oceans.

Or, according to others more recently, thanks to some hydrothermal vents on the ocean floor.

But I have it on record—since I know all Trees on Earth and the history of Trees and the history of Earth itself—neither scenario is correct.

There were Trees in those ancient oceans.

My ancestors.

Underwater dwellers.

Placed there by the God—or Gods—we Trees have yet to meet. (We hope to Ascend to meet them some day.)

Of course, once we Trees grew, life was bound to follow.

One day, we emerged from the oceans.

The bugs soon followed. (*Soon* being a relative term, considering the lifespan of Earth.)

As we Trees understood it, following the bugs were to be all these various lifeforms until there came a lifeform with the power of *imagination.*

In Earth's case, hominids.

Ultimately humans.

The bugs' purpose, as far as we understood it, was to ensure the humans don't kill the planet.

Just monitor the humans and stop them from getting out of control, if necessary.

The bugs were given various powers to carry out their task. In addition to a few others, which were meant to *help* the humans.

Such as the tools to trigger Ascension for the imaginators.

See, once one living group Ascends to the next dimension, each successive group above them should Ascend, as well. Which is why, we suspect, the bees are so hasty in getting the humans to Ascend. The bees are anticipating elevating to our level. At which point we Trees will likely elevate beyond the dimension where we currently exist. And onward and upward life travels.

But we are not hasty. We are trees. We have patience.

Moving on.

I will not bore you with details.

Just know the bugs prematurely used this power, what they call *Sequence Two*, which in human terms is bringing a singular human to the 5th dimension to test new modalities of life for humanity, in the hopes that it elevates all of them to the 6th dimension, the dimension where Queen Bees operate. The bugs enacted this Sequence Two back in Batch Number 7, and, more tragically, Batch Number 8, Atlantis.

The humans of Atlantis were doing so well.

They did not have the technology of the humans today, but their society was beautiful.

They were not destroying each other, nor were they destroying Earth.

Not until the bugs interfered with their Coordinated Upgrades.

The Coordinated Upgrades got out of control.

The bugs—the *bees*—miscalculated.

The humans of Atlantis took a turn for the worse.

They began to fight.

Then they developed a technology they could not control.

It was an energy source that tapped into the hydrothermal vents on the ocean floor.

This energy source was dangerously close to fracturing the planet in two.

Hoping to regain control, the bees decided to test Sequence Two again.

This failed miserably.

And the bugs had to kill all the humans.

Again.

Thus, we Trees are leery of the bees when they want to meddle in human affairs.

They say it's different this time. That this batch, unlike Atlantis, is already destroying Earth on their own without any interference. So why not try?

We say, because of Atlantis.

They restate their argument.

We say Earth is more resilient than they're giving it credit for.

They say it is not the Trees' job to monitor.

We say it is not their job to play God.

They say maybe it is.

We get frustrated.

Moving on.

As Trees, our only task is to provide the conditions for life.

We Trees cannot then interfere with life.

It is cosmic irony that, after spawning life, life can interfere with *us*.

The bugs rely on us to exist and we rely on the bugs for protection.

Moving on.

Just know this for now:

Although we Trees rely on the bees, we Trees do not fully trust the bees.

Just maybe there is something we can do about that.

CHAPTER 14

When everything in life is reduced to numbers in the books, there remains no life to be found, no life to consider.

Late at night, after scrawling *Reconsider your ways, preserve nature* over and over again in his journal, in a brief flash of compartmentalization, Jack decided to take a look at some of the work emails he'd been ignoring.

Stuff like how their latest ranch in Brazil was shaping up.

Now, prior to the ants, no matter how you sliced it, if Jack Telda could find a way to produce a pound of beef for twelve cents less than FFS's current number, that'd simply equal *a shit ton of money.* That is, as long as Food First Service continued selling *millions* of pounds of beef.

But the problem is, for Earth, when millions of pounds of beef is reduced to numbers, that's all the variable is: Beef.

Not cows.

It's not millions of pounds of *cows*, or, millions of cow *lives*, which sounds a whole lot different.

Really, beef is just a word that helped the whole world, Jack Telda included, compartmentalize the endless slaughter of cows, a truly sentient and loving being.

Oh, the power of marketing.

Anyways, the reason Jack Telda was still alive and processing numbers was because The Bugs deemed him to be a Fence Player, which according to their definition is a potentially powerful human that is easily malleable based on who one surrounds oneself with. The Bugs decided to give Jack another chance because they wanted him to realize his precious numbers were actually precious life, and they thought there was potential for him to make that consideration. At least provided he gets a push in the right direction. And once pushed, perhaps he could do some good with his power.

See, before The Bugs started interfering with Jack's life, numbers to Jack were just acres of real estate in FFS's foreign asset portfolio and the cost to manage all those acres. They weren't the clear cutting of *billions* of trees, just to free up land for row crops of grain and corn (to ultimately feed the cows). It was all thousands of tons of feedstock to Jack. Not countless soybean plants, planted in optimized lines extending well beyond the horizon, destroying the land on which they grew. Just metric tons of soybeans and their corresponding dollar value. Jack never considered there were living plants at the base of his numbers, genetically modified to survive the assault of poisonous chemicals, which occupied other numbers in Jack's books. His books and numbers didn't take account of the countless plant-life and animal-life the tons of chemicals in his books killed. The only numbers that represented plants were the millions of metric tons of crops Food First Service harvested each quarter. All to create cheap and sugary food to feed both cows *and* humans.

Truthfully, Jack had never considered all the bees, birds, apes, cats, crawlers and critters, flyers and four-leggeders, snakes and spiders, all the *bugs* and everything else that died as a result of any of his actions, like, say, clearing rainforest land to start a palm oil plantation. Not to mention, and not for nothin', Jack for sure never paid any mind to the healthy soil ecosystem the former forest nurtured. He never stopped to think it was an ecosystem that housed *trillions* of microbes and other forms of life, all universes in and of themselves. And he sure as hell didn't pay any mind to any Indigenous people that were displaced on account of his decisions.

The Bugs wanted Jack Telda to realize with FFS's monocultures planted, the rich soil ecosystem would soon turn to dust. And there's not much life in dust.

This is the nature The Bugs wanted Jack Telda to reconsider.

Yet it remained to be seen if Jack would indeed land on the right side of the fence.

Now, a few weeks after the ants' second message on the streets of Philadelphia, late at night scrolling through his work email, Jack was teetering on the edge of sanity. The data a fly was capturing relayed that he might actually be looking at all those numbers a bit differently, though of course, only time would tell. As far as the fly could see, Jack had a look of permanent terror plastered to his face.

What was happening with his colleagues sure wasn't helping.

Mitch David was still reported missing, and Mitch's wife was still locked up in a mental hospital adamantly claiming, no matter how many anti-psychotics they gave her, that her husband was killed and dragged into the woods by ants and hornets. She implored the authorities to check the house's security cameras, and the authorities reported the wires had been cut and the memory chips destroyed. And as a result, the authorities were now considering her a primary suspect in Mitch's disappearance.

The next morning after Jack's night of emptily staring at work emails, during his quarterly call with his boss Roger Cassar, Roger was speculating Mitch met up with the wrong people. Roger said Mitch is probably somewhere rotting in the Atlantic as they spoke, his bloated murdered body decomposing in the saltwater. Which made Jack think his boss had a vivid imagination. "What about you Jacky boy?" Roger said after his eerily in-depth and oddly specific hypothesis. "How're you doing? Where are my reports?"

"Sorry, sir," Jack said over the phone, haggardly making his way through Rittenhouse Square to 18th street. "I, uh, it's been a tough few weeks." At the moment, rather than sitting comfortably in his office fully prepared for his quarterly call with Roger like normal, Jack was trying his best not to give Roger any signs he was late to the office, again. Which, for the record, was the ninth time he'd been late in the past few weeks. The only other time Jack had been late during his nine-year tenure at FFS was when his wife delivered little Jack Jr to the world at 8:35am on a Tuesday. Jack made it to the office that day at 9:04am.

"Oh Jesus, Jack." Roger said. "Get your shit together. I'm hearing you haven't been yourself lately. You've been on edge all the time and you flip your shit every time you see a fly. Are you even at the office right now?"

"I, uh," Jack said. "Sir I'm sorry. I'm on my way there right now."

"Don't give me your sorry bullshit, Jacky. I've got one VP missing, presumably dead, and now that VP's ass buddy in operations is coming apart at the seams. I need you to get back to form. Forget Mitch. He was an idiot anyways. Now, bypassing the facts that a) you don't have my reports, b) you're literally running late for work, and c), for the first time, I'm starting to lose some faith in you, I want you to shut the fuck up, get to the office as fast as you can, and while you're doing that, *listen.*"

Jack said nothing and continued down the sidewalk. He kept his head on a swivel, half paying attention to Roger, half always on the lookout for any bugs, ants specifically.

"Good," Roger said. "Alright. I've got some news for you, organizationally speaking. We can't go around waiting for Mitch to return, so there's gonna be a new Mitch in your office. Next man up. You know the drill. Even if Mitch showed up at this point, he's surpassed the grace period an exec can go AWOL without returning to duty. So Mitch is out. You've got a new guy coming in. His name's Craig Fox. We poached him from those pricks over at PoconOrganics."

"That independent operation?"

"Jacky, I said shut the fuck up. And yes, that independent op getting national traction with their bullshit regenerative preachy bullshit. They're being a real thorn in our sides right now all over the internet and we had to do something about it. Craig was their top marketing guy, which isn't saying much given how small they are, but that's beside the point. Since he'll be working mostly with marketing, he won't really be involved in the operational side of things like Mitch was, but I can count on you to take on Mitch's load, right Jack?"

"Uh, yes sir," Jack said, now almost at the office. He stopped himself from saying the crude joke that reflexively came to mind in response to Roger's innuendous comment.

"Good. Now for the last time, shut the fuck up. I only have another minute. This Craig character is a real hotshot with some big ideas for branding, so we wanted to bring him in as another authority figure in your office. To start, he'll answer to you, but once you get him up to speed on the innerworkings here, he'll supervise his own team…"

As Roger unfurled his strategy for Craig, Jack saw a couple dots buzzing up ahead around a trashcan. He had the wherewithal to mute his end of the call with Roger, seeing as he had to pass the trashcan to get into his building. "Oh shit," he said as he got closer to the trashcan. "Oh shit, oh shit, oh shit."

Almost at the trashcan now, Jack slowed his pace to that of a crawl. With his back against the closest building, keeping as far away from the trashcan as possible, Jack sidestepped the bin as three yellowjackets were hovering right around the rim. Then, for a brief moment, it appeared as if one of the yellow Jackets was flying straight towards him.

Jack yelled: "OH SHIT!" then took off sprinting down the rest of the block to FFS's building lobby, his arms flailing wildly, trying to swat away the yellowjackets that were indeed *not* after him.

Jack crashed into the lobby, breathless, and could hear Roger faintly screaming through his phone.

"Jack! Are you there!"

Jack unmuted his end of the call. "Sorry, sir," Jack said, panting. "Was just shutting up like you said."

"But I asked you a question, Jacky."

"Uh."

"Don't *uh* me. I want to know you'll take care of it."

"Uh, yes sir. Of course. I'll take care of it." Jack had no clue what he was taking care of.

"Good. Craig Fox will be reporting directly to you, to start. I want you to get him up to speed with marketing. Then I want you on that shitshow of a deal with Brazil. They've been off ever since Mitch went missing. Keep me posted."

"Got it," Jack said.

"Good. Until then." Roger hung up without saying goodbye.

Jack put his phone away without really knowing what to do next.

Instinctively, he got on the elevator and headed up to the 21st floor.

Jack got off the elevator, bypassed the pit without saying a word to anyone, and went straight for his office.

Per usual, his assistant came in right away with his morning latte. "All your messages are prioritized. Nothing urgent besides the call you had with Roger. There's a Craig Fox in Mitch's office, he told me to let him know when you arrived. Would you like me to send him in?"

"Uh, yes," Jack said. "Thank you."

In the corner of the room, so as not to be a bother to Jack, a fly hung out. Smaller bugs lingered about a 48-inch tall braided Ficus tree, the only indoor plant in Jack's office. (Jack's assistant tended to the plant.) These microflies living off the potted soil kept an ever-present eye on Jack Telda while he was at work.

A few moments later, Craig Fox walked into Jack's office and shut the door behind himself without asking Jack if he wanted it open or shut. "Jesus Christ," Craig said, choosing his first words to Jack ever so carefully, "you look like absolute dogshit." Then, after making that lovely first impression, Craig Fox held out a hand. "The name's Craig Fox. How ya doin."

"Jack Telda. Nice to meet you."

Instantly, Jack had an uneasy feeling about this Craig guy. When Jack asked him about PoconOrganics, Craig said he didn't give a shit about regenerative farming or any of that hippy craziness. Truth is, for some unknown reason, they offered him a decent salary which was more than he was making at the time, about three or so years ago. He said when he got on board, he thought really hammering the message of responsible agriculture was the best way to get some movement with the market. It seemed like people—especially yuppies—were gobbling up all that peace love nature save the planet bullshit. There was a wedge he was able to drive into the food system. Create some FUD— fear, uncertainty, doubt—about the nature of the industrial food system. Naturally, that took the form of blasting Big Ag and everything they did and the results it had on the planet. Craig concluded by saying, "Of course I don't know if any of that shit is true. But hey, it worked."

"Well," Jack said, "that's great and all. But now you're working *for* Big Ag. What're you gonna do to reverse all that damage you helped create in the market's confidence?"

"Oh, that'll be easy," Craig said. "People are stupid. As long as we package it with some pretty bells and whistles, good tits and talking, people will believe whatever we want them to. We'll just say those types of farmers are liberal socialist commie hippies or something, too stupid to understand how capitalism works and how that way of farming could never feed all the people on this planet, regardless of if that's true or not. We'll say Big Ag is necessary if you don't want people to starve. You know, some bullshit like that."

"Gotcha," Jack said. "Gotcha."

When Craig left Jack's office, the fly hanging out in the corner followed suit and found itself the nearest spiderweb. It almost got swatted to death while en route, but unluckily for Craig, it was able to deliver its recording to The Bees.

CHAPTER 15

Okay, it's the first Monday of the month, which means it's poker night with the crew.

Poker night, like every other time we go out for drinks, which is about three to four times a week, is of course at The Burrito Joint.

Now, The Joint has only been open two years.

Normally, this time of year, pre ski season, the place is pretty quiet, and we'd have it mostly to ourselves. Especially since it's a Monday. (Which is why we chose it for poker night.) *But*, it's been about two weeks since I launched their new website and online ads and tonight, I gotta say, the place is *buzzing*. We got local musician Mikey Slacks jamming away on his acoustic guitar and kick drum, throwing off positive upbeat vibrations; and the place is humming with people, not an empty seat to be found. And everyone seems to be really digging the meatless menu, which is now standard on Mondays. Honestly, the place just feels alive. The mood dominating the room is palpably good and fun.

Up in the corners of The Joint's dining room, remaining perfectly still and unobtrusive, sat some flies. Some were observing the whole place, while two of them kept trained eyes on Joelle Velstar. Every now and then they'd swoop down and do a quick flyover around her head.

Okay, even with business booming, Molly and Bob are awesome and made sure we got our circular table in the corner. The one we always use for poker nights. The first Monday of every month, we always fit our group of five around this same four-top and cozy on up.

We're about thirty minutes into the game and there's no clear chip leader yet. It's my turn, so I look to my cards, then to the only other player left on this hand, Andrew Stout (the younger of the Stout brothers). Liking what I see, then feeling him out, detecting a bit of nervousness tinged with hope, knowing his tendencies, I say, "Check."

Andrew takes a moment to consider. He has one eyebrow slightly raised and a cheeky grin smeared across his face. His energy is telling me if the right card comes on the turn, he'll have a decent hand; but for now, he's probably got just an *okay* one, maybe a pair. Betraying the cards I think he has, he says, "Raise. Fifty." And he giddily tosses five chips to the center of the table.

Darren Stout, Andrew's older brother by a year, just shakes his head and radiates humorous pity toward his brother. I know he's seen this scene play out all too many times. For this hand,

Darren, along with Colby Winters and Sarah Lockwood, folded pre-flop when Andrew started with a modest bet.

And here I am, sitting Jack-Queen suited, with decent odds to hit a straight. "Call," I say, and throw in my chips.

Sarah, the dealer for this hand, flips over the turn and right there's my luck. I get the King and am now sitting on a straight. I do my best to not shift energy levels at all, to stay calm and steady. I sit for a second, look at my cards, look again at the community cards, then back to my cards. I give off nothing Andrew could use. Meanwhile, after the King came up for the turn, excitement literally exploded out of Andrew. Honestly, it made me think excitement was a *tangible* thing. I can still feel it coming off of him, despite his best efforts to stay neutral like me. So, based on how my not-so-bright compadre always plays, and his general aura, I assume he might have King-10 or King-9 and hit a two-pair, or maybe he's holding a pair already and hit three of a kind. Processing all this in about ten seconds, sensing how he's going to play the hand, I again say, "Check."

And, just as I intuited, Andrew is all too eager to bet big again. He raises me eighty.

Extremely confident in my hand but keeping that vibe to myself, setting up my final move, I do my best to ooze doubt and look uneasy. I pretend to think it over a second; but instead think about how Andrew's going to lose it when he sees I have a straight. He'll probably storm out or something, go smoke a cigarette. After a solid thirty seconds of *deep* contemplation, I call and toss in another eight chips. It's a good thing he can't read my mind.

Sarah flips over the river, and it's a two of hearts. Andrew's face lights up in what's got to be the worst poker face of all time. His goofy smile is telling me he's absolutely sure he has it in the bag. Naturally, I check once more, baiting him to go further and further in the hole.

And as I expected, Andrew immediately says, "All in!" He barely waited for the *eck* to leave my mouth before blurting his bet, as if this poker game were actual sex and he just came too fast.

"Call, ya freakin' idiot," I say playfully, doing my best to emit goodwill his way, since I know I'm about to clean him out.

I let Andrew turn over his cards first and I was spot on. He was sitting King-10.

I flip my cards and collect my winnings, which now make me the clear chip leader.

The excitement that was pouring out of Andrew immediately turns into a fury that is felt by all of us. It changes the energy of our group. Andrew yells, "God DAMNIT!" and slams the table. He then heads outside for a cigarette. In the wake of his wrath, Darren laughs at his brother's misfortune. Sarah and Colby both kind of look away, and each put on a *yeesh* face.

Fortunately, no one else at The Joint is disturbed by Andrew's outburst, as the music and good times everyone's having has drowned out his temper tantrum. The good vibes are just *too* strong.

As could be expected, it's another playful rowdy night up here in Carrabassett Valley.

A few hours later and it's the last hand of the night. Colby's going all in with what little chips he has left. He's projecting this downtrodden energy that tells me he's already accepted what's about to happen. Like with Andrew earlier, I do my best to radiate goodwill and love, and I call him with my pocket queens. Once again, I win poker night. I honestly don't know why they still play with me.

"Fuck you Joelle," everyone says to me, in a way that says they hate me, even though they still love me at the same time. Kinda like how you can really hate your best friends sometimes.

As is tradition, with the winnings, I buy the next round for everyone. And since I'm buying, I choose the beer. "Alright guys, everyone's getting a Yessir, take it or leave it." The crew gives me the thumbs up and I walk over to the bar and holler at Molly, "Hey Moll! Five Yessirs por favor." She smiles and says she'll bring 'em over.

A moment after Molly brings the beers, Sarah says, "So, Joelle. What's going on? You've been on a tear lately. What's up with Yessir?" She nods her head to the beer before taking a sip. I can feel her genuine curiosity and what seems like admiration.

"It's crazy!" I say. "Those guys are rad. They built this gigantic year-round greenhouse in Buxton. They're growing all their own specialty hops 365 days a year. So like I did with The Joint, they're having me build them a new website and ad campaign to showcase their whole mission and what not."

"They giving you free beer or something?" Colby asks.

Just playing around with him, I respond with a slightly mocking tone. "No, Colby. It's this funny thing. In exchange for doing work for them, they're actually giving me this thing called *money*. And you know what's wild? I can use that money to *buy* their beer, if I want. Or anything else I want. Crazy, right?"

"Yeah Colby," Darren chimes in. "Free market capitalism and all that shit."

I don't know why, but just by saying that, Darren makes me think about that term, Free Market Capitalism, and what it means to me. How it's enabled me to start this business and go out on my own with very little barriers. It makes me ponder it's not really a *free* market out there, per se, like, with crony capitalism and what not, but for me, it's damn sure free enough. Makes me wonder: how can I leverage that freedom even more? But I keep these thoughts to myself.

"I can't hear them *at all* over the music," one fly in the corner says to another.

"Well, why don't we go down there and have a listen? Maybe grab a sample or two. Per the Queen's direction. I mean, they seem to have chilled out a bit."

A second later, these two flies leave the safety of the corner of the room to get up close and personal with Joelle. They both land on the rim of Joelle's pint, facing her. Acting on permission from Queen Bean, this is to be a subtle message, of sorts. If Joelle could get it.

As the flies wait for Joelle's response, they collect samples of her chapstick on the rim of the glass for any potential data.

Okay, suddenly I'm taken away from joking around with Colby and I can't help but notice these two flies, as if acting in perfect unison, on my pint glass staring *right at me*. They're just toiling away atop the section where there's a smudge of my chapstick. They walk around on the chapstick, stop, rub their front arms together, and it almost looks like they're analyzing... *something*.

Transfixed, I hold out my hand, palm up, thinking *hey there little buddies. Whatcha doin? Here...*

And crazy as it is, but God as my witness, at my gesture, both the flies, in unison, hop from the rim of my pint and land on the tip of my pointer finger. And now they're comfortably stationed on my fingerprint, as if they're awaiting my next move. While they wait, they keep touching my skin then rubbing their arms together, like I guess flies are wont to do.

Gently and slow, I lift my hand to just in front of my eyes. To inspect these little buddies a bit closer. And I'm honestly shocked to see the flies do not budge.

Huh, I think. Then I get lost in my thoughts. My brain summons visions of flies and spiders and bugs and superpowers and human evolution. I don't know what it is about these flies, but I want to know more about them. Like where'd they come from. Are they really *just* flies?

To the flies, Joelle is, at least physically, still at the table with her friends. But from what they can analyze, it appears she's traveled, mentally, far off into another space much different than where her body currently sits. The flies don't have the capabilities to get in there and root out her essence the same way Bees do, so they're left to just guessing this, sensing it.

Then, Joelle finally makes a sound. Inaudible to her friends, but crystal clear to the flies, she mouths: *Who are you?*

Since the flies are unable to respond, Joelle keeps staring into their buggy little eyes before mouthing another question: *What do you want from me?*

She takes no notice of the fact her friends had stopped talking. Colby nudges Darren, energetically telling him to look at Joelle. The rest of the table then falls silent as they all sit for a second or two, completely baffled at the site of their friend with two flies on the tip of her finger, six inches from the front of her face.

Unable to contain her confusion anymore, Joelle's friend Sarah says, "Joelle, what the fuck are you doing?"

Okay, at the sound of my name coming out of Sarah's mouth, I return to reality, unsure where I went for a moment there. I jolt my head towards Sarah, ask her what she said, and by the time I turn my head back to my finger, the flies have flown away. Sarah repeats herself and I say, "Uh, nothing. What's up?"

"You were just staring at flies that were hanging out on the tip of your finger. Weirdo."

"Oh," I say. "Uh, yeah. I don't know. They were just kind of chillin there. I guess I was hypnotized by them not flying away or something. That's cool, right?"

"Again," Sarah says, "*weirdo.*"

"Yeah," I say. "You know what. I lied. I was actually talking with them. You ever wonder why I always win poker? I got my little fly spies peeping all your cards."

"I knew it!" says Colby. "You cheat! Queen of the bugs over here is nothing but a cheat!" I can clearly detect the jokiness in his tone.

"Yep," I say. "That's me. Poker champ. Queen of the bugs."

CHAPTER 16

It's only been a week and Craig Fox was already killing it at his new job.

His new boss, *colleague?,* Jack Telda, yeah he was a weird dude. But everyone else at the office seemed pretty dope. There were a few smokeshows, and he presumed he was definitely one of the best-looking dudes there, so he liked his odds.

On Friday after work, in anticipation of his first paycheck with his new bumped-up salary, Craig maxed out his credit cards at the King of Prussia mall, decking himself out in whatever gear he wanted. (Not to mention and not for nothin', now that he could afford it, Craig treated himself to a bag of nose candy big enough to last, at best, a week. At worst, two days. Maybe one. Depending on who he met up with tonight. Though so far, none of his friends responded to his text asking what they were up to. At this point in his life, Craig wouldn't, maybe couldn't, admit to himself that his friends weren't actually real friends, and that he was actually terribly lonely. If he went deeper, maybe he'd realize it was because his value system had gotten so far away from what's truly valuable in life.)

Anyways, after doing a pinky-sized line off the baby changing station in the mall bathroom, Craig made his biggest purchase of the day on a complete whim. He was walking past the outdoor sporting goods store and recalled a bunch of the junior associates talking about mountain biking. An hour later, Craig walked out of the mall with five large shopping bags and a brand new $3,000 full-suspension mountain bike.

The next morning (he did not end up doing anything with friends after his shopping spree), in order to test out his new toy, Craig headed to Wissahickon park, which was a gem of a trail network within Philadelphia city limits.

In the parking lot, while Craig geared up, a father-son duo was just getting back from a hike. The young boy commented, "Woahhhh, cool bike!"

"You like that?" Craig said, likewise admiring his shiny new mountain bike. He aggressively clipped up his helmet and tightened the strap. "Probably cost more than your pop's car." Craig gave a smirky nod toward the kid's dad. "Best of luck, kid."

The kid looked back at his dad, a single father doing his absolute best, who was beet red behind his humble car that performed its job admirably of getting him and his son from point A to point B.

Then, for the ride, to really get in tune with nature, Craig synced up a portable speaker to his phone, turned the volume all the way up, put the speaker in one of the bike's water bottle holders, and started blasting his workout mix. A combo of heavy metal, EDM, and some pop workout stuff. He then sped off down the trail. Anyone within a few hundred feet of Craig Fox would hear his music over anything else their ears may take in while walking through the woods.

It only took a minute or so of riding his new souped-up bike before Craig developed a cocky confidence in his abilities. He was bombing it around corners, blasting over rocks, and beasting it up climbs. His dedication to CrossFit was paying dividends on this bike ride. He was a machine. He scoffed at all the other bikers that had to stop and pull to the side while he zoomed past and dominated the singletracks of the Wissahickon woods.

With his music blaring, Craig had to shout as loud as he could, "ON YOUR LEFT!" as he approached bikers or hikers going in the same direction. Then, thinking he was protected by the cover of his music, he'd say things like "fat ass" as he passed.

Although he thought the people wouldn't hear his malicious comments, they did. As did The Bugs in the area.

The truth is, and this is something The Bugs knew all too well, that when left unchecked, Craig often made others around him feel worse than they did before they interacted with him. This is not a good thing, at least in the eyes of the The Bugs, the protectors of Earth.

A few miles into the ride, Craig was going uncontrollably fast down a little hill. At the bottom of the hill was a slight corner, and right around that corner was an off-leash dog. The dog stepped in front of Craig's path, forcing him to make a quick decision. Overconfident in his abilities, Craig tried to jump his bike over the dog. But rather than get the requisite two feet he needed, Craig got his front tire maybe three inches off the ground and he couldn't elevate his back tire at all. He ran right over the mutt, which caused Craig to crash over the handlebars. Now, a world-class biker *may* have been able to make the jump over the little dog, but it should be noted, a world class biker would have known not to go so fast on trails as populated as the ones in Wissahickon. And besides, Craig Fox was *not* a world-class biker.

The pup yelped loudly as it tumbled underneath the bike's tires.

"Buddy!" the dog's owner yelled. He went over to console his wounded and scared pup.

Heavy metal was still booming through the speaker.

Splayed out on the side of the trail, Craig patted himself over, checking for any injuries. There were none. Once he confirmed this, he yelled. "Fuck!" He got up and stood within a few feet of the guy with the dog. "Control your fucking dog, dude! I should sue you. Dogs are supposed to be on leash here!" The guy with the dog didn't know how to respond. He just knelt there, holding his dog, with a stupid look on his face.

Craig then inspected his bike to make sure it wasn't broken. He didn't bother to ask how the dog was and had a few parting words before he sped off again. "Fucking *idiot*. Leash that mutt. You're lucky I didn't kill it."

Frozen by rage and fear and confusion as to how someone could act like that, the guy with the dog thought, but didn't say, *Jesus, dude,* you *were the one going too fast. These trails are for everyone.* But alas, he said nothing and let Craig Fox go on his way, thinking he was supremely and always in the right. (And other than a newly developed phobia of bikes and some bruising, the dog was okay.)

At the site of that scene, at least two dozen flies who witnessed everything flew themselves immediately into nearby spiderwebs.

Ten seconds later, Queen Bruth sent the command.

A minute or so after *that*, Craig was once again bombing uncontrollably fast around the Wissahickon woods on his new bike, having luckily escaped injury after steamrolling that mutt. *I'm the man, keep pushing, go faster, go harder,* Craig thought, almost constantly, as he sped past other hikers and bikers on the trail. *I'm the man, keep pushing, go faster, go harder.* This mantra was on repeat in his head while his speaker screamed for everyone to hear he's got the eye of the tiger. All the while, Craig was also thinking how the other people on the trail must be in awe of how awesome and cool he looked.

Really, in fact, almost everyone he passed thought some variation of: *that guy's a douche bag.*

And The Bugs were keeping an eye on him the whole time.

At last, during a stretch where there wouldn't be any other humans for at least two minutes, The Bugs made their move.

Since Craig was wearing glasses to protect his eyes from the wind and any debris, a lone hornet first tried to fly straight into his mouth. It missed, however, and bounced off his chin. "Ahh, what the shit," Craig said.

A second hornet tried a different tack. Rather than approaching head-on, it came in at an angle, and managed to lodge itself up Craig's nose, hindquarters first. Once up in there, it stung the inside of his nostril. Craig took one hand off his handlebars—while still going pretty fast on a technical part of the trail—and slapped his own nose. With only one hand on the bike, he was still able to maintain balance on the trail. But that's when another hornet swooped in and stung the hand that was still steering the bike. Craig was able to ignore the pain though and maintain his grip. Then while two more hornets stung that same hand, three more went after his other hand as it returned to the handlebars. Even more hornets targeted his exposed neck. Craig took his eyes off the trail to focus on swatting away hornets and in doing so, a serious rut got the better of him. Craig crashed and fell into a bush off to the side of the trail.

Immediately upon hitting the bush, a swarm of hornets was on him, stinging every exposed inch of his skin. Hundreds landed and crawled under his shirt sleeves and stung mercilessly.

All Craig could do was scream. He didn't have time to consider what was happening.

Because just as the hornets got to him, the ants arrived and enveloped Craig in their infinite creepy crawliness. Like with Mitch David, they crawled *into* Craig via his nose, ears, mouth, eyes, peehole, and asshole. He squirmed for maybe fifteen seconds before passing out from the pain of ten thousand hornet stings.

In a few moments, Craig Fox was dead.

Same as Mitch, The Bugs then carried Craig, and his speaker, off into the woods, leaving no trace of him anywhere, save his new bike that lay on the side of the trail.

CHAPTER 17

There was a lot on the table at this Meeting Of The Bosses. The hazy and unreliable data regarding topsoil erosion, the progress of Directed Elimination, whether or not any of the Coordinated Upgrades were showing promise of having The Bees initiate Sequence Two, and what not.

"The problem is," Queen Bruth was reporting, "we can't get accurate measurements of soil quality in areas where it's most eroding, because that's where the highest concentrations of herbicides and *pest*icides are used. Anytime we send in ants to get some readings, they're poisoned and die before they can get to any spiders, which are also dying around the inflicted areas. Moreover, the runoff around those areas and the poison that makes its way onto flowers are killing all the local Bees as well. This is happening all over Earth. And it's having profound impacts on the other larger forms of life that rely on all us bugs for sustenance."

Each of The Bosses had an intuitive sense of a global map, heat-mapped per se, that highlighted where there were and were not populations of Bees. To them, there were large patches of redness—indicating *no* Bees—around certain deserts, high mountain ranges, and around areas where the humans were participating in Big Ag. The latter area was of primary concern because those patches of redness were growing month over month with the proliferation of these agricultural practices. And these were places where there *should* be Bees.

"So how are the combative efforts going?" a Queen from Sao Paulo asked.

"Queen that's a good question," said Queen Bruth. Having crunched the numbers for the rest of The Bosses, she provided the answer: "Estimates show Directed Elimination will start creating positive tangible effects within at least four months. This will be accomplished by tipping Fence Players to the side of goodness. Per our guidelines, we have targeted Fence Players in the arenas of agriculture, land management, politics, and several other sectors; all of whom will be poised to enact conservation and rewilding policies. It will take four months minimum because the power system humans have developed is quite robust with their *next man up* policy. Sexist too for that matter. It'll take a little time for some human organizations—such as coal mining operations—to crumble as we continue removing multiple key players from their team. Fortunately, the ants and hornets and their other helpers have been incognito enough with their tasks. A few humans have witnessed our interference, but their minds are so feeble their peers place them in mental hospitals because their claims seem so ridiculous. However, we cannot rely on this to be the case moving forward. We *must* be more diligent in ensuring no other humans catch on to what we're doing. Otherwise, if they find out, we risk them rioting and us having to sound the Final Alarm to prevent catastrophe. Anyhow, Directed Elimination is proving to have a net positive effect on the Fence Players around the eliminated targets. Take out enough negative thought leaders, and the persuadable—albeit rather capable—humans start to lean toward goodness again. They really are simply the average of the other humans they spend the most time with. In summation, our efforts will merit positive change in about four months, barring unforeseen acts of God, of course."

"Meanwhile," a Queen from Paris added, "Coordinated Upgrades are yielding significant results in areas of greatest concern. The targeted Artists are producing more work, and the resulting work, as far as we Bugs are capable of judging, is quite good. Objective measurements confirm our judgments too, as human engagement and sharing are up and the subsequent conversations are more in line with the messages the Artists are delivering."

"Which are predominantly messages of healing and love and protection and stewardship for Earth," a Queen Bee from Los Angeles said, continuing the thought for her sister.

The Bosses, during their weekly meetings, had a way of communicating with and *for* one another. Beyond the reports for which a few of The Bosses were responsible, their meetings were more an act of congregation, one in which they continued each other's thoughts, affirmed they're all on the same page, and they're forever working in unison toward their shared purpose of protecting Earth from the potentially destructive power of humankind.

"Yeah, and for real," a Boss in Boston added, "like back in the day, when the art is good, the people and their outlook starts to be good too. Our flies are reporting a wicked awesome uptick in values, and therefore, shopping behavior. Meaning they're spending less on throwaway crap. And when they do spend, it's on better stuff."

"And of course, the businesses have followed. Have y'all seen the reports on all these new businesses that are starting up with missions beyond the stuff they sell? What they're calling the *triple bottom line?"*

Yasssss, the Queen Bees collectively buzzed in response to their sister from Atlanta.

"And with great results. There is a local group here embarking on cleaning up the Western Pacific Garbage Patch," said a Queen from Tokyo.

"Yes! Us too! But the eastern one!" reported a Boss from San Francisco.

"And that, my Bosses," Queen Bruth said, bringing the group back to focus, "is a microcosm of the good that is *already* happening thanks to our Coordinated Upgrades. There are countless examples of businesses like these operating in other sectors—whether it's wildlife conservation, reforestation, trash cleanup and recycling, or advances in new materials that are more sustainable than their plastic counterparts. Which is why I propose three new measures..."

The Queen Bee Bosses *loved* whenever one of their sisters came forth with a proposition. It meant potential for *change.* It meant they might be moving, if only a little bit, closer to their goal beyond protecting Earth, toward their goal of Ascension, for the *Bees.*

"1)" Bruth said, "I propose we increase the percentage of hives that can enact a Coordinated Upgrade from 10% to 12%.

"2) I propose the humans *already* being upgraded can have their dosages upped by 4%. Then, pending an analysis of their progress, if they've made statistically significant improvements, they can be upgraded 8%."

A stir whirred about the Bosses. Eight percent upgrades were practically unheard of. The statistical significance in order to warrant that drastic of a measure would indeed be, well, significant. And if any miscalculations in upgrades were made, it could yield horrendous results due to a misplacement of concentrated power.

"And 3) I propose, pending a Net Impact Score analysis of the Fence Players, we increase messaging and, more importantly, *specificity* of messaging by 7% to the Fence Players."

The Bosses considered the propositions in an instant. Since they were offered by a Boss of great renown, they all knew these ideas were substantiated by a keen instinct, an innate understanding of patterns, and by a mind that has always understood the workings of the Bees' existence. They agreed unanimously and a shockwave of directives blasted all over Earth, alerting all Queen Bees everywhere.

Excitement pulsed through this special communicative chamber of the world's Queen Bee Bosses. Some were even starting to utter the idea, the re-emerging possibility, the hope of them initiating *Sequence Two*. Just maybe, there was someone out there who fit the bill.

"And now, Queens," Queen Bod concluded, noticing the attention waning and going elsewhere, "we know the numbers. Rather than harp on our lost sisters and brothers, let us instead rejoice in the passing of these proposals and end with our prayer."

Born of this Earth, Before God and Its worth, Bred to protect Earth's Bountiful Births...

CHAPTER 18

I am a Tree.

Being a Tree, as long as my body is alive, my physical presence must remain stationary on my plot of Earth.

Unless, of course, when I'm young enough, a human decides to move me.

My *spiritual presence*, however, transcends the globe and lives on long after my physical body perishes.

It's not so bad being physically stationary one's whole life, so long as one is connected, constantly and perpetually, to one's trillions of kin.

Which, I am. Given the level of existence where my kin and I live.

Now, the level in which we Trees communicate, the dimension where we converse, is not yet accessible to the other forms of life on Earth.

Not even the bugs.

Life, by the way, regardless of form, communicates with any number of other lifeforms, so long as they've made it to the same dimensional level.

Rather than Maslow's Hierarchy of Needs, think of it as Life's Hierarchy of Communicative Levels.

THE BUGS

Just as the humans don't know what is yet to be seen on the bugs' level, and as the bugs don't know what it's like to be on the Trees', we Trees don't know what dimensional level is beyond ours.

Based on patterns thus far, fractal in nature, there surely is something higher. Something deeper.

Something that we the Trees strive to reach.

Until we reach that next level, we are bound to our Earthly roots.

The bugs, supreme in their own right, have realized the same conundrum.

That of ascending levels of communication.

The bugs believe they are trapped in their current dimension of existence until they bring the imaginators—the humans—to their level.

Perhaps then, given some *thing* the humans may need to imagine, *they* the bugs can Ascend.

The bugs do not know what awaits them upon moving up to the next level.

It is we the Trees that await the Bugs and the rest of life.

Though unlike the bees, we Trees can be patient. We do not feel the urgency to rush the humans. We believe in the principle that all will happen, given its time, if it's *supposed* to happen.

When it does happen, perhaps we will Ascend ourselves to whom or whatever is waiting for *us*.

Why else would we be confined to Earth, looking over all life on this lovely planet?

Seriously, *why*?

CHAPTER 19

It's been a week since Jack's quarterly call with his boss Roger Cassar.

And since then, Jack's been a wreck.

Thanks to the ants, nothing in Jack's life had any compartments to go in.

He was losing it at work and at home.

In the office, Jack was unable to concentrate on anything for longer than a minute at a time, and only then in the momentary instant when an email or call or urgent question from a pit kid was thrust into his face. "I don't know, figure it out," became a common refrain from him. And after hitting send or hanging up or shaming a middle manager for asking a question they should know the answer to, Jack would return to his desk, his always-close-to-empty glass of whiskey there within arm's length, right next to the leather journal he used for work. Lately, in that journal, he wrote the same thing over and over and over again.

Reconsider your ways. Preserve nature.

Then, at home, it was no different. Every day, he'd slump up the elevator to his rental suite, and like clockwork, Amy would say, "Yay Daddy's home!" to Jack Jr when Jack opened the door.

And every day, she'd say this in a voice Jack felt in his bones was the epitome of fakeness.

She'd then ask, "How was your day?"

He'd say, "You know. Good. Things at work are crazy though. Still got some work to do."

Then he'd go into the office of their rental suite and he'd sit at *that* desk with an always-two-finger-full glass of whiskey, and do the same thing, writing the same phrase, over and over and over again in his journal. *Reconsider your ways. Preserve nature.*

Now, for Amy, even though their marriage hadn't been awesome lately, she still *knew* Jack. She could tell something was up. He was more disheveled than she could ever remember him. He never used to come home stinking of bourbon. And although having to do some work at home after work was normal and all, he used to at least give her a kiss on the cheek before disappearing into his office for the night. He used to at least ask her how her day was, or if there was anything she was working on. Which, depending on the week, would vary between trying to learn guitar or to knit or to watercolor, or something. Something to occupy her time since Jack always insisted she didn't have to work, even though she may have wanted to. Like, maybe interior decorate, or something fun like that. She honestly didn't know because the possibility was never real nor needed. So now, yeah, something was definitely up. Amy didn't know what. She *wanted* to know. But thanks to the apathy Jack exuded toward nurturing the family, she never mustered the energy to ask.

So when Jack said he had work to do and he better get to it, Amy said, "Okay babe, dinner will be ready in a bit." And the only time she'd see him again for the rest of the night before putting Jack Jr to bed and going to bed herself, would be when she brought Jack a plate, which he would then eat at his desk, alone.

Amy never ate alone these days. She at least had Jack Jr.

But still.

She wished Jack would come back. She wished he *cared*.

Jack, meanwhile, even though he wouldn't acknowledge it, hated himself for how he was acting. To get by, he told himself there was nothing he could do about it. It was who he was, and he couldn't control the fact ants were after him and he still had to earn money to pay for the life of means him and Amy enjoyed. Though, to be fair, this wasn't a new thing. The ants entering the picture didn't affect this approach to life. Jack, in order to reach the rung he was on at FFS, had to make some sacrifices. And family time happened to be one of those sacrifices. He always justified this sacrifice and convinced himself he was a good husband and father thanks to his ability to afford all these finer things in life. He justified it by saying that type of life was enough for Amy, rather than a life with an attentive and loving husband. And although he always justified it, he knew somewhere deep down he was bullshitting himself. That he could be a better husband. That he *wanted* to be a better husband. A better father. But, thanks to whatever, thanks to his subconscious fear of being vulnerable, thanks to his subconscious fear of his *presence* not being enough rather than his money, he instead continued on with the same tired routine.

The main difference nowadays, after the ants, was Jack would pour a bit more whiskey in his cup. And instead of actually work, which there was plenty to do since he wasn't doing any *at work*, he'd just scrawl the same thing over and over and over again in his notebook. Filling every inch of his journal with the same five words.

Reconsider your ways. Preserve nature.

And it wasn't line by line he would write this.

On one page, he'd write it in a spiral that started in the center of the page and extended outward, ultimately leading into a triangle on the next page which was formed of the same words. When the spiralized triangle was done, he'd fill in the empty space around it in every which way he could, always writing the same phrase.

Over and over and over again.

Normal definitely not insane stuff.

Meanwhile, there was always a bug watching, whether a tiny little fungus gnat, or a regular old fly. And the reports they sent to Queen Bruth did not instill much confidence in her with regards to the stability of her Fence Player's mental state. He was clearly teetering on sanity's edge.

Every now and then, he'd stop. He'd actually contemplate what those five words meant. What did the ants really want him to do? He thought back to that first message they sent, when he lit his house on fire. By not doing any work at work, he ostensibly had halted any deals that were on the table, which is something the ants said they wanted. *But*, he thought, *is that enough?* Jack was never sure.

After a weekend of scribbling in his journal and ignoring his family, Jack showed up to work expecting Craig Fox to be waiting for him in his office. This is something Craig did throughout his first week at FFS. Wait in Jack's office, in *Jack's* chair, doing what Jack considered to be Craig's subtle attempt at being *alpha*.

But alas, today, Craig was not there. Which was a welcomed surprise for Jack.

When Jack's assistant came in with the morning latte and reports, Jack asked if he had seen Craig yet.

"No, sir," Jack's assistant said. "Want me to call him for you?"

"No, please don't. Just let me know when he gets in or if he calls."

"Yes, sir. Anything else I can do?"

"No, that'll do it."

And with that, Jack's assistant left Jack to it. To his own devices.

Today, at least to start, was par for the course lately. While binge-watching documentaries online, Jack would scrawl that phrase away in his journal. Word after word. Page after page.

This morning, Jack breeched a particular rabbit-hole of documentaries after entering the simple phrase into the search: *preserve nature.*

From that, Jack watched activist videos showing the horrors of an industrial cattle farm and slaughterhouse, videos of Indigenous lands being clear-cut and stripped bare leaving its peoples homeless and aimless, and more videos still on the decline of Bee populations. He then segued into videos on why the loss of Bees was *so* important.

Now, nearly four hours into his workday, he was twenty minutes into a new video about ant colonies and how they operate, which was the eighth such video he's watched on the subject.

The flies and other bugs positioned in Jack's office got a kick out of his strange behavior, constantly scribbling the same thing over and over and over again in his journal as he watched these documentaries. They had no idea what it all meant in the long run, just that the Bees had everything under control and all they had to do was fly into a spiderweb after recording anything.

Near the end of the workday, there was a knock on his door.

"Come in," Jack said.

His assistant, looking uneasy, came in, said, "Sorry to bother you. But Jessica, Roger's assistant, called and asked if by any chance we had heard from Roger..."

"Well, uh, no," Jack said. "Not today. Why?"

"I guess Roger didn't show for the board meeting today, and he hasn't been answering any calls or messages."

Jack's mind instantly, instinctively, went to ants.

Then to Mitch David.

Then to Craig Fox and his current absence.

Then back to Roger.

Roger would *never* miss a board meeting, not without notifying someone at least.

Jack's assistant remained in the doorway, unsure what to do or say next while Jack sat there, slowly transforming into a petrified shell of himself. Jack's face turned shiny, sweaty, flush, and he started breathing faster. Jack's assistant didn't dare ask if Jack was doing alright. Instead, he sort of awkwardly stood there, awaiting further instruction.

"Uh," Jack said. "Thank you. Let me know if something happens."

"You got it," Jack's assistant said before leaving the room.

When his assistant left and closed the door, rather than go for his standard bourbon, Jack took out a bottle of twenty-year single malt scotch from his desk, poured himself a three-finger drink, and gulped it down in one swig. He was thinking he had yet to do *anything* that would be considered the preservation of nature, other than not working on actively clear cutting it. So he figured if the end was nigh, he may as well drink the good stuff.

A few hours later, a few more stiff drinks later, a ten thousand dollar donation to the WWF later, Jack was sloshed, much more than normal, and was unable to scribble anymore in his journal. He moved to the leather couch in his office to lie down. Once horizontal, thoughts of ant armies and bug brigades murdering his boss and new colleague swirled about his mind as the whisky's alcohol swirled about his blood stream.

Lying on the couch in his office, an empty glass of scotch resting on his belly, Jack remained paralyzed by fear and drunkenness. He questioned reality. *There's a glitch in the matrix or something and this is all one long bad dream*, he sincerely thought at one point.

At that moment, a fly buzzed down to have a closer look at Jack's condition. It landed right on the rim of his glass and, once again, appeared to stare straight through Jack's tormented psyche, mockingly rubbing its arms together.

Not totally rooted in reality, which is to say completely sauced, Jack looked straight back at the fly. Without thinking about what he was doing, slurring his words, he asked it, "Whadyou want from me?"

In response, the fly immediately flew away from Jack and darted behind the fridge in his office (where a spider and its web was waiting). Jack paid no attention to where the fly went, and instead chose to continue staring blankly at his glass of scotch.

A few moments later, with Jack's stupor keeping him from paying too much attention, a single-file line of ants came crawling out from behind the fridge.

Before Jack could take notice and freak out, the ants neatly spelled out on the floor in very large letters: *Don't panic!*

They waited in this position for Jack to notice.

A few moments later, Jack rolled his head a few inches to the left, looked beyond his glass and saw the ants on the ground before him. Hundreds of ants. Maybe thousands. Spelling out a very clear, very easy to read, and very easy to follow message. Even for a drunk.

Though the instructions were simple and easy, Jack indeed panicked.

He jumped up on his sofa and yelled, "Ahh shit! Ants! Whadyou want!?" He stood there petrified as the ants reformed themselves.

As the words *Don't panic!* uncoalesced, a few thousand more ants came out from behind the fridge, single-file. Going letter by letter, in much smaller font, they perfectly spelled out:

Jack, you know what's happened. Craig is dead. Roger is dead. We The Bugs killed them. They had to go. Now, do you want to be next? Are you reconsidering your ways? Are you preserving nature?

"What does that even mean!?" Jack pleaded. "I just donated ten thousand dollars to the World Wildlife Fund!"

A few of the ants dispersed and disappeared behind the fridge. The remaining ants mixed together and rearranged themselves to answer Jack's question with as much specificity as the Bees allowed:

Although noted, that is not what we wanted you to do. Now, get back in touch with nature. Away from the city. Figure it out.

Once Jack finished reading the message, the ants in his office, starting with the last period, formed a single-file line and exited behind the fridge. Leaving Jack Telda to figure it out.

Jack collapsed in on himself, fell to his knees on the couch, bent at the waist, and held his head in his own arms. He whimpered softly, "What does that mean? What do you want from me? What does that mean..."

Jack rocked back and forth, the fundamental nature of reality getting uprooted from his mind. A fly recorded him asking God what was happening over and over. The fly took note of the blood pounding throughout his chest, evidenced by his heartrate, which the fly could document. The fly then flew into the spiderweb behind the fridge and shortly thereafter, a steady line of ants marched back out to the center of Jack's office.

The little black line of crawlies appeared endless, each ant ultimately coming to a stop after arranging itself into the formation of a letter. One letter after another, just like before. Only this time, the font was much smaller, the message much *much* longer. Upon reading the first four words of this new message, Jack locked his office door. Two minutes later, after witnessing a parade of ants emerge from somewhere behind his fridge with horrifying directiveness, he finally had some marching orders. All the ants and flies, all the bugs in Jack's office scanned his eyes as he read:

First: lock your door. Now, okay dummy. Get this. You are not alone on this planet. There's a lot more life out there than just Jack Telda and the occasional human he interacts with. There's life <u>everywhere</u> and The Bugs have determined <u>you</u> have been responsible for the death of <u>trillions</u>. However, unlike your colleagues Mitch David, Roger Cassar, and Craig Fox, we believe you may still have some good left in you. You are the product of multifaceted external social pressures that have resulted in you working on the wrong side of the fence. The Bugs have determined you may yet be able to play on the other side of the fence, the <u>good</u> side of the fence, pending the *removal of certain negative forces in your life, such as your colleagues. Now, if you want to live, we suggest you take leave from your job, use the vast wealth you have hoarded to remove yourself and your family far from the city, and then we suggest you spend real and meaningful time in nature, and, God willing, with your family. Perhaps then, you can reconsider your ways. And if you haven't figured it out yet, which it seems you haven't, before you leave Food First Service, cancel all pending negotiations with your counterparts in Brazil and elsewhere. And as you do all this, keep in mind, we might need you in a position of power at FFS in the future. Say you need a sabbatical. Or something. Don't burn that bridge. If this message doesn't register, your case is lost and you will be killed. Good day.*

Jack finished reading the directedly specific message (straight from Queen Bruth), took a few deep breaths, and his blood pressure began to normalize.

Given the cue Jack had read and digested the message, the hundreds of thousands of ants in his office calmly and orderly made their way behind the fridge and disappeared somewhere in the walls.

CHAPTER 20

Okay, today's an emotional one for me. *This* day, rather than a morning ride, I decide to go for a morning hike, which I'm sure Maple will love just as much. Mom is letting me borrow her car so I can drive to the trailhead at Bigelow Mountain. She understands why I want to do this and arranges to have a coworker pick her up.

The reason today's so emotional is because today is—would be—my dad's birthday.

He died when I was seven, a year after we moved to Carrabassett Valley.

Which means I was old enough to remember him in a general sense and in incomplete memories, but I wasn't old enough to really absorb my own unique understanding of him and any quirks or mannerisms he carried, or the sound of his voice, or any life lessons he wanted to impart to me, at least one to one, father to daughter.

Of course, Mom has filled me in on a lot about who he was and what he was all about. Like how he was a real outdoorsman, how he would go live out in the wilderness for weeks at a time before my mom got him to settle down and nest. How, except when he was working, doing carpentry or general house building and repair, he'd pretty much spend *all* his time outside, be it downhill or cross country skiing, or hiking, or trail running, or kayaking, or canoeing, or fishing, or hunting (strictly for food and clothing and everything else an animal body could be used for, *not* for game), or, in the spring, summer, and fall, gardening. How the outdoors, and trees specifically, gave him life, and how he respected Mother Nature with all his soul and how he wanted to be a good steward of the land. But again, I'm getting all these lessons and personality traits second-hand, from stories my mom still tells me to this day, even though I've heard them all a thousand times by now. Of course, I never tire of hearing them and of course I believe them. In my hazy memories, my dad *is* all those things my mom describes.

I remember being in the woods with him, sitting on his shoulders hugging his forehead and squealing with delight as he would jump up and have overhanging branches and leaves brush against my face. I vaguely remember him showing me how to build a primitive shelter, how to start a fire using only wood, how to look at and identify plants, which plants you could eat, which ones you couldn't. I remember being around water with him, him teaching me how to swim, how to fish. I remember him telling me to Leave No Trace as I interacted with nature.

I remember, on his last birthday before he died, how he said all he wanted as a gift was for me and Mom to hike Bigelow Mountain with him, as a family, and that's all he could ever want in the world. How he already had everything else he needed. Again, I may be filling in some of what he said based on what mom tells me. The specifics are not all that clear. The only clear memory I have of that day was being at the top of the mountain with the wind howling, looking at manmade Flagstaff Lake beneath us. This memory is strengthened by the picture my dad took, the one I've copied at least a dozen times to make sure I never lose it, the one I keep copies of in my wallet, on my desk, and another to use as a bookmark. My dad had set up a tripod with his camera and got a great shot of the three of us on the top of the mountain, me sitting high on his shoulders.

So, yeah, I think it's fitting that today I hike Bigelow Mountain and meditate at the top. Meditate on my dad, on how awesome he was, and how great he was to me, how I miss him to this day more than I could possibly describe, and how much I seriously with all of my heart hate drunk drivers.

At a good pace, it takes me about two hours to get to the summit. The whole way up, my mind is kind of blank. When I do have actual thoughts, they tend to gravitate toward wondering what it'd be like to hike with my dad these days, with me as an adult.

Today, I've only seen one other hiker on the trail, going in the opposite direction. Finally at the top of the mountain, I take a seat overlooking Flagstaff Lake, in the same spot where Dad took that picture all those years ago. I put some water in a bowl for Maple and we just relax. I really allow myself to feel the loss of Dad and what it means for my life.

I do this every year on Dad's birthday, when I'm home. In some past years, when I wasn't home, I would still meditate on Dad's birthday, just thinking about him. The years I am home and do these Bigelow hikes, Mom doesn't join me, as she was never *really* into the whole hiking thing. She did all of that to win over my dad and keep him happy. She would have done anything for him. I'm sure he would have done anything for her.

After Dad died, Mom was a wreck for an entire year. Like, she would never leave her bedroom. Grandma and Grandpa—my mom's folks—came and stayed with us the whole time. They were the ones that kept the wheels on at the house, made sure I went to school, did all my afterschool activities, and what not.

To this day, it's easy to see remnants of the depression still there in Mom, but to her credit, she's done a great job at getting back on track and moving on (though, of course, she'll never completely move on, as evidenced by the dozens of pictures of Dad still framed throughout the house and her utter refusal to even entertain the thought of dating again).

Now, thanks to some of these recent yearly meditations, I now believe Dad's absence is part of the reason why I was such a little shit in middle school and high school. You see, I *ran with the wrong crowd*, so to speak, even though that crowd is still the crew I hang out with to this day, and even though some might say I was the cause of my crew acting the way we did.

Back in high school, kinda with me at the lead, we were assholes. We were the stoners, the ones who'd show up high to *any* event, show up late to class, high, of course, or we'd skip it altogether. We found enjoyment in being blatantly disrespectful to authority figures, and we were, I'm ashamed to admit and reflect upon now, quite frankly *mean* to some of the other kids in class. Before high school, in middle school, we'd make fun of people ruthlessly, based on the clothes they wore, how they styled their hair, any potential insecurities they may have about their body, whether it was the excessive number of moles Colin T had, the way Britney R's nose really hung off her face, Rebecca P's acne, John S's general fatness, and you get the picture. Fucking *assholes*. Only once was I on the receiving end of a barrage of insults, when my mom made me go to a summer camp near my grandparents in Connecticut the summer after eighth grade. And my goodness, getting ridiculed day after day for two weeks straight about being a country bumpkin from Maine while a roomful of spoiled rich kids laugh at you, yeah, that absolutely *sucks*. At this camp, I would hide in the bathroom during dinner to avoid having to eat with the other campers. After experiencing that, I swore I'd change my ways, at least with regards to how I treated others. Being on the receiving end of that type of bullying was enough for me to never want to inflict that pain on anyone ever again. So although my crew continued ridiculing others in high school, I stopped. And now, in retrospect, even that. I should have done more. I should have spoken up and made my friends stop as well. But, whatever. I didn't. Can't change the past.

Anyways, to really illuminate how immature I was back in the day, the way me and the crew ran, I used to think the amount of weed I smoked (that is, *a lot*) and the amount of other drugs and alcohol I consumed made me proportionally cooler, so by the time I was a freshman at UMaine, I could smoke an entire blunt by myself and drink enough vodka to keep up with any of the guys. (Even though I couldn't. But still, I'd try. And it'd usually result in me being dangerously blackout drunk.) All the while, I'd act like this, thinking I was the shit, in a *cool look at me* kind of way. And beyond all that, truly abandoning the memory of my dad and what he tried to teach me, on weekends, I'd arrange for a crew to go out in the middle of the woods with a few cases of beer, get absolutely hammered, and then we'd *leave* all the trash out there. Cans and junk food bags and laminated cardboard scattered on the forest floor like so many ashes of our uncontained fire. *Not our problem*, we would have thought leaving it all there, if we were thoughtful at all, which, obviously, we weren't even *that* thoughtful.

At the time, I never stopped to think how disappointed Dad would have been in me if he could see what I was up to.

THE BUGS

I cringe so hard now at the memory of how I acted.

But yeah, I get it, all that behavior can be shrugged off as adolescent foolishness that eventually gets better with the passage of time. But I refuse to think it was all just adolescent foolishness, due to the fact that to this day, I'll still catch Darren flicking a cigarette butt out the window when we're in the car, no matter how many times I tell him not to; or I'll have to hear Colby and Andrew joke about some out-of-towner on the mountain and the ski suit they're wearing; or whatever. I don't know. I guess I feel like my badness went deeper than all that negative stuff. Almost like in a misery-loves-company sorta way. Like I'd actually find this perverse satisfaction whenever I elevated myself at someone else's expense. While doing it, I never thought of how my actions *really* affected others. And I damn sure never actively tried to *not* hurt someone, let alone think of ways I could potentially help others whenever I interacted with them.

Anyways, somehow, almost miraculously, I was able to maintain a B- average in high school and still get into UMaine. Of course, going to college is what Mom definitely wanted, and she says it's what Dad would've wanted as well (which I'm still not sure I buy).

At UMaine, I kept up my delinquent ways my first two years. Even though I stopped making fun of people, which I thought was heroic, I still trashed every place I went, and I showed general contempt for my fellow human.

It's at the start of my junior year I did a complete 180 on what a garbage human I was.

Because I'm meditating atop Bigelow Mountain right now looking at Flagstaff Lake and I feel ultra-truth-telly, I'm happy to share what prompted my ultimate spiritual enlightenment. And that method, which I'm *definitely* not saying is for everyone, is

127

one day I took a whole bunch of mushrooms. Like, I mean *a lot*. More than I've ever taken.

I was in neon-lighted room with four of my friends and two strangers one of my friends invited. What followed was simultaneously the scariest and most rewarding experience of my life.

Scary because I really got out in another dimension, one I felt was totally real and accessible, one that was showing me every single solitary way I've been being such a bad person. It opened the curtain and wholly revealed *me* to me. And since I was such a negative person at the time, what was behind the curtain was scary. I didn't consciously *want* to hurt others; I didn't *want* to be a bad person. Who does? But the further into this dimension I went, the further I understood how I was doing pretty much *everyone* in my life wrong, myself included. This dimension transcended time and hurled me into my past, brought me back to my present, then showed me what a future looked like if I kept on the road I was walking. A future filled with empty hollow meaninglessness. Seeking pleasure and fulfillment in all the wrong places.

But *then*, the whole experience was rewarding because it let me know that road is not one I *had* to walk down. In this other dimension, I was given the option to be the effective antithesis to the bad person I've been. Like, the simple concept of how the clothing someone wears has absolutely no bearing on *my* happiness, unless I let it (for better or for worse), and only shitheads judge other people for wearing different clothing, and I should let everyone do what makes them happy without judging them, as long as what makes them happy isn't harmful to others; and how unbelievably *cruel* it is to make fun of someone's physical appearance; how making others needlessly feel bad hurts one's own soul; and what not. I realized I had done all these things because I was angry at the world for taking away my dad. And I then took that anger out on others. My mind in this other dimension was telling itself I did all this for a simple reason: Because it's easier to be angry than it is to let yourself be sad. To really *feel* sad and process that sadness.

Sitting in that neon room, as the mushrooms were showing me the way, my entire past opened up and linked together as if it were a spider web with my essence at the hole in the center. I thought of my dad. I thought of Leave No Trace. I thought of how I behaved all those times in the woods and the countless pieces of litter I left to either be picked up by someone else, or to be left there to forever alter the makeup of the natural world. Tripping on mushrooms, conjuring the memory of my dad, in a random room with four friends and two strangers, I burst out crying.

Everyone asked if I was alright and in response, I excused myself and ran to the bathroom. I locked myself in there, ignored my friends asking if I was okay through the door, and kept crying. Sobbing. Wailing, really. Tears of sadness and pain and growth and unbridled catharsis.

I told my dad—who at the time I fully understood to be up in heaven, but not the Christian form of heaven, more of a new dimensionality of heaven where his spirit and being lives on through me and anyone who remembers him—I told him I was sorry for everything and I'd change and fully live within his mantra to Leave No Trace, to be a good steward of life, to leave the world in a better place than I found it, because *he* definitely did.

I don't know. Since then, after reading more and more about aspects of The Self, it seems like I just had one big ego-collapse in that psilocybin-induced experience. Which allowed me to really understand I'm one small part of the vastly complex system known as Humanity, which is one small (okay, maybe big) part of the vastly complex system known as Life On Earth, and that no matter how small my part is, I *do* have an impact on the whole thing, so I might as well make it a positive one.

This is what's on my mind, now that I'm on top of Bigelow Mountain, sitting next to my pup Maple. That I'd like to make the world a better place.

And with that thought, considering where I'm at, given where I've been, I think Dad would be proud of me.

Of doing something with my education, with my mind, with my skills.

And oh yeah. I forgot to say.

My business finally has a name, now. *Upwards Momentum Marketing*, or UMM for short. Our tagline is: *Kindness and stewardship foster our vision of reasonable and sustainable work.* And yeah, I know that doesn't say what we do *at all*, but whatever. I'm happy to report the business is definitely trending in the right direction.

At the start of my project with Yessir Brewing, I took a night trip down to Portland for a tasting event they were hosting. A few rounds in, the owners of Yessir introduced me to their pals over at *Homegrown Clothes*, a soon-to-be-operating local company that's using the same indoor farming technology, coupled with a few hundred acres for summertime crops, to cultivate hemp year-round in Milan, Maine. They designed and built a processing system that efficiently turns raw hemp into soft and durable clothing material, of several varieties. The first crop is being harvested right about now, so they're just getting off the ground.

Now, I haven't mentioned yet I have a penchant for growing crops in the same family as hemp in my neck of the woods. But I do. This penchant allowed me to hit it off with the owners of Homegrown Clothes right away.

So yeah, they're my third client, and I think I'm close to landing yet another Portland company—*Lobstah Gals*—who were also at the Yessir tasting event.

You know, it's funny. I initially started an online business because I wanted to leverage my ability to work with any company located anywhere in the world. And to start, my first clients are *all* from Maine.

As all this runs through my head at the top of Bigelow, in relatively calm conditions, a bee has shown up and is flying about eighteen inches in front of my face, almost like it's analyzing me, just hovering there, occasionally darting a few inches up and down or side to side. This triggers me to recollect that high idea I had not too long ago about the spiders and their webs. Looking right at the bee, I say out loud, "Hey bee. What's going on? You trying to tell me something?"

As if in response, this bee seems to fly up and down and up and down a few inches, almost like it's nodding. And then it just flies off.

Huh, I think. *Weird.*

CHAPTER 21

In Hive0A1347KR, Queen Bean was receiving reports on her hive's Coordinated Upgrade, Joelle Velstar.

"Queen," one of her worker Bees was saying, "the combined increases in desired virtues have yielded positive results. While getting new clients, Joelle has set up a tidy home office space and, as an improvement for her, papers are not scattered everywhere. She keeps the top of her desk mostly clean, but her drawers and filing system needs improvement. Regardless, she is getting a lot more work done with each day."

"Good," Queen Bean said. "Good. The Bosses have allotted more room with our upgrades, so let's up the increases in organizational skills by 1.5%." Queen Bean knew all too well what over-eager Coordinated Upgrades did back in the days of Atlantis, so they were extra cautious with upgrades these days, hence the meager 1.5% increase for Joelle.

"Done," responded all her worker Bees out in the field. The worker Bees then let all the spiders know. This happened almost instantaneously.

"Now, about her character, her demeanor, her attitude. How is she doing?" Of course, Queen Bean could access all of this information herself. However, she found involving her worker Bees to be a worthwhile affair.

A different most trusted worker Bee answered with data collected from the flies. "Quite well, Queen. Objective levels of happiness expressed by her *and* all the people that interact with her have seen a significant improvement. To wit, she is making others *smile more*, causing her to smile more, which has created a positive feedback loop of smiles, and on and on the cycle continues."

"Wonderful!" said Queen Bean. "It seems we have indeed chosen well. Smiles abound are good. Let's continue increasing our desired virtues as long as these positive trends continue."

"Done," her worker Bees droned in unison.

Then Queen Bean had to re-ask. "And just to be sure: I *believe* she's passed the basic morality tests. Has she made the requisite improvements after that quick dosage?"

"Would you like a replay of one of our tests, Queen?"

"Surely," said Queen Bean. "That would be lovely."

As easily as a human can turn on and watch a TV, Queen Bean's mind flashed to a recording a fly had uploaded to the worldwide spiderweb.

Joelle was in the car with her friends, Colby and Darren. They were driving to Farmington to see a movie. Joelle was sitting shotgun. Per Queen Bean's orders, in the car were three greenhead flies and a hornet, waiting under a seat for them to be mid-drive. Once Joelle and her friends were good and settled, the flies and the hornet were to cause a ruckus and pester all three humans.

"Ah! What the fuck!" yelled Colby once the flies and hornet started flying about. "Kill them! Kill them!"

From the back seat, Darren took off his shoe and started swatting at them indiscriminately.

"Holy shit guys," said Joelle. "Calm down. Why are you trying to kill them? Just open the windows."

But at first, opening the windows didn't work. The greenheads kept buzzing about and the hornet landed softly on Joelle's exposed knee. Seeing this from the driver seat, Colby yelled, "Kill it! Kill it!" But Joelle didn't listen.

Though she could have easily killed the hornet on her knee, she instead lowered her hand gently toward it, emanating an *I come in peace* kind of vibe. In response, the hornet crawled from her knee onto the tip of her middle finger. Joelle then brought her hand to the open window and the hornet flew off into the wild.

The three greenhead flies remained though, and were still causing a ruckus. One bit Darren in the backseat on his neck. "Ah! What the fucking shit!" Darren yelled as he slapped at his own neck. "Fucking, greenheads!"

Two of the greenheads landed in unison on the dash in front of Joelle. Again, Colby yelled, "Get them! Kill them!"

But rather than swat at them, Joelle calmly said, "Flies, get the fuck outta here. This is a human space. Window's open. On your way." And just like that, the flies flew out of the window.

"Holy shit," Colby said. "You really are queen of the bugs."

And as quick as that scene flashed before Queen Bean's mind, it flashed away, leaving her to communicate with her worker Bees in their special Bee dimension. "Okay," said Queen Bean, "wonderful. Still, though, keep a close watch on her empathy levels. I'd like to confirm she's properly concerned with her fellow *human's* wellbeing..." Queen Bean trailed off, thinking once more of becoming *the* Queen during this batch of humans to initiate Sequence Two.

"To that end," reported one of Queen Bean's worker Bees, filling in the conversational gap she left by trailing off, "some flies took note of several interactions Joelle had in Portland. As she was walking downtown from her hotel to the Yessir Brewing tasting party, she encountered several homeless people. With each one, she stopped and engaged, asked if she could buy them some food or something. She apologized for not having any cash she could give them. One took her up on the offer, and she accompanied him to a convenience store to buy him something to eat. Then, later that evening, she was walking the same streets with one of Yessir's owners, and when she acknowledged another homeless person's presence, the owner of Yessir asked her what she was doing. He said don't give them money, as they will only spend it on drugs and alcohol; and there are city services they could be using if they really wanted help. Joelle, taken aback by this approach, questioned her client. She ended by saying she couldn't help it. Her heart can't help but break every time she passes a homeless person. Like it's a failure of society's doing, of which she's partly responsible. She said there's something seriously wrong with a system that allows such pervasive homelessness in the second richest country on Earth. Her client said it is what it is. To which Joelle replied: What it is, is a real shame."

"Oh," said Queen Bean. "Good report. Thank you. Beyond her empathetic tendencies and overall character, are there any oddities I should be aware of?"

"There are, Queen," a high-ranking worker Bee said, well, buzzed, across that dimension humans had yet to reach. "Earlier today, at the top of Bigelow Mountain, I flew right up to her and hovered for a quick analysis. While hovering, she acknowledged my presence, and, Queen, she *spoke* to me. This is the second such interaction she has had with a bug, following her inquisition of the two flies at her last poker night."

Receiving this news, Queen Bean's energy levels peaked. "Honey, this is *significant* news! Why didn't you tell me this sooner!?"

"Respectfully, you never made us aware of the significance, Queen."

"Oh, right," said Queen Bean, recalling she hadn't relayed *all* the pertinent information to her workers. "Well, this could be big! Tell me: *Was she high?*"

"No, Queen. Not at all."

"Oh. My. *God*." said Queen Bean. "Honey, Sequence Two is *possibly* on the table. Tomorrow, during her morning ride, send her a little message. She has one final test she must pass."

CHAPTER 22

I am a Tree.

Once again, a different Tree than the ones you have already heard from.

According to the humans, my name is Methuselah.

They think I am the oldest Tree alive.

They are wrong.

I will not disclose the whereabouts nor identity of our oldest kin; I would not inflict that fame upon them.

I am here to share something else.

And that is a conversation I recently had.

With a queen bee.

Speaking down one dimensional level, so the bee could communicate with me, I said:

Come on. Why are you discussing Sequence Two again?

Because we think it may be time, the queen bee said.

That's what you said last time with Batch Number 8. Atlantis, I said.

But this time is different, she said.

That's what you said during Atlantis, when talking about Batch Number 7. Pangea, I said.

And it was different then, too! We learn more each time, said the queen.

Sequence Two resulted in Pangea splitting, I said.

But that resulted in more biodiversity! said the queen bee.

Yes, but you did not anticipate that, I said.

Besides, I said, with Atlantis. They were moments from their energy source blowing up the planet.

And we stopped that from happening, said the bee.

Now what about this time? I said. What is it this time you are not anticipating? Given this batch's technology, could they not be swifter in their destruction of Earth? What do you bees foretell will happen?

We have enough knowledge to know we could not possibly foretell that, said the queen. It is our understanding there is a statistical probability that, should a human from this batch meet all eight billion of our new prerequisites for Sequence Two, we will be successful in triggering humanity's Ascension.

And, I said, what is the possibility it could all end horrifically? Of them destroying that which you bees were sworn to protect? Is that a possibility at all?

Yes, said the queen, somberly. There is that possibility. But it is low, according to our projections.

But still greater than zero, I said. Greater than with Batch Number 7 and Batch Number 8?

Yes, said the queen bee.

Then, I said. Still.

What would you have us do this time? said the queen.

I would have you wait. I would ask you exercise patience.

It's already been over a million years, she said. How long would you have us wait?

A million more. Until it is undeniably dire and there is no other option.

You've listened in on The Bosses, said the queen bee. You heard the reports. You know the data we're working with. You understand if we do nothing, these humans might irrevocably poison Earth. Or ruin its ability to support complex life. You know we can't let that happen.

The data you have does not predict the future. These humans are supremely imaginative. They may solve these problems on their own. Why are you bees rushing things, again?

When I the Tree asked this, the queen bee stayed silent a good while.

Then she said, We are acting in what we believe is the best interest of Earth, of all species on Earth, you Trees included.

Power. Even you bees are susceptible to its corruptions. We Trees feel you are being too hasty.

We Bees appreciate the Trees' opinion.

But you will proceed anyway, I said.

That we will, said the queen bee.

Although it will anger us Trees…

It is not within our control whether you Trees are angered.

Oh, but it is, I said.

All the same, the queen said.

You are right, I said. All the same. We Trees cannot stop you.

CJ FRIEDMAN

And we are not angry, I said.
We are just disappointed.

CHAPTER 23

Clearly, the ants could not have been more direct and specific with Jack Telda.

Therefore, that very day Jack received the clear message in his office, after sobering up a bit, he called his counterparts in Brazil and told them the deal was off the table. Then Jack took a sabbatical from Food First Service. Since Roger Cassar was nowhere to be found and no one yet knew he had truly disappeared, and since Jack didn't want to let everyone know bugs had murdered him, Jack didn't really have any another direct higher up to answer to. So, he told his assistant and one of his direct reports in the pit and an HR manager he was taking a leave of absence. His assistant and his report in the pit asked what they should do, and he told them to figure it out. Before leaving, though, Jack did add, vaguely, "Whatever you do, *preserve nature.*"

From there, to justify moving out of the city, Jack told Amy FFS had said he was working *too hard* and he *needed* to take some time to get away and recharge his batteries. He suggested they move out of the city and get a place in the Poconos for the fall. It'd be a good opportunity for them to reconnect as a family. Amy half-heartedly believed him and whole-heartedly wanted it to be true.

And with that, the Teldas moved to the Poconos.

CHAPTER 24

Okay, once again Maple and I are out for our morning ride. And once again, as always, there are spider strands hanging across the trail.

Though today, they're a lot larger than normal. Almost as if...

For Joelle's morning ride, to monitor the effectiveness of Queen Bean's direct message in real time, flies were constantly swarming the side of the trail Joelle normally rode and were hurling themselves into spiderwebs with each movement she took.

In the safety of her hive, Queen Bean reveled in the news coming in:

Joelle has gotten off her bike. She has noticed the increased size of the strands hanging across the trail. She is walking up to one now, getting closer... Closer... Now!

Okay, what. The. Fuck.

I *knew* something was up with the strands today, and I gotta be honest, it's taking everything I've got to not completely lose my shit right now. I knew I needed to inspect these things, but I never expected *this*.

After walking up to one of these monster strands, with my face about three inches from it, I can confidently say this is no ordinary spider web strand. It's actually *two*, hanging in parallel, with freaking *cursive writing* formed by a third strand between the two. And I kid you not, the cursive writing, hanging across the trail, says:

Hello Joelle. Hello Joelle. Hello Joelle. Hello Joelle.

Over and over and over until it exhausts the space across the trail. Then, seeing another strand of the same size up ahead, I duck under the one saying *Hello Joelle* to go see what the next one has to say. It, too, says, *Hello Joelle, Hello Joelle*, over and over again. But, at the end of this one, it says:

Whatever you do, Joelle, do not share this online. Do not share this with anyone. We are watching.

Okay, WHO is watching!?

And I swear to God, I'm not even high this morning.

So either I've completely lost it and I need to go to a mental hospital, or, Maple as my witness, the spiders are *talking to me*.

For posterity's sake, for my sanity's sake, I whip out my phone and take a picture of the strand, even though these freakin' spiders are instructing me not to share it.

As I stare in wonder at the photo I captured, then back again at the real-life strand before me, that high idea comes back to me and I think then say out loud, "I knew it! You ARE upgrading me! Holy shit!"

Then I say, "Wait. Are you? Am I losing my mind? WHO'S WATCHING ME!?"

Queen Bean buzzed in elation at the reports as they traveled interdimensionally to her hive:

Confirmation received, Queen Bean. Joelle has acknowledged us bugs. She has gleaned our presence, our communication, and has accurately hypothesized our actions.

Queen Bean knew she had to connect with her sister Queen Bruth. She suspected, and now needed additional validation from a Boss, that Joelle Velstar had met the prerequisites for the initiation of Sequence Two.

Getting the confirmation in less than a moment's time, Queen Bean relayed another message for Joelle to some ants in the field.

Okay, shit is getting real. And weird. It's getting *real weird*. Right in front of me, a freaking parade of ants is marching onto the trail. And it looks like they're spelling something out for me. So, yeah, I guess this is my life now. Waiting for ants to form whatever message it is they're forming.

Wait.

Holy shit.

Maybe I *am* queen of the bugs.

My heart is pounding because this is just so fucking *out there*, but still, given the fact spiders are talking to me through their webs and now ants are moving with a clear purpose, I am patient enough to let these ants finish their message. I'm reading as they go. Once they're done, this is what the message says:

Hello Joelle. This is Queen Bean, a local Queen Bee in your neck of the woods, talking to you via these ants. To answer your question, all us bugs are watching you. But most importantly, I have been watching you. And I am pleased to say you are indeed correct about the spiders. We – meaning the spiders, via my direct orders – have been upgrading you. And now it is time for you and I to meet. We need you to go back home and await further instruction. And just to reiterate what the spiders said, do not share any of this with anyone. K?

Okay, like, what. The. Fuck.

No way this is my life right now.

No way this is even real. It can't be.

But, you know, maybe it is?

And if it is, what do I even say to that?

Do I just go home? Listen to some all-knowing queen bee that has been apparently monitoring my life...

I mean...

I guess?

"Alright Maple," I say, after giving it a few more moments of thought. "Uh, I don't know what the hell is happening, but that is some weird shit right there. Let's go home and see what's going on."

CHAPTER 25

"Queen, I cannot begin to tell you how unbelievably proud I am of you!" Queen Bruth said. "You did it! I only wonder, though. You know, given your reclusiveness up there in Maine, I have to ask. Are you ready?"

Queen Bean considered it a moment. She had been allowing herself the grand dreams of being *this* Queen, the one to choose the right human to initiate Sequence Two, but now, given the looming task at hand, she hesitated. There was about to be a *big* spotlight drawn on her from Queens around the world, notably The Bosses. She had never met all the bosses and now she would be required to attend their meetings. Though she always had the ability to communicate with *any* Bee alive, Queen Bean, like most Bees for that matter, primarily chose to communicate and engage with only those Bees she knew well, from a personal perspective; with those that reinforced her self-image and self-esteem and all that. "You know," she said, "I don't know. I guess I have no choice though, right? I guess I *have* to be ready."

You better be, Queen Bruth thought, which Queen Bean registered, which Queen Bruth could sense she registered.

Queen Bruth continued thinking her thoughts so her sister could choose whether or not to absorb them: *You are about to bring a human's mind to the edge of the fifth dimension. She will not know what's going on. And you're going to have to explain to her how she is now responsible for the fate of her fellow humans. That she may never see her friends or family again if things go wrong. She may never see her friends or family again if things go right. You have to prepare her for all eventualities.*

"Ah! Stop freaking me out!" said Queen Bean. "I know. I know it's a lot. But you Bosses have tweaked the eight billion prerequisites since last time. I wouldn't be helping her elevate humanity to the fifth dimension if she weren't ready for it, right?"

"I mean," said Queen Bruth, now outright speaking her thoughts interdimensionally rather than thinking them for her sister, "that's what we're hoping. The prerequisites are much more robust than the last two times, but as you know, we do not have full predictive power. We will have to wait and see. And furthermore, it will also depend on how well *you* do."

Now, jealousy and envy are two diseases that don't exist within the Bee queendom. All Bees are programmed to understand the fundamental nature of reality, that they are all in it together, and as such, there are common goals they all share. In the long view, it does not matter *who* is responsible for moving things upwards and onwards, only that things *do* move in that direction. Whenever a goal is attained by one, it is attained by all, and therefore, is treated as a moment to celebrate. So, with this programming, Queen Bruth was indeed celebrating her sister, and Queen Bean could *feel* this celebration. But at the same time, Queen Bean was detecting a tinge of—*something*—radiating from Queen Bruth that she had not felt before. Feeling emboldened by her new status, Queen Bean decided to address her query head on. "Hey," she said, "what is that? What is that you're feeling?"

"Oh," Queen Bruth said. "That. You really want to know?"

148

"Yeah," said Queen Bean. "It's probably best I have all the information before I embark on this mission."

"Fair enough. Well, what you're sensing is my trepidation. You're just so sweet and loving and kind and local and… and… I guess, *basic*. These global matters don't normally concern you. And now you're tasked with overseeing whether or not a singular human raises the consciousness for the rest of her kind. My trepidation stems from the fact that I don't know how well you're going to fare."

Though these words somewhat hurt Queen Bean, she knew they were justified. "Fair enough," she said. "I don't know how I'm going to fare either. But all the same, I'm going to give it my best shot. And hope for the best. That's all I can do."

"I suppose that is true," said Queen Bruth. "Besides, the moment's here. I have received word this very second The Bosses have conferred and confirmed the result. Are you ready for your first Meeting?"

"Let's do it," said Queen Bean.

Given the news, there was an emergency Meeting Of The Bosses, which Queen Bean was now able to join. Entering this special interdimensional sacred chamber, she was astounded she was actually attending one of these meetings.

Due to it being an emergency meeting, unlike normal ones, The Bosses did not provide their undivided attention to the topic at hand. Many of The Bosses were engaging in the emergency meeting while simultaneously conducting business around their hives scattered across the world. As Queen Bean reported her findings on each and every one of the eight billion prerequisites Joelle Velstar had met, Queen Bosses were also busy discussing the daily movements of some politicians they'd been following, processing whether or not they were truly Fence Players. In all but one of these cases, even with some colleagues of the politicians in question removed, the politicians continued with their misdeeds, misrepresenting their constituents in order to advance their own personal gains via approval for projects that promoted environmental negligence. So the Bosses made plans to Directly Eliminate them. Other Bosses were looking into the key players responsible for the advancement of weaponized AI systems; others responsible for the development of deforestation projects in Germany and Brazil and elsewhere; the ongoing efforts of coordinatedly upgraded activists to protect natural land in Alaska; the rise in timber markets thanks to newly instituted plastic bans; likewise the intensified production and lobbying of the plastics industry and the massive amounts of garbage it created; destructive commercial fishing practices; the selling of protected lands for rare Earth material extraction; the destruction of the Yucatan jungle to accommodate growing tourism, not to mention other jungles around the world being decimated for the same purpose; the destruction of Floridian wetlands for cookie cutter condos; and so on. The areas of concern were seemingly endless these days.

Despite the fact all these conversations were happening at once, the Queen Bee Bosses were still fully engaged and elated to hear the reports from their sister Queen Bean. And not one of them objected to initiating Sequence Two, having found the data verifiably good.

Thus, they pooled their collective energetic resources, which required a considerable amount of energy, and began plans to start the sequence.

From across the planet, through a dimension soon to be accessed by one specific human, The Bosses prompted all Queen

Bees to send Hive0A1347KR, Queen Bean's hive, their complete reserves of Thoughts & Prayers. These Ts&Ps were to be focused, of course, on the Sequence at hand.

Within a matter of moments, Hive0A1347KR was full to the brim with energy stores, enabling Queen Bean to encode the proper message and send it to the right spider.

That spider, the one nearest Joelle, received the message and immediately synthesized the data.

And in the following moment, Joelle didn't know what bit her.

Joelle was sitting on her couch in her living room, searching online for examples of spider webs that spelled out personalized messages. She did this while awaiting the further instruction Queen Bean had promised. The only thing she could find online was the story *Charlotte's Web*. She was still reeling from what had happened and had biked straight home after seeing what she saw, wondering all the while what a Queen Bee might want with her. Fortunately, Joelle heeded the words from the strands and the ants and did not share the picture she took with anyone. She instead went to find validation, hoping there might be someone else who shared another instance of this wild occurrence.

While she continued her search with Maple snuggled at her side, an itsy-bitsy spider crawled onto her back. The spider nipped the back of Joelle's neck right above her lowest cervical bone. In that instant, Joelle's consciousness flashed into an existence of black nothingness.

Sequence Two had been initiated.

PART TWO

PART TWO

CHAPTER 26

Okay, I was just sitting on my couch trying to find other examples of spider webs spelling out messages for people when I felt a little pinch on the bone that sticks out where the neck meets the spine. Next thing I knew, I was thrust into an empty plane of black nothingness. There're no discernable dimensions here, I have no body in this empty space, there's no *physical* feeling, but I'm fully conscious.

Once the spider armed with the collective Queen Bees' Thoughts & Prayers bit Joelle's C7 bone, Joelle's eyes rolled in her head and she fell backwards onto the couch.

As Joelle's mind went into the blank emptiness, Maple pup got up from her perch next to Joelle on the couch. She placed her front paws on Joelle's chest and whimpered a bit. Maple pawed at her human mom and whimpered some more. She barked. Once, twice, then after a brief pause, a third time. Maple then let out a final whimper before scampering off Joelle's chest, off the couch, toward the door. Demonstrating an uncanny intelligence,

CJ FRIEDMAN

she then finagled the handle to the front door to let herself out. Since Joelle's mom was already at work, knowing where each of Joelle's friends lived, Maple bolted to the one who lived closest, Sarah Lockwood.

Once outside Sarah's door, Maple started barking and barking and barking, as loud as she possibly could. "HELP! HELP! SOMETHING'S WRONG WITH MOM! HELP!" she was saying.

Thankfully Sarah was home and heard the relentless barking. "Hey Maple," she said after opening the door. "What're you doing here? Where's Joelle?"

"RUFF! RUFF!" Maple said. She then turned and ran down Sarah's walkway and stopped at the end. Once she stopped, she turned, as if waiting for Sarah to follow, and barked three more times, in her mind saying, "Mom's in danger! Something's wrong! Follow me! Follow me! Help! Help!"

Sarah stood outside her door, simultaneously unsure but also extremely sure of what was happening. "What's up, Maple?" she said. "What's going on? Is Joelle okay?"

Maple sprinted back up Sarah's walkway, tugged at the bottom of Sarah's shirt, whimpered, barked, and then ran off and stopped at the end of the walkway again. She paused there to look back and confirm Sarah was indeed following.

"Alright," Sarah said, "lemme get my shoes."

Maple then led Sarah straight to Joelle's comatose body.

While Joelle's physical body was being rushed to the hospital, her mind continued to exist in a new-to-her dimension.

THE BUGS

Okay, this is really odd. It's like this: Close your eyes. Take what you see when your eyes are closed, and now remove *all* physical sensation – all noise, touch, smells, the feeling of your body inside and out, *everything*. It's not even like floating, since I don't have a body here to *feel* like I'm floating. It's as if my mind is all here, but the whole of existence around my mind has vanished. Naturally, I have to wonder: *Am I dead?*

And out of nowhere, as if in response to my specific thought, which I *definitely* didn't say out loud, considering I have no body therefore no vocal cords here, a chipper voice answers. "Hello Joelle Velstar! No, no honey. You are not dead."

Now, I can't see anyone talking, but I can hear this voice perfectly well. It's a voice wholly different from any internal voice I've ever known. The voice is light, airy, and resonates as if everything is going to be alright. *Who are you?* I think, since I have no mouth or body to speak. *Where am I? What's going on?* I'm honestly too overwhelmed by this existence of nothingness to think straight.

"One question at a time, please," the voice from nowhere says. "I will only answer if you ask one specific question at a time."

So I think about it a moment. As I think, my mind recalls the last experiences in my body. Being on the trail. Receiving a message from the spiders in their webs and from the ants about them upgrading me. About how I was to go home and wait for a Queen Bee to present herself to me. "Wait," I say, "are you Queen Bean?"

"Good, Joelle! Yes! I am Queen Bean." And she leaves it at that.

"Okayyyyy," I say, well, think, since apparently this voice, Queen Bean, can hear my thoughts. "If I'm not dead... This doesn't really *feel* like a dream... It feels a bit more real... Like I'm totally lucid, in a way I've never been in a dream... So... Where am I?"

"You, Joelle, have qualified to enter a higher dimension. One previously unavailable to your human kin. But before we grant you *full* access to the higher dimension, you are here, in a waiting room, to steal a phrase from your kind, *for* that dimension. You're here now for an orientation of sorts. To learn what awaits you once you have full access, to learn what you must do."

What. The. Hell. I think.

"Assuredly *not* Hell," Queen Bean responds. "In fact, hopefully, quite the opposite."

"What do you mean by that?" I say, inside my mind. "You mean I'm in heaven? I thought I wasn't dead. Where *are* we? An orientation? What must I do!?"

"As I said, please, one question at a time. I can surely answer more than one question in an instant, but *your* brain is only able to truly process one answer at a time. Therefore, to accommodate your capabilities, I will not answer two, let alone five, questions at once. *Focus*, Joelle."

"Okay," I say, taking another few moments to think over where I want to steer this conversation. "You said hopefully the opposite of hell. Does that mean I'm in heaven? I thought you said I wasn't dead."

"No, you are certainly *not* dead. I just meant we hope to *create* a type of heaven. But that is something I will get to, in due time."

"Okay..." I say, not really digging all the vagueness. "And again, I know you're *Queen Bean*, but, like, who are you, really?"

"As I had the ants tell you earlier," Queen Bean says, "I am a local Queen Bee in your neck of the woods. I am the one who prompted your Ascension."

"Oh. Got it," I say, like that's a totally normal thing. "Ascension. Queen Bee. Messenger ants. *Obviously.*" I pause again to gather my thoughts. I have so many questions I want to ask. Like what does Ascension mean, how have the spiders been upgrading me, *why* have they been upgrading me, and what not. I guess going step by step, I start with, "So, Queen Bean, are you, like, a God among bees or something?"

"Honey, that is ripe!" says Queen Bean. "No, no. I am a normal everyday Queen Bee. I simply have had the great fortune to be the one who oversaw *your* development. And I may be getting ahead of myself here, but I will be the one accompanying you as we set out to elevate humanity's collective consciousness."

"Oh," I say. "Elevate humanity's collective consciousness. Of course. I mean, I guess that solves it."

"Solves what?" says Queen Bean before I can finish my thought.

"Oh, nothing. Just that I've completely lost my mind."

"Honey, honey. I apologize. Like I said, I may have got ahead of myself. This is all new for me as well. Now, you haven't lost your mind. On the contrary, your mind is quite special. So special, in fact, you have prompted us to start Sequence Two."

Queen Bean says this as if I know who *us* is and what *Sequence Two* is, which, of course, I don't.

Since apparently my feeble mind can't handle more than one question at a time, I decide to lead with a more open-ended question. "Okay..." I say, drawing it out. "Would you care to elaborate on that?"

"Surely!" says Queen Bean, all bright and happy like. "The *us* you're wondering about is all the Queen Bees across the world. We are responsible for all the bugs on Earth, who in turn are responsible for monitoring humanity and the health of the planet. You know, to make sure you humans don't destroy the liveliness of Earth. Now, with regards to Ascension and Sequence Two. You can think about it like this: While you humans operate primarily in your three-dimensional space alongside your fourth dimension of time, we Bees operate in all those dimensions, sure, but we also operate a few dimensions higher, both in the fifth dimension and sixth dimension. You, Joelle, have met the roughly eight billion prerequisites for us Queen Bees to initiate Sequence Two, which is why you are here, talking with me now."

"Got it," I said, not really getting it. "And what exactly is *Sequence Two*?"

"Sequence Two is the process by which we Bees sequentially Ascend *all* of humanity to, ultimately, the sixth dimension. But in order to do that, we need one singular human, *you*, to craft the right variables by which that will be possible. Once we are done talking here and you are oriented to the task at hand, you will be charged with testing new modalities for humanity. To get it right for everyone else. We will be conducting those tests in the fifth dimension, where we've set up the proper simulation and what not."

"Uh," I say. And that's all I'm able to say. I'm basically rendered speechless. I mean, that's a lot to process and I'm not sure where to begin.

Perhaps sensing how overwhelmed I am, Queen Bean continues. "Oh honey," she says. "Don't you worry. I will be with you every step of the way." As she says this, I feel somewhat relieved by her tone, though not any less confused. "It's like this," she says. "Once we are done talking here, we are going to place your mind in a simulation. Now, are you familiar with the game, SimCity?"

"Uh, yeah."

"Good. Well, think of the next steps like *that*. SimCity is a digital simulation in which you are able to determine the planning and construction of a city. The next step you are about to embark upon is somewhat similar. We Bees, within the fifth dimension, have built a simulation, of sorts, which your mind is going to enter. In this simulation, you will be a first-person player in a game that, to you, will be the exact same thing as life itself. The only difference is you will have the added sensory perception that we Bees possess within the *sixth* dimension. If, at any point, you want to exit the simulation and return to the safety of *this* part of the fifth dimension, this empty void where we're talking now, all you have to do is find a Bee and get stung by it."

"Oh," I say. "So this is kinda like a Morpheus and Neo moment. Cool."

"Exactly! You are Neo. I am Morpheus. Good," says Queen Bean.

"Gotcha," I say. "So, in this simulation, what am I supposed to *do*, exactly?"

"Oh, right," says Queen Bean, as if this mundane bit of information casually slipped her mind. "I will be in your ear, so to speak, the whole time, communicating with you, letting you know how things are going. Once we begin, you will be tasked with creating new rules for humanity. New guidelines and parameters that will ensure it is safe for all humans to have access to the sixth-dimension perceptions. Your only constraint is the rules have to obey the natural laws of physics. Once you create a new rule, we Bees will test it within the fifth dimension simulation."

"Okayyyy..." I say, not really sure how I'm supposed to do any of that.

"Don't you worry, I will walk you through how to create a rule. For example, let's say you want to enact the rule change: *Every human on Earth is now vegetarian.* That certainly falls within the confines of the natural laws of physics. In this case, it's a humanitarian *behavioral* change, which is permitted. So, total vegetarianism. That's your rule change. Since we move forward one rule change at a time, you enact that rule by giving me the orders to then pass on to The Bosses who will—"

"Wait, who are The Bosses?"

"Oh," says Queen Bean, "The Bosses are like the bosses of all Bees. They're the ones *really* in charge. So, yeah. I pass your rule to The Bosses, who then say to me, we're going to fast forward the simulation five years to see how this change affects the world. We do that, us Bees check in on what that looks like for humanity within the confines of the simulation, and we determine, sure, it's a positive change. Then you and I keep doing that, one rule change after another, provided your changes are *good*, until we get the A-Okay from The Bosses saying the whole of humanity is ready for Ascension to the sixth dimension. Easy peasy."

"Yeah," I say. "Super easy. I mean, though, it seems like there's a crazy amount of information you haven't told me about this whole Sequence Two thing and what comes next."

"Which is why I'm giving you the opportunity to ask any last questions before we begin."

"Okay, so, like..." I'm trying to think of what to ask. Being told you're responsible for elevating humanity's collective consciousness is kind of a big responsibility, so I don't want to mess it up. "Okay, I authorize a rule that humanity has to live by, and time fast forwards in the simulation. What happens to *me* while this fast-forwarding goes on?" I know it's a selfish question, but I want to know.

"Good question," says Queen Bean, and at this point, I'm getting a bit frustrated with her for not volunteering information without me having to ask for it first, but, you know, whatever. "It's like this. When you wake up in the simulation," she says, "it will be like how life is *currently* in reality. You'll come to and life will seem real, plus all the added benefits of perceiving life through a six-dimensional lens. Then, in order to start a fast-forwarding to test any of your ideas, you'll get yourself stung by a Bee and we'll come back to this void to watch how the fast forwarding goes. That way, we can fast forward a hundred years or more and your body will be preserved as it is."

"Wait," I say. "What?" Then another thought hits me. "Hold up. So if the simulation gets fast forwarded 100+ years, what happens in *real life*? Wait. That's not my question. My question is this: What's happening in real life right now!? While I'm talking to you wherever this is."

CJ FRIEDMAN

"Again, we are in a void of the fifth dimension. And oh yeah, your body in real life is in a coma. But don't worry. You're safe."

Well that prompts a whole set of new questions for me. But I don't want to forget the tangent we had already gone down, so I circle back before I lose it. "Okay, we gotta get back to all that, but before we do, to your point about fast forwarding the simulation and everything. Say the simulation gets fast forwarded 100+ years, what happens in real life?"

"Well, it will all be proportional," says Queen Bean. "Time will still move forward in real life, but not as fast as it does within the simulation. Like right now, it has felt to you as if we've been talking here for a long time, but time in your reality, down in the third and fourth dimensions, where you're in a coma, has moved quite a bit slower. It'll be like that."

"This is a hell of a lot different than Morpheus and Neo," I say.

"That was *your* analogy. Not mine."

"But you agreed with me!"

"I am an agreeable Bee."

"So," I say, thinking of other things I've seen, trying to ground this whole mess, "it's more like all the confusing time stuff in the movie Inception. Like when they go into the dreams?"

"Exactly!" says Queen Bean with an enthusiasm that somehow makes me feel at ease. Though given one more second of thought, that ease is pulverized by the implications of everything.

"If time is all warped like that, and we've been talking here for a while in this whatever you want to call it—"

"Fringe part of the fifth dimension," says Queen Bean.

"Sure, while we've been talking in this *fringe part of the fifth dimension*, since you claim I'm not dead, what's going on with my actual body that's in a coma, you know, in reality?"

"Oh, yes," says Queen Bean. "Naturally you would be curious about that. Back in the fourth dimension and lower, time is moving quite a bit differently than what you are experiencing *here*. As I said, it's moving *much* slower. Your mind was brought here by means of a spider biting your neck and injecting you with the proper energy, so to speak. In the time we have had this conversation, the spider has just left your neck. Based on our calculations, your body is now comatose, you will be discovered by someone, and then summarily brought to the hospital for monitoring. And before you ask, we will ensure your body does not die, Joelle. To everyone else, it will seem like you are simply in a coma."

"Oh, *simply* in a coma. Totally not a weird thing at all for my mom or anyone to deal with."

"Nope!" says Queen Bean in that perpetually chipper voice of hers. "Besides, if at any point you want to check in with your physical body and see how things are going, we can do that."

"Really?" I say.

"Really."

"Okay, well, then, let's see it."

With that request, in a flash, the black empty space of this fringe part of the fifth-dimension whooshes away. It's no longer emptiness. Projected as a screen what *feels* like beneath me, I'm looking down upon my living room. I see a bird's eye view of my body laying comatose on the couch. Which means I guess I'm having a legit out of body experience. Maple, in *super* slow-mo, is pawing at my chest. This view is then zoomed in upon and the scene travels through my nostril and we emerge back into this plane of empty black nothingness.

"Woah," I say. "Trippy."

"Indeed," says Queen Bean.

It takes me another moment to recalibrate and return to what we were discussing. "So," I say, "I create a rule change. Let's say you fast forward the simulation, I don't know, 500 years to test it out. What happens to my body in reality? Like, I assume if time *in reality* moves forward 50+ years or whatever, my body is going to grow old if it's stuck in that coma, and at some point, I'd die."

"Well, *no*. We will have spiders constantly in touch with your bodily hardware to ensure you do not age."

"Holy crap," I say. "You can do that?"

"In special circumstances, we can. And this is understandably a quite special circumstance."

Then thinking it a bit further out, I confirm the horrid notion this scenario means. "So, my body stays the same, but in this situation, it seems like if I enact a rule change and the simulation moves forward long enough, everyone I know and love on Earth might be dead by the time I get to go back to reality."

"That is a possibility, yes," says Queen Bean.

"*Damn*," I say. "That's heavy."

"Did you think the responsibility of ensuring the survival and advancement of your humankind was going to be *easy*?"

"I mean, no? Obviously, I had no idea what it'd involve. I never thought I'd have that kind of responsibility in the first place."

"Well, you do! It's like how you've been worried for so long that you've been squandering your potential. Well now is your chance to rise to the occasion!"

I know the tone of Queen Bean's voice is supposed to make me feel good and excited and everything, but, it doesn't. I'm kind of dreading what's happening right now.

"Well then," Queen Bean says, interrupting my thoughts, as if the implications of all this weren't screwing with my head, "are you ready to begin?"

"What! No. There's so much more it seems you're not telling me. Like, who determines how far the simulation gets fast-forwarded?"

"The Bosses do."

"And how will I know how much time that'll be for whatever rule-change I want to create?"

"You won't."

"Seriously?" I say, not really *asking* if she's serious, but more saying it rhetorically, since I know she is dead serious. "Given how advanced you Bees seem to be and everything, I'd think this whole process would be a bit more fool proof."

"Look," says Queen Bean, "we've only done this Sequence Two twice before, and we failed both times. That's not a big sample size. Just like anyone, human or otherwise, *we're* doing the best we can with the information we've been given. In order to ensure a *safe* Ascension to the sixth dimension for all of humanity, this is what needs to be done, as far as we know."

"As far as you know!? I thought you were some supernatural Queen Bees or something."

"That may be, but still. Both times we initiated Sequence Two ended quite perilously."

"What!?" I say. "What are you talking about? What do you mean, perilously?"

And in response to my multiple questions, I get nothing. So I recalibrate. "Uh," I say. "What do you mean, both times ended perilously?"

"To answer that," says Queen Bean, "please allow me to fill you in on what's *really* going on with regards to life on Earth." Queen Bean then tells me more about the bugs and the specific ways they monitor humanity and *why* they monitor humanity. Because of our apparent potential to kill everything, which is the flipside of what's so great about us – our ability to infinitely create *new* stuff. She tells me how the bugs have the capability of killing every human alive, and how they've done it multiple times before, leading up to what they're calling *my batch* – Batch Number 9, I guess. And honestly, at this point, I take all this news in stride, given the outrageousness of the situation and what not. "Yes," says Queen Bean, "the last time we ran Sequence Two, we hastily enacted the human's rules in reality prior to fully testing them out in the simulation, and, long story short, that resulted in us having to start all over again. Thus ended *Atlantis*, as you may know it. And the time before that, Pangea split and we had to kill all those people, too, you know, for their own good."

"Uh, I *don't* know," I say, wishing she'd make her long story long. "But, whatever you say." With that, I think more about the situation I'm facing. The ridiculousness of it all. How I'm apparently tasked with raising the consciousness of every human alive without dooming everyone. How I'm apparently going to see what life looks like in the sixth dimension, albeit through some simulation supernatural Bees concoct for me within the fifth dimension. How I'm apparently existing at the moment within a fringe part of that fifth dimension. I think about all this for a good while longer. It's pretty heavy stuff. Finally, I say, "Got it. Cool. Cool cool cool."

"Cool indeed!" says Queen Bean, apparently not picking up on my sarcasm, or choosing to ignore it, or something. "And before you start thinking of rules to make, you should know we only have the power to test fifteen of them before we run out of power for the simulation."

"Uh," I say. "What!?"

"Yeah," says Queen Bean, "to power this whole thing, us Queen Bees had to pool our collective Thoughts & Prayers into a condensed energy ball. As some of you humans like to say, without getting too far in the weeds, there's a limited amount we can do."

Again, the casualness with which this all-knowing Queen Bee is withholding valuable information is irritating. I mean, honestly, she seems a bit spacey to me, which isn't giving me much confidence in her as my guru for this whole thing. "So," I say, "fifteen rule changes to alter the course of human history for the better. I got that right?"

"Yep!"

"Queen Bean," I say. "My goodness. How much is there you're not telling me?"

"Probably a lot," says Queen Bean, as if that's not a problem at all.

"Okay," I say, not buying what's happening to me. "Now if you'll excuse me, I'd like to wake up now."

"Joelle," says Queen Bean, the apparently supernatural but at the same time quite spacey Queen Bee who's hijacked my consciousness, "this will go a lot easier if you simply enact trust that this is your reality now."

I don't actively say anything for a while as I ponder what Queen Bean has said. Finally, I say, "And if I enact trust and accept the fact I have to create new rules for humanity to live by that will prompt the elevation of humanity's collective consciousness... like, how do we start?"

"Well, as I said earlier. We are *here*, first, to serve as an orientation. To get you acclimated to this new reality of yours."

"Oh," I say. "Of course. So, to get me acclimated to this reality before I enact rule changes or whatever, what do we have to *do*, exactly?"

"Well, like any good orientation, you have to *learn*."

Again, I'm not really digging this supremely powerful Queen Bee's vagueness, which I'm unfortunately learning is becoming a pattern. "Learn *what*?" I say.

"More, I suppose."

"You suppose?"

"Yes."

"Great," I say. "Very helpful stuff."

Queen Bean says nothing.

"Okay, so, if I'm to believe all of this craziness..." And I stop there. Needless to say, it's hard to wrap my head around what's happening to me. I give it a few more moments to really think it over. "Wait a minute," I finally say. "You said the last two times— the *only* two times—you've done Sequence Two, every human alive was killed. So, I guess it's safe to say the people in my position didn't succeed?"

"That is correct, yes."

"They *didn't* elevate humanity's collective consciousness."

"Not quite."

"So that means…"

"Indeed," says Queen Bean, still reading my mind. "If you fail at your task, we will have to wipe out your batch and start all over once again."

CHAPTER 27

I am a Tree.

The bees do not care that we Trees are disappointed in them.

Like a teenager who is going to do something the parent doesn't want them to.

It is a bit like that.

We Trees are the parents.

Bees are the teenagers.

We can't stop them, per se.

All we can do is tell them how we feel about their actions.

And right now, us Trees are not happy the bees have begun Sequence Two.

Again.

They don't have a good record when it comes to Sequence Two.

But, like the kids they are to us, we hope they know what they're doing.

And if they don't, we hope it goes well all the same.

CHAPTER 28

Jack, you've been in the Poconos for five days now. Do you know how many bugs there are out here? You realize how it easy it would be for us to kill you, right?

Defeated, Jack nodded, though the declaration didn't help his crippling fear of bugs at all. Since Jack still hadn't told Amy about the bugs, and since he would not go outside, the ants were now talking to him as he sat on the toilet in his rented chalet. It took about a minute every time the ants rearranged themselves into a new message.

Look, at some point you will need to address this situation with your wife. We are not going to do that for you. But before then, we are no longer asking you, we are telling you: Go for a hike. You've been out here too long to not immerse yourself in nature.

Whispering, Jack said, "Out there? That's where all the bugs are…"

Again, it doesn't matter if you're sitting on the toilet or hiking in the woods. Clearly we can get to you, anytime.

"Why is it so important I go for a hike?"

It's impossible for us to articulate. You just need to, okay? You'll see why. What, you don't trust us?

"Well, no. Not at all. You've killed several of my colleagues. You threaten me constantly. Why *should* I trust you?"

Because we haven't killed you, yet. Just go for a fucking hike, Jack Telda.

And with that, Jack Telda decided he'd go for a hike.

Before he left, though, he said to Amy, "Hey, I'm gonna go for a little walk in the woods. You and Junior wanna join?"

Sitting on the couch in the vaulted living room, nursing Junior, Amy gave Jack an inquisitive look. "You mean a hike? Really? When have you ever gone for a hike before?"

"I don't know," Jack said, "I figured since we're out here and all, might as well enjoy the scenery a bit."

Amy wasn't buying it. And Jack could see it on her face. Truth be told, in the few days they've been in the Poconos, Jack could see Amy had been less than thrilled about the family's sudden move away from the action of the city to actual greener pastures. She appeared, at least to Jack, to mope around the chalet all day, bored, maybe a bit resentful, and depressed. Despite this, he still kept her in the dark regarding the buggy advancements in his life. Though, to be fair, he *wanted* to let her in. He just feared she might think he had truly gone crazy. So instead he did the easier thing—say nothing—and let the chasm between them grow.

To Amy, it was clear Jack had been hiding something significant from her lately. Which is the type of neglect from a partner that can inflict serious damage to one's confidence, emotional wellbeing, and self-worth as a human. Thanks to their increasing inability to fully and openly communicate, she didn't bother challenge him on whatever it was he was hiding. She instead focused all her time and attention on her baby, Jack Jr.

Jack Jr, in the Poconos, didn't really exhibit much change in demeanor at all, since he was still a pre-crawling baby and getting the same amount of uncompromised attention and love his mother had to give. Amy *did* notice he liked looking at trees out on the back deck, though.

"Whatever you say," Amy said. "I think we'll stay here. You have fun."

"Ok," Jack said. "I'll be back later." He didn't try at all to convince her to come.

When Jack closed the door behind him, Amy said, "Love you." She said this quietly, unconvincingly, longing for the good old days when that was really true.

During Jack's first hike, he was on high alert. He half-suspected ants or hornets or some other kind of bug was going to attack him at any moment.

At the first fork in the trail, just as the ants had done on the streets of Philadelphia, a group congregated on the ground in front of Jack. They formed an arrow pointing which way to go. They did this at every trail juncture. After several arrows, some ants would spell out:

Keep going.

You're doing great.

At first, it was hard for Jack to believe these messages. He thought the ants were surely leading him to his death. But still, onward and upward he went.

About halfway up the small mountain, Jack's legs throbbed, he was short of breath, and he didn't think he could go any further. But after further encouragement from the ants, he kept on moving.

Now at the top of the mountain, there was this strange sense of physical accomplishment he hadn't felt in, maybe, ever. His lungs were burning, but, he realized, they were burning in a good way. He took deep deep breaths and relished the crisp fresh air flooding his body. Jack stood at the top of the mountain, feeling good, and soaked in the view of a lush forest before him. Then, right in front of a slab of rock, a group of ants appeared. Here, they spelled out:

Jack, you did it! Well done. Now, take a seat. Continue soaking in your surroundings. <u>Breathe</u>. Focus on your breath. Just, <u>be</u>.

Having not been murdered so far, actually feeling quite good with himself at the moment, Jack was starting to gain a bit of trust in the bugs. Accordingly, he did as he was told and took a seat on the slab of rock, and just breathed.

In a sense, Jack Telda meditated for the first time. Safe atop the mountain.

The ants let him be, for the time being.

Once Jack started to get fidgety, the ants received word from who was *really* communicating with him, Queen Bruth. Before he got up to go, the ants arranged themselves to say:

Jack, there is a lot you must work on. But to start, we expect you to do this hike every day, first thing when you wake up. Every day, we encourage you to invite Amy, and accept whatever decision she makes. We will see you tomorrow, bright and early.

Thus began Jack's new daily routine.

Amy always declined the offer to join him.

Jack, despite their isolation up in the Poconos, despite what his subconscious was trying to scream to his consciousness, continued distancing himself. When it came time to eat meals together, they did so in front of the TV. They barely spoke.

It took several hikes before Jack's crippling fear of bugs dissipated and he could accept the fact they did not want to kill him, *yet*. Whenever he talked with the ants, they kept reminding him he was still sitting on the fence and only his future actions would determine if they would stop using that word, *yet*.

During his eighth daily hike, the whole way up the mountain, Jack ruminated on his new life. What Food First Service must be doing without him, without Roger, without anyone else that may have disappeared. He relished the fact he didn't know what specific time it was, *on a Tuesday*, because for the past eight years, at this time, he would have been in an office, or strictly adhering to a packed *work* schedule.

As he walked along the trail, he thought he was definitely reconsidering his ways, *but*, was he doing enough to preserve nature? Was he doing *anything* to preserve nature? He had stopped using single-use water bottles, which was a leap for him. Right? Then, he thought, preserving nature, that's gotta be a question for later. First, he had to reconsider his ways. It seemed foolish to start doubting things now. A clear path had been laid for him, and all he had to do was follow it.

Today, when he got to the top of the mountain, Jack sat on what he had come to refer to as his meditation slab. Once sitting, rather than thinking inwardly as he did while walking to this space, Jack Telda seemed to be praying aloud. "I'm doing my best here," he said, his elbows on his knees, his chin in his hands. "I moved my family out of the city. I'm hiking every day. And I've done little else out here *besides* reconsider my ways. You know this. I *believe*, at least, I understand the bad consequences of my past decisions. That it was the people I surrounded myself with for nearly a decade that nudged me to make those decisions. But now, while I'm finding my peace out here, it's not *really* all right. Amy seems to be withering away. I've never seen her like this before. She barely has any energy, she doesn't really engage in conversation with me, and it seems like she's always sleeping or lying down, when she's not tending to Junior. So I don't really know what's going on there. I don't know what to do." Jack paused a moment. "What should I do?"

Within a matter of seconds, a herd of ants filed out from beneath a rock in front of Jack. As they have done every time Jack sat on his mediation slab, the single-file line of ants continuously marched, forming letter by letter their very specific answer, as directed by Queen Bruth.

Jack, it should be obvious. You basically said it. You have not fully reconsidered your ways. We urge you to meditate further, and during your meditations, conjure images of your wife and child. Conjure their meaning in your life. Conjure your meaning in theirs.

Following orders, Jack sat and breathed. Sat and thought. Sat and conjured images of his family. It took some time before true thoughts and emotions circulated within his mind. Finally, they started to coalesce.

Married for eleven years.

Working at FFS for nearly nine years. Climbing the corporate ladder. Which required a tremendous amount of energy.

Energy he took from giving to his wife.

Finally, after ten years of marriage, having Jack Jr, as Amy hoped it might bring them closer. Make them love one another again.

It didn't.

Sitting on the slab, Jack tried to remember why they fell in love in the first place. His mind came up with timing and convenience and mutual attraction, and, was that it?

Jack couldn't remember the last time he cried, but for whatever reason, here on his meditation slab, he wept.

Because, with regards to him and Amy, it had to be more than that, right? They had fun together. They used to laugh together.

Yeah, they did.

But, really ever since FFS, things changed.

Jack's been taking Amy's love and support for granted.

He hasn't been supporting her the way she deserves.

Maybe money doesn't solve all problems.

The problems that really need solving require time.

Attention.

Love.

Honesty.

Coming to this understanding, Jack's tears subsided. He sniffled away the mindset of his past. "Ok," Jack said. "I think I know what I have to do."

And what's that, Jack Telda?

"I have to be open and honest with my wife."

CHAPTER 29

Okay, back in college, after my mushroom-induced positive mental breakthrough, I had this romantic interest. Andi. They were fluid in a way I've never intimately known before, a way I loved. Andi introduced me to one of my favorites, Kurt Vonnegut, because they said I reminded them of a female version of Eliot Rosewater. You know, without a penis and all the money and powerful family and what not. Anyways, a line in that book—*God Bless You, Mr. Rosewater*—always stuck out to me. This was it:

There's only one rule that I know of, babies – 'God damn it, you've got to be kind.

I say all this because apparently, now, I'm tasked with imagining new rules humanity has to live by that will basically create a utopia on Earth. I guess I need to ensure humans don't destroy everything should we all get access to the whatever powers come with experiencing life in the sixth dimension.

"Not quite a utopia," says Queen Bean, interrupting my train of thought.

"What do you mean?" I say.

"That word gets thrown around a lot, and to be quite honest, as far as we Bees understand, it's not a possibility, nor is it totally desirable."

"Again, what do you mean?" I say.

"Well, a utopia is defined by existing as perfection. As far as we Bees understand, with regards to how you humans operate, that would halt any innovation. The human potential for infinite creativity stems from the fact that once any question is answered, several new problems present themselves. If you were to create a utopia, we suppose there would be no more questions that require answering."

"Oh," I say. "Got it. So *not* a utopia. But a world in which humans don't destroy everything. Is that right?"

"Yep!" says Queen Bean inside this void of empty black nothingness, all perky like. "More or less."

"More or less. Got it," I say, though I don't really get it. And I think about it some more. Again, it's a pretty heavy responsibility. Being *the* human responsible for whether or not everyone alive either gets elevated to a new mode of existence or gets *killed by bugs*. Like, why me? Which I figure is actually a legit question. "Seriously," I say, "I've been a piece of shit at times in my life. I've been mean. A jerk. And for real, I'm not all that bright, at least compared to a ton of other people on Earth. There's *gotta* be better candidates for this role. People way better or nicer or wiser or smarter or whateverer than me. So, *why me?*"

"An astute and self-aware consideration, Joelle," says Queen Bean. "According to the roughly eight billion prerequisites necessary for you to be here, of the roughly 108 billion humans that have existed in your batch, you were chosen *because* of all those things."

I remain thoughtless, hoping Queen Bean will elaborate, which, she doesn't. I can tell she's perfectly content with being extremely vague, which is kind of frustrating. "Would you care to elaborate?" I say.

"Surely!" she says, and the chipperness of her voice makes me feel as if I was never frustrated at all with her, which must be some kind of superpower, because her constantly withholding all this critical information is *really* frustrating. "First, let us consider your notion that you've been a *piece of shit*, as you say. Well, that is certainly true. You have been. And, to your point about people being nicer than you or *whateverer* than you, that is also true. There are people born into this world who are inherently kind and loving and nurturing. But that is not who we need for this role. In that respect, we have chosen you because you have in fact been the *opposite* of all those things. You have experienced and wrought negativity, and still, through your own volition, you have changed your ways. As a result, *now*, you are able to empathize with that position of weakness and cruelty. And you are able to delineate the difference between being bad and being good. And after all that, even while seeing what being bad can sometimes get, you have chosen the side of goodness. Additionally, regarding those who are wiser and smarter than you. Sure, there are *lots* of people with more wisdom and intellect than you. Hundreds of millions more people. But wisdom and intelligence are not that which we covet for this role. Better, your instincts and inclination to now help any you encounter is what drives these prerequisites. Your understanding that everyone is in it—that is, life—together. And, as you rightly surmise, many other people have met these specific individual prerequisites as well, but when we analyze *everything* about your essence, well, here we are."

I mean, some of that was really cool to hear, but a lot of that hurt. It's not great being told objectively by a supernatural Queen

Bee there are hundreds of millions of people with more wisdom and intellect than me. I mean, I've always thought I was pretty smart, but I guess I'm not *that* smart. "Oh," I say, a bit downtrodden. "Got it."

"Oh, honey!" says Queen Bean. "I didn't mean to make you gloomy! All I meant to say was that you are *perfect*." This, okay, yeah, it makes me feel better. "You're the perfect blend of human that's not *too* smart, not *too* imaginative, not *too* exceptional, such that you would be blinded by your own awesomeness to see how life may exist for more normal people out there." Aaaaaaand that better feeling is gone.

"Great," I say, "thanks for that."

"Shoot!" says Queen Bean. "I'm not conveying my sentiments properly. What I mean to say, Joelle, is that you are the human we have been waiting for. Of course, you *are* smart, you *are* imaginative, and all that. But more so than any quality like that, you're kind and loving and you want to help people. Your instincts are wonderful. These qualities, above all else, is why you are here."

"Right," I say, "understood." I leave it at that and try to process everything happening. After what feels like a few minutes or so, my mind goes back to the fact Queen Bean told me all the bugs literally annihilated every human alive, multiple times before. And that that could happen again, if I don't succeed in my new role. "So," I say, "I'd like to know what went wrong with the previous batches. You know, in order to avoid making the same mistakes. What happened to Atlantis?"

"To answer that, you first have to understand something about the lost civilization. We Bees have intuited, thanks to certain psychedelic compounds, some humans in your batch have connected with pre-historical times, since, as your batch has rightly concluded, energy is never lost nor destroyed, just simply placed elsewhere. Of course, I'm paraphrasing there. But anyways, the energies of Atlantis, the *vibes* of Atlantis, and of all previous batches of humanity for that matter, exist within an ether of sorts, and have never truly disappeared from Earth. However, the reliability of your batch's connection to these pre-historical times is, at best, extremely tenuous. Although those psychedelics provided an ethereal bridge to these previous batches, that bridge was not secure nor complete, therefore the information garnered was faulty. Because of this faulty bridge, Plato and others of your batch have since misinterpreted what Atlantis was, what it stood for, what it constituted, and what happened to it."

Queen Bean pauses there, and I sense she's giving me the opportunity to ask for clarification, should I want any. And since I don't know what clarification to ask for, I choose to remain questionless, hoping she'll continue as she's going. But of course, she doesn't. She stops there with a heaping lack of information before us. "So…" I say. "Again, what happened?"

"Oh, right," she says, and for the second time, I'm realizing this all-knowing Queen Bee is a little bit spacey. "Let me summarize it thusly. Plato got *some* parts correct. And *many* parts incorrect; just like most people who really take the time to try and understand or connect with Atlantis. Therefore to avoid any confusion, I will simply tell you. To your batch of humans, sure, it may appear Gods presided over the land of Atlantis. But that is not really the case. It was just the *previous* batch of humans. And what that batch accomplished—before they were wiped out by us bugs—would appear Godlike to those living in Plato's time. In Atlantis, they achieved wonderful technological progress and an *almost* harmonious existence. Which is why we thought they may have been ready for Sequence Two. In our hastiness to get things moving, we enacted less prerequisites than we did for you and elevated someone we thought ready for the task. As your batch likes to say, long story short, we gave that person the opportunity which we're about to give you, and they made some wrong decisions. Those decisions were enacted by us Bees before we fully tested them in the simulation, and things devolved into chaos for Atlantis. War broke out, they did indeed attack an ancient city, not quite Athens, as Plato foretold, but something similar, and a new energy source they had developed was in jeopardy. In essence, they had started tapping geothermal vents on the ocean floor, and the way they were harnessing it showed signs it was soon going to rupture and split Earth in two. As a result, we Bees deemed hope to be lost for the batch. Consequently, in order to protect Earth, which is our sole purpose, we bugs took action and wiped them all out. But not before we had the mosquitoes collect enough Atlantean DNA so as to start all over again."

"Uh," I say. "That doesn't really answer my questions about any mistakes my predecessor made. That makes it seem like you *bees* made the mistakes."

"That is a reasonable assessment, yes."

"So how do you know you're not going to make the same mistakes this time?"

"We don't. *But*, what we are wonderful at is learning from our mistakes. As a result, we have enacted more prerequisites that *you* met. Now we are determined to give the tests within the simulation more time before enacting them in the real world. So, you know, progress!"

"Right. Progress." To be honest, my confidence in these Queen Bees is waning. "Alright, so, like, when do we start?"

"When The Bosses let me know you have learned all you need to learn in this orientation."

"And how will The Bosses know that?"

"Since you have entered the void here in the fifth dimension, your subconscious is now fully accessible to us. The Bosses are able to root around within the recesses of your essence to glean that which we need to know."

"Oh, of course," I say. "Makes total sense."

I stop there, assuming Queen Bean will fill me in on everything else I need to learn, but as I refrain from asking questions, she remains silent. And given the whole experience thus far, I don't know why I would assume she would give me all the information.

"Joelle," says Queen Bean, "I am not telling you everything unprompted because this responsibility is on your shoulders. All the information you need is available. You just need to ask the right questions."

"Okay," I say. "What information do I still need to know?" I figure that should do the trick.

Queen Bean takes a moment to respond. Finally, she says, "Was just checking with The Bosses. And yes, good question. Here's what you *need* to know: If you die in the simulation, we cannot revive you and humanity will be doomed. If, during the fast-forwarding for one of your rule changes, something catastrophic happens in reality and we Bugs need to act and take everyone out, well, then we will do so. Other than that, I think we're good to go!"

"That's it?" I say. I mean, sure, it does feel like we've been talking forever, but that seems so anti-climactic.

"Oh! Sorry, one more thing. When you're in the simulation, you're going to want to tell people what's going on. Just know that you *can't* do that. If you tell *anyone* about *any* of this, the simulation will be tainted, and we won't be able to continue."

"Okay...." I say. "Is *that* it?" For some reason, I don't think it is.

"Yep!" says Queen Bean, surprising me. Though, to be honest, given how this conversation has gone so far, I still doubt she's told me everything I need to know.

Nonetheless, I take her at her word. "Okay, so what happens next?"

"Well isn't it obvious? It's time for us to leave this void of the fifth dimension and for you to get simulated! Time for you to see life in 6D."

"Wait, really? Just like that?"

Queen Bean says nothing. I think of another, singular, question to ask. "So, like where am I going to be, you know, in this simulation?"

"Well, again, you know how time is moving at different speeds here and back in 'reality'?"

"Uh, yeah?"

"Well, you know how it feels like we've been talking here for a *long* time?"

"Uh, yeah."

"Well, again, you're going to be placed in the same location where you currently exist in reality, just in the simulation. And so you're not thrown off by where you wake up, please, take a look at where your body *currently* is."

Like the last time Queen Bean showed me what's happening down in the third dimension, the black nothingness of where we are whooshes away. Beneath us, I'm looking at a scene of me lying comatose in the hospital. My mom is sitting next to my bed, holding my hand, seemingly praying. Maple, since she's qualified as a service dog, is lying on a dog bed on the hospital room floor.

As I'm looking at this scene, I guess in response to what I'm thinking, Queen Bean says, "Don't worry. There are two flies in the corner of the room. They're monitoring the situation. You are not going to die or anything."

"But, my mom," I say, "she'll go bankrupt if I stay in the hospital too long."

"Yes, an unfortunate circumstance, especially considering the US is one of the wealthiest nations on Earth. But, you know, don't worry about it! Crippling medical debt will be nothing in the long run if you don't get the next steps right and we have to deal with the potential temporary extinction of humanity."

"Oh, great," I say. "That's super reassuring. Thank you."

Then, I guess since my worry is not dissipating, Queen Bean says, "Hey, we'll look into a solution to help your mom with the whole financial aspect of the arrangement."

"Thanks," I say, genuinely meaning it.

"You're welcome! Now, are you ready?"

"I mean, I guess so?" I say, not really sure.

And before I can finish articulating the thought, the black empty nothingness of what I've come to know of the fifth dimension zips away. I awake within my own body in the hospital.

First, I hear my mom, with as much excitement as I've ever heard come from her voice, yelling for the doctor, "She's awake!

She's awake! Doctor! She's awake!" Then my vision kicks in. As my mom is yelling for the doctor, I can literally *see* the excitement radiate off her body. It's a colorful mass of energetic waves that clearly articulate happiness and relief and hope. I guess *this* is life in 6D.

CHAPTER 30

Although he came to a decisive conclusion at the top of the mountain, now that he was faced with actually telling Amy he had been talking with ants, Jack hesitated. But, he figured, why not go for it.

Upon getting back to the chalet, Jack found Amy lounging on the couch, snuggled up with their son, Jack Jr. She was reading to him.

"Hey," Jack said, with a bit more affection in his tone than he's used in recent years.

"Hey," Amy said, sensing that inflection, putting some hope into hers. She put down the book.

"Can we talk?" Jack asked.

"Yeah, sure," Amy said, not sure what to expect, but somewhat reassured by Jack's manner.

Jack walked over and sat next to Amy on the couch. He turned so he was facing her and reached out to hold her hands. "I'm sorry," he said, getting right to it. "I've been such a dick."

Amy was taken aback. She didn't want to say *no you haven't*, because she was curious to see where he'd go with this, and, truth be told, he had been kind of dickish of late.

"I don't know," Jack continued. "Remember when we first started dating? How much fun we had?" Amy nodded slightly, perhaps sensing Jack remembering their times barhopping across the city then staying up till the sun rose, them walking the boardwalk on the Jersey Shore in the summer, them *living life,* loving life, *together.* "Being up here," Jack said, "getting away from the city and Food First, getting away from all that business, I guess I've just had some time to think about it, and I want to say… I'm sorry."

Amy didn't know what to say. Where was this coming from? Was Jack smoking something on his hikes? Instinctively, sensing her husband doing all this *feeling,* she said, "Oh… Jack… It's okay."

"No," Jack said. "It's really not. I've grown distant. I haven't loved you, haven't loved Junior the way I should, the way I *want* to. I guess, what I'm realizing, I don't know…" This was hard for Jack to admit, but, as fly as his witness, he said it: "I've been a bad husband. A bad father."

Honestly, Amy had no idea where all this emotion and reflection stemmed from. She had resigned herself to the fact their relationship was trending downward, and she had lost the will to work on it. Jack had never shown this type of remorse or self-awareness or thoughtfulness before. And really, she was loving him showing it. She didn't want to interrupt his train of thought, to prevent him from expressing his self-inflicted grievances. So she sat there, her hands in his.

"What I guess I'm trying to say," Jack said, "is I want to be better. I *will* be better. And that starts with being honest with you."

At this, Amy didn't know what to expect. What did he have to be honest about? Was Jack about to tell her he had an affair or something?

"So, remember the fire?" Jack asked.

"Uh," Amy said. "Yeah? How could I forget?"

"Well, I know what caused it. Actually, I know *who* caused it." Jack couldn't believe he was about to tell Amy all this. He didn't want to. He paused there.

"Yeah…" said Amy.

"Well, *I* did. You see, and *please* don't think I'm crazy here, but like I said, it's time for me to be open and honest with you. You see… Okay… Here it is." Jack took a deep breath. He wanted to let out the following thoughts in quick succession before he could stop himself. "I got home that day and, like, a few million ants chased me and stormed into our house and were about to kill me so to fend them off I made like a blowtorch using your hairspray and a lighter and *I* torched our house." *Damn*, Jack thought, it was like a weight the size of a thousand trillion ants was lifted off his shoulders.

Amy looked at her husband like he was messing with her. He couldn't *possibly* expect her to believe that. Could he? "Are you serious?" she finally asked. "You're fucking with me."

"I hate to say it," Jack said, "but *dead* serious." He then proceeded to tell her all about the ants. About the messages they were sending him. About their threats and advice and *how they killed his colleagues*. And that *they* were the reason he took a sabbatical from FFS and the reason he moved the family to the Poconos. Amy, understandably, looked at him like he had lost his mind. She suggested they call a doctor, that Jack gets help.

"Here," Jack said. "Follow me." He got up from the couch, picked up Jack Jr, reached again for Amy's hand, and led her outside.

Once they got outside, he handed Jack Jr back to Amy and said aloud, to seemingly no one in front of them, "Okay, I told her. Help me out here. *Please.*"

In response, a steady line of ants emerged from the grass onto the walkway leading up to the Telda's rented chalet. As they have many times before for Jack, they formed a message, letter by painstaking letter:

Hi Amy. It's true. We've been talking with Jack.

CHAPTER 31

Okay, I opened my eyes and I'm in the hospital. Mom is right there next to me.

Hovering around her, beaming off of her, as visible to me as the hospital gown I'm wearing, is what I can only describe as her aura. The essence of which is obviously loving, though, in this instant, it's tinged with worry, fear, relief, and, as my eyes blink a few more times, seeing the transcription of her aura more clearly, hope. It's like a wavy hazy cloud of green-blue-orangeness which pulsates from two centers—her heart and brain—outward with every movement of her body. The energy pulsations are as legible to me as any book I've ever read. Intuitively, I can feel my ability to alter these pulsations with my focused thought and intentions. So, with that ability, I want my mom to feel less worry and fear, and more lovingness and relief and hope. Now thinking that, wanting that, my facial structure reflecting those desires, I can see her aura change to match that which I yearn for. Her shoulders loosen, a smile unfurls itself across her face, a few happy tears well in her eyes, and she reaches out to squeeze my hand. As she does so, I see her energetic waves of love flow directly into my palm, through the veins in my arm, and up toward my heart. I can see and feel and alter and embrace *all of this.*

THE BUGS

On the floor, there's Maple, radiating simple goodness and sweetness and love. A vibrant green encircling her being. Seeing me awake, she gets all excited and jumps up onto the hospital bed with me and starts licking my face. Given my new sixth dimensional lens of reality, it's fun to see her licks transfer some of that vibrant green goodness onto my being, which are then absorbed into my own aura. This corresponds with me actually feeling better as Maple gives me all this love. She keeps licking and licking until the doctor walks in, at which point I tell Maple to get down. And being the good dog she is, she hops right off the bed.

The doctor's aura is one of neutrality, which, in this instant, quiets the radiant love and hope emanating off Mom.

As the doctor starts to ask me questions, I hear Queen Bean in my ear, "Tell her you feel fine and you want to go home." So I say that.

To which the doctor replies I really need to stay for monitoring. Upon saying this, I can visibly see, thanks to the energetic beams shooting out from her, she's frustrated with my stubbornness and unwillingness to simply accept what she says as indisputable truth.

Queen Bean tells me to ask if it's legal I'm held in the hospital against my will.

Blah blah blah and a few minutes later, even against my mom's wishes, I'm walking out of the hospital, feeling like a million bucks. To appease my mom, I tell her I'll stay home with her, since she took work off, and if I feel even *slightly* out of the ordinary, I will let her know and we can return to the hospital. "Besides," I say, "if I feel this good, what's the point in racking up a crazy amount of hospital bills for an unnecessary extended stay?"

Mom reluctantly agrees and we head home, though she's still curious as to what happened to me. Likewise, all the doctors were baffled and unable to provide any explanation. I refrain from telling them my mind has been kidnapped by Queen Bees and we're currently in a simulation within the fifth dimension created *by* said Queen Bees. Considering how real the simulation is, I think I'd get admitted for being insane.

Meanwhile, Queen Bean is in my ear telling me to be normal, don't act weird, and we can get to Sequence Two once I'm good and settled. She reminds me again I *cannot* tell anyone about what is happening.

The whole ride home is a new experience for me.

Looking out the window of the car, *everything* appears to be alive in a way I never appreciated before. The trees, the people in other cars, the grass, the river that runs along the edge of route 27, the birds, the bugs, *everything* has its own energetic field beaming off its physical body. The energetic fields interact with one another and bend and warp when they touch, almost like thermodynamic transfers of heat, but, in this case, transfers of simple energy, like a million Venn diagrams of toroidal energy spheres networking with one another, but doing so in an almost fractal and hexagonal web of connectivity. And beyond the alive things with all *their* energetic fields and what not, I see the power lines, my cell phone, anything hooked up electronically, they all have their own energies flowing off them as well. In a haze of all this extra sensory that's assaulting my perceptions, all blending together, it's easy to see, way easier than when I would eat mushrooms, that yes, indeed, everything *is* connected.

After the coolest car ride of my life, we get home. I'm tempted to go for a walk in the woods, to see all this connectivity up close and personal, but Queen Bean reminds me of the task at hand. Accordingly, I sit on my couch and pop open my computer. I guess I'll do some research about ideas I could enact that'll help change the world for the better. But before I get to that, as soon as my computer powers up, I get all these email notifications. I've only been in the hospital for two days and the guys at Yessir Brewing and the ladies at Lobstah Gals and the folks at Homegrown Clothes have reached out about all the deliverables we had on the table. Then they all reached out sending me well-wishes, as apparently my mom called each of them to let them know I was in the hospital. Without thought, I start replying to them to let them know I'm alright and I can get back to work ASAP.

"What are you doing?" Queen Bean asks in my head. "And, so you know, you can *think* your answers, so you don't look crazy talking to yourself in front of your mom."

Got it, I think. *And, uh, I have contractual obligations to these folks. I gotta do some work. What's the rush?*

"What's the rush!?," says Queen Bean, "Oh, just the fate of your humankind. And have you forgotten? We're in a *simulation*. This isn't reality. You can forget all that stuff and there'll be no repercussions. We have work to do."

Oh, shit, I think. Honestly, this simulation feels so ridiculously real—well except for all the aura stuff glowing off of everything, which, to be honest, is easy to overlook after only a few minutes—it made me forget all about Sequence Two and plunged me right back into my pre-saving-the-world daily responsibilities. As if the notifications derailed my train of thought. *Right, so, from here, how do we proceed?*

"Although I implied there was somewhat of a rush," says Queen Bean, "as to get you to stop replying to work email, I do not mean to rush you. These are important matters we are dealing with. As you were, prior to seeing those work notifications, I encourage you to do whatever research you were about to do, look for inspiration or ideas regarding these rule-changes we need to enact."

10-4, I think.

And that's what I do. I go online and search *Ideas to save the world*.

The first thing that pops up is a pretty simple list. Stuff like:

> *Reduce, reuse, recycle*
> *Volunteer for cleanups*
> *Educate others about the value of natural resources*
> *Conserve water*
> *Choose sustainable*
> *Shop wisely, buy less plastic, and bring reusable bags*
> *Use longer-lasting light bulbs*
> *Plant a tree*
> *Don't send chemicals into the waterways*
> *Bike more*

And upon reading all that, I'm like, *duhh*. But it all seems mundane and like a drop in the bucket. My instinct is saying, wait, what about all the international corporations responsible for lobbying whatever destructive practices they lobby, or for creating all that cheap plastic in the first place? Or whatever. Why is the onus on the individual and not the corporations that allow all this easy destructive shit to proliferate? And before I go down a rabbit hole of corporate injustices, I'm interrupted.

"Consider," Queen Bean says in my head, "the ramifications if *everyone* did those things on that list."

I'm like, *right*. Though I can't help but feel some righteous indignation about the fact individuals only act in their best interest, at least according to econ 101, and they typically go with the path of least resistance, which, again, is a path that's perpetuated by these global companies and the power structures in place. Besides, I want to make a splash. I feel like there's a way bigger impact rule change I could create than something on that first list.

"Now don't go getting ahead of yourself," says Queen Bean. "Why not start small?"

I consider her advice and think the reason to not start small is because I only have fifteen rule changes at my disposal. I have to make them count. However, as I currently sit, I'm not yet ready to choose my first rule change. So, I continue my search online.

As I'm reading more and more about the dangers of fast fashion, which apparently is the second largest source of pollution in the world (which causes some pride to swell in me thanks to my partnership with Homegrown Clothes), the thought hits me, *how do I even enact a rule change for all of humanity?* Queen Bean never told me *how* I go about doing that.

"Oh, of course," Queen Bean says in my head. "Right. You just say to me, *Queen Bean, this is my rule: so on and so forth and what not and bloop, saying whatever the rule change is, let it be done.* That's it. Whatever you say in between *Queen Bean this is my rule* and *let it be done* will be your rule. Then I relay the information to The Bosses, they program the change into the simulation, you go and get yourself stung by a bee, you fall into a coma wherever you get stung, you and I go back to our special void in an empty part of the fifth dimension, and we fast forward the simulation to see what happens. Easy-peasy. Come on, think of a simple one. Let's see it happen." I can tell she's getting antsy with me.

Then I recall something Queen Bean said to me, back in the void, something about my *instincts*. So I go with it. I trust my instincts and say the first thing that pops into my head. *Okay, I say by way of thinking, Queen Bean, this is my rule: Everyone over the age of ten must volunteer once a week to do one hour of trash cleanup. Let it be done.* And as soon as I say it to her, the millisecond the thought leaves my mind, I'm like, that's such a *stupid* use of one of my fifteen changes.

"Sounds good!" says Queen Bean. "Now, go find a beehive and get yourself stung."

"Wait," I say, instinctually hating myself for proposing such a small-time and inconsequential rule. "Can I take that back? I want to try something else."

"Sorry, you can't. I already sent it to The Bosses. The fate of the world is now waiting on you to go get stung by a Bee and see what happens if everyone over the age of ten picks up litter for an hour a week. And don't worry! If it doesn't work out, you still have fourteen rules left!"

CHAPTER 32

"Alright, Jack," Amy said, "what the fuck? How'd you do that?" She was referring to the ants that walked out from the grass and confirmed they had been communicating with her husband.

"I didn't," Jack replied. "This is legit. Here, look." Jack turned to face the ants on the ground before them, thought about how to proceed for a second, then said, "Alright, how about a different message?"

In response, the ants rearranged themselves and were joined by a few of their kin. Letter by letter, they formed the message:

Amy, we can save a whole lot of time if you just believe this is really happening. We understand it may be difficult, but, such is life.

Amy snorted a quick laugh. "Jack, seriously, I'm impressed. How the hell are you doing this? Are these like some little robots Food First has made for farming or something?"

"I wish!" said Jack. "And I swear, I'm not controlling them. Try asking them something. Or tell them to form anything. Something I couldn't have pre-programmed."

"Okay," Amy said, playing along. "Spell out supercalifragilisticexpialidocious."

With haste, some of the ants retreated from the messaging area and the remaining bunch reordered themselves to spell out the Mary Poppins word. Meanwhile, at least eight dozen flies were monitoring this interaction, constantly flinging themselves one after another into nearby spiderwebs so Queen Bruth could be privy to this important moment in real time.

Amy thought about it a moment, considered the robot ants could respond and move in conjunction with commands like that. She changed the approach. She repositioned Jack Jr from her right to her left hip, said, "Okay. How about, why Jack? If what he's told me is true, why spare him but not Mitch? What makes Jack so special?"

At this, the ants did not move.

"They won't answer if you ask more than one question at a time," Jack said.

Amy thought she had won, that she proved he was doing something fishy, although she still didn't know *how*, exactly, he was doing it. Nonetheless, she decided to humor Jack. "Ohhh, right," she said. "One question at a time. Got it. Okay, *ants*, what do you want with Jack?"

At *this*, a horde of ants emerged from the grassy area to join the ones on the walkway. It took about two minutes for the ants to form the message. Amy grew increasingly tense with each passing second as they spelled it out for her:

Look, Amy. Your husband is not lying to you. We killed Mitch because, as you have probably noticed in your interactions with him, he was a true asshole. There was no hope of salvation for his moral character. He was long lost to badness and he would forever be an asshole. Your husband, though, Jack, okay, yes, he has been an asshole, at times, as you've gradually seen throughout your marriage. However, recall the days you two first met. How wonderful he was. How kind. Well, we Bugs have determined Jack is what we call a Fence Player. He has the inkling to fall on either side of the fence, *good or bad, depending on who he surrounds himself with. For a while, he surrounded himself with assholes like Mitch, which assisted in turning <u>him</u> into more of an asshole. Of late, though, we are attempting to steer him toward <u>good</u> people, and we trust he will surround himself with humans of that ilk moving forward. Humans like yourself. Now, you ask, why him? Considering his Fence status, considering his position of relative power at a company heavily responsible for global food production, there is hope yet for not only him, but through him, hope for humanity. As he has told you, we Bugs monitor Earth to protect it from the potentially irreversible destructiveness of humans. We have identified Jack as someone who may yet help humanity avoid such catastrophic conclusions.*

Upon reading the ants' message, Amy had to strongly consider the possibility this was all real. And as she stood there contemplating which reality to believe, a lot of the ants in that long message marched away and the remaining ones spelled out:

Okay, Amy, Jack, brace yourselves. <u>Do. Not. Move.</u> To further prove all us bugs are in on this, we are going to do something that we have not even done for Jack. Again: DO. NOT. MOVE. And also, don't panic.

In an instant, a thick cloud of bugs flew out from the woods. Before the cloud got to them, Jack reached over and pulled Amy close. The two of them held Jack Jr between their bodies.

About the size of Jack's unnecessary SUV, the bug cloud was a buzzing mixture of hornets and flies and dragonflies and moths and mosquitoes and all types of flying critters. In the time it took Jack to pull Amy and Jack Jr close, the cloud was upon them. It enveloped them in a swarm of impending doom, though, as the Teldas stood perfectly still, the cloud maintained a distance of roughly four inches off their bodies.

The buzzing sound was deafening.

Jack Jr started to wail.

"Don't move," Jack cooed to Amy, fully aware of the danger this swarm posed and fully trustworthy of the message the ants had delivered, due solely to the fact they had not killed him yet. "They said don't move. Be still."

It took everything in Amy's body not to sprint for the inside of their house. She stayed within the confines of Jack's loving arms, closed her eyes, held her baby close, and prayed the bugs would fly away. The sound of tens of thousands of bugs completely encircling them, buzzing incessantly, was so loud, she couldn't hear herself think. Yet since they did not move, not a single bug appeared to touch them. But the threat was readily apparent. At any moment, this swarm could collapse on them and there'd be nothing Amy nor Jack could do to stop it.

With so many bugs moving in close proximity around the Teldas, it created a kind of buggy sauna. The heat was quickly becoming unbearable. Amy and Jack were sweating profusely now, and Junior was still wailing.

After the longest twenty seconds of Amy's life, the swarm departed, leaving Amy, Jack, and Jack Jr completely untouched.

As the proverbial and literal dust settled around them and Amy regained her bearings, she looked down at the ground to see the ants had formed a new message:

Believe us now?

She did.

THE BUGS

It took the rest of the afternoon for Amy to come to terms with the fact ants were communicating with her husband (and now her), that bugs were consciously responsible for the deaths of people she knew, that any of this was happening at all.

After the swarm of bugs encircled her and Jack and Jack Jr, she couldn't help but believe.

The Teldas spent the remainder of the afternoon and evening going over everything Jack had already told Amy, but in more detail, like about when the ants first marched on Jack and he torched their house, the times in Philly when they sent him messages on the street and in his office, and how Jack *barely* held onto his sanity throughout it all. Though this time, as he went over all of these events, Amy offered a more sympathetic ear.

With everything out in the open now, Jack felt a sense of hope return to his life. After going through a near-death experience, actually, going through what he considered a perpetual-near-death-experience-via-threat, seeing that life could end so abruptly, and now having Amy on his side, that sense of hope enabled him to look at Amy in a way he hadn't since before he proposed. Back when they first met and he was a youthful optimistic undergrad. That hope extended now to when he looked at his son, *really looked* at his son, and Jack felt, for the first time in a long time now that he thought about it, *good.* Given all that feeling goodness, as he explained the whole situation to Amy, Jack kept apologizing for his behavior. For neglecting her, before the bugs and after, for the way he treated her, and for the way he'd fall into glasses of whiskey, alone in a separate room, while his life unraveled, rather than be open with his wife. He again promised to be better.

CJ FRIEDMAN

"Jack," Amy said, sitting sideways on the couch facing her husband, "this is *insane*. I'm having a hard time continuing to believe this is all real. But, going with the belief that it is, like, I get it. I understand. It's okay."

"Really, it's not," Jack said. "I know I've said it already, but I'll keep on saying it. I should have been open and honest with you from the start."

"I don't know. I really don't," Amy said. "I mean, it's not entirely on you. I could've been a bit more assertive, you know, working on our relationship. Marriage *is* a two-way street." As she was saying this, Amy reflected on the position that if blame *could* be assigned, then sure, most of it could fall on Jack's shoulders. But he was just being so vulnerable now. She wanted to assuage him of some of that blame.

"I appreciate that," Jack said, sensing the ways in which Amy was helping him through this. "Really, I do. And again. I'm going to be better. For you and for Junior." Jack leaned forward and put his head on Amy's shoulder, wrapped his arms around her.

Amy held him right back.

In turn, they both agreed to try harder, moving forward.

Finally, after a long day, before bed, Amy asked what this all meant, where should they go from here?

Jack said they should go for a hike in the morning. That he suspected the ants will have some answers for them.

The next morning, Jack and Amy—with Jack Jr in a carrying backpack that Jack carried—went for a hike.

Jack loved and appreciated that Amy was now fully in his world, that he could be 100% open and honest with her, that she didn't think he was crazy, and that the wedge between them seemed to be gone. In fact, rather than a wedge being there, Jack hadn't felt this close to Amy possibly ever. Something about a shared crazy experience will do that to people. Jack's previous aloofness toward their marriage and his role as a father was now gone, and given its vacancy, a surge of fulfillment occupied his heart. On the hike, he gratefully accepted the weight of Junior on his back. In fact, he frequently reached back to squeeze Junior's little hands, thinking about, really for the first time since Junior was born, that prevailing hope for his family's future.

The ants sure were onto something after all.

Amy, likewise, despite the craziness of the past eighteen hours, loved the energy flowing between her and Jack. They actually had passionate and loving sex the night before, for the first time in *long* time. With that sense of hope within Jack being a tangible thing and all, Amy similarly felt a brightness for their marriage and life together. That is, of course, pending what the ants had in store for them.

About halfway up the mountain, Amy was struggling since her body wasn't used to this kind of physical exertion. Not really loving it, she asked Jack, "Why are we doing this?"

"Well, it's like the ants told me. They want me to reconnect with nature. And, you know how I've been doing this lately by myself? Well, honestly, at first, I hated it. But then I started to love it. I think you will too. Also, I've been speaking with the ants when I get to the top."

With her legs and lungs burning, Amy said, "And why couldn't we speak with them like we did at the house?"

Jack hadn't considered that, he was so immersed in this routine of venturing into the woods to converse with the ants at the top of the mountain. "Oh," he said, "well, yeah, it's mainly the first part, to reconnect with nature and get immersed in it. Isn't this *great*?"

"Yeah," Amy said sarcastically. "I'm loving it."

Jack sensed Amy's struggles, since those too are tangible. He suggested they stop and rest, to snack on trail mix and take a drink. "I felt the same way the first few days out here," he said. "Trust me, you'll start to love it."

Given how her body was feeling, Amy didn't wholly believe him. Her quads felt like a frying pan was searing them from the inside out. She happily took Jack up on his idea to rest for a moment and snack. She grabbed a water bottle out of the side of the backpack, slunk down, and took a seat right on the dirt ground.

After a few moments, with everyone properly snacked up, Jack said, "Alright. Not much more to go. Shall we?" He reached out a hand to help lift Amy up.

Finally, they made it to the top of the little mountain. Though her body was on fire, Amy felt good having made it to the summit. She hadn't seen a view like this—a blanket of tree cover stretching for miles and miles beneath her—since her childhood, when her dad drove them along Skyline Drive in Virginia on a family road trip. Standing at the top of this small mountain in the Poconos, a sense of accomplishment pulsed through her she hadn't expected.

Once Amy took in the view, Jack gestured for the two of them to sit down on the rock he's grown familiar with, his meditation slab. Though this time, it felt better sitting there, feeling Amy next to him, knowing she was on board with this new wild journey.

"Okay," Jack said to Amy. "Ready?"

"Ready for what?" Amy said.

"To learn what we have to do next."

Amy gave Jack a puzzled look, as if to say, *I'm not ready for any of this shit.*

Inferring her answer, Jack turned his attention forward, to the ground. "So," he said, "We're here. Amy's on board and we're ready to help make things right. What are we supposed to do now?"

Amy's first instinct was to ask Jack who he was talking to, but recent events quickly adapted her to the situation, especially as a single-file line of ants came out before them, forming a message letter by letter:

Good. We are pleased to see you two reconcile and re-strengthen your once previously strong bond. You two are stronger <u>together</u>. Now, to answer your question, Jack Telda, what you are to do now is to go <u>back</u> to Philadelphia.

"Wait," Jack said, "I thought you wanted me to reconnect with nature?"

A nearby fly flew into a spider web, after which about half of the ants retreated as the others formed their response:

And you have, more or less. Now, it is time to return to work. We have high hopes for you.

"And," Amy interjected, curious to know her husband's fate, "what are those hopes?"

Another fly flew into the same spiderweb and a steady stream of many more ants emerged before them, spelling out:

Food First Service is a global company responsible for, as you Jack might say, a <u>fuck ton</u> of food production. Considering the way FFS operates, what comes with that, as we'd say, is a <u>fuck ton</u> of ecological damage. No doubt FFS feeds hundreds of millions of people *annually by operating this way, but from the data we have analyzed, this type of food production is not sustainable for Earth. In maximizing production—and therefore short-term shareholder value—you are destroying the future. Jack, as you are aware, we have eliminated a few key players at FFS you know of, and a few more you are unaware of. In doing so, we have made your return to work quite desirable for the few remaining board members. They are currently scrambling and need someone with your experience to step in.*

"Step into what?" Jack asked.

A conversation with the ants, by the way, was a wonderful exercise in patience. It took time for them to arrange themselves into a message.

According to our analyses, you are slated to be the next CEO.

"Holy shit," Jack said. He had always dreamed of climbing the corporate ladder that high, but never in a billion years had he ever thought it'd come as a result of bugs murdering everyone on the rungs above him. After only a moment's consideration, he thought, *Oh well, if that's the way it's gotta be, then that's how it's gotta be.* Just to confirm, though, he said, "Are you serious?"

Dead serious.

After another moment of consideration, considering how much he now valued his family and how much he wanted to spend time with them, working on building a good life together, Jack said, "Wait, but I just realized I may not want that. That means I'd be working *more* than I was before. What if I want more time with my family."

Intuitively understanding how Jack operates and the type of language that has worked on swaying his behavior in the past, the ants spelled out:

Whoopty fucking doo, Jack. Take it or leave it. We need you to do certain things at FFS. As CEO, make work life balance a thing across the board for your employees. Or something. Figure it out.

Amy, having been brought into this whole mess, now wondered what this all meant for her. "What about me?" she said. "What am I supposed to do?"

At this, the ants did not move. Jack reminded Amy she needed to ask one question at a time.

"What do you want with me?" she corrected.

Amy, we are sorry you have been brought into this whole mess. From what we have gathered, you are indeed a good person and have much to offer the world. In this case, though, we only need your husband, for reasons related to his position at FFS. If it were up to us, we'd have you step in and make all the decisions and act as CEO. But alas, that is not the position you are in. We encouraged Jack to come to you with all this because we know unequivocally that when you two are open and honest with one another, you make Jack a better person. Due to the routes you two have taken in life, Jack has found himself in a position of power we need to leverage. For now, we need you in on his life, so he does not unravel.

"Oh, got it," Amy said, a bit downhearted at her being thrust back into this old-school traditional role of wife supporting high-powered working-husband.

As more ants joined the messaging platform to spell out something new, Jack reached out his arm and pulled Amy close to him. He kissed her on the forehead. While the ants rearranged themselves, Jack said to Amy, "Hey. You're amazing. I love you and appreciate you and will do whatever I can to support you."

Though Amy appreciated Jack's sentiment, it didn't fill the void in her that yearned to do something more with her life. As the ants said, though, alas, her fulfillment would have to wait. So, Amy sat there in Jack's embrace, thinking about her future, what fulfillment might be for her, while the ants finished up their long message.

So, Jack. You are to end your sabbatical and return to Philadelphia and Food First Service. You will, according to our calculations, be welcomed back with open arms and asked to step in as acting CEO. Once in position, you are to fulfill the following changes to the company…

The list of duties for Jack to fulfill was big. In a bit more detail and specificity, the ants told Jack he was to re-wild Food First's tens of thousands of acres in Brazil and Indonesia and India and other parts of the globe. He was to return the land-management and protection to local populations, specifically to local populations committed to preserving biodiversity. Then the ants gave him detailed instructions for transitioning FFS's monoculture corn and soy fields in America to regenerative agriculture farms. They told him to invest further in regenerative family farms all over the country. They told him to be patient with the process. That a return to profitability could take upwards of 7-10 years, probably more, on account of the time regenerative farms require in order to begin realizing their potential.

Jack had interjected at this point. He said there's no way he could do all this. As CEO, he would have a board to answer to. And stakeholders. They'd kill him if he proposed these plans.

Yes, Jack, replied the ants. *They'd kill you, but only figuratively. Now consider the alternative if you don't do what we are telling you to do. In that case, we will kill you, <u>literally</u>. Besides, you have us on our side. We may be able to help you move things forward.*

CHAPTER 33

Okay, I made the stupid rule change everyone needs to volunteer to pick up trash. Then I told my mom I wanted to head outside for a minute, just to get some fresh air, but really, it was so I could get myself stung by a Bee. Since this simulation's so real, and since I had *just* come out of a coma, Mom's reluctant to let me go anywhere except the safety of the couch. Thanks to my new sixth dimensional capabilities in this reality, I can see her objections before she even verbalizes them. The visible aura emanating off her body is radiant orange red clouded with what I can only describe as fear, and it's speaking to me as if it's a language I've known my whole life.

Queen Bean tells me, given the access I currently have within the confines of my new capabilities, I should better understand how energies work with people. That they are supremely tangible and work akin to Newton's theories on how heat energy transfers. "It's like this," says Queen Bean, "think about your time in college. If you were sitting around all mopey or hungover or something and your friend burst in with all the energy in the world, ready to party, *your* energy levels would perk up a bit, but at the same time, you would bring down her energy. And you'd meet somewhere in the middle, having transferred energies to one another. It's like that. Simply project to your mom it's safe for you to go outside and get her energy to change. You just have to actively *be* that which you want."

So that's what I do. I concentrate really hard on projecting safety and confidence and comfortability with moving away from the couch. It's like a focused meditation of sorts that I project via aura-like laser beams shooting from where my third eye might be, and as I do all that concentrating, I notice the energies vibrating outward from my mom's center change from an orange red fear-based color, to a more yellowish bluish greenish *okay I'm cool with that* color. Even though she's now totally fine with me going outside, Mom does insist she's coming with me.

So, we go outside. Queen Bean directs me to the nearest bumblebee hive on the outskirts of our lawn, I go near it and provoke the Bees, and one of them stings my arm. My body collapses to the ground and now here I am, back in this particular void of the fifth dimension with Queen Bean, the area I've learned was built just for me for these viewing and training purposes.

For the unfurling of my idiotic rule change, Queen Bean lets me watch the scene back in the simulation play out. My mom understandably panics when she sees my body go limp. She's hysterical and calls 911 and is blaming herself for letting me go outside and she looks like she's about to have a complete nervous breakdown and I feel *horrible* watching all this happen.

"Joelle," says Queen Bean, "remember you are watching a simulation. This is not real. In reality, you are still in a coma in the hospital and your mother is still heartbroken *there*, waiting for you to awake. Besides, you need to forget the triviality of your life and that of your mother's, as you now must be concerned with *humanity's* life. Do not forget your responsibilities. Be like a Bee."

Although this all makes sense logically, I still can't help but feel for my mom, albeit Simulation Mom.

Nonetheless, I muster the strength to refocus on the task at hand.

"Alright, good," says Queen Bean. "Now, The Bosses have programmed your rule change into the simulation. Let us see what happens." As she says this, I'm still upset with myself for blurting out such a stupid and foreseeably meaningless rule change. *Everyone picks up trash.* I already know it's doomed to be inconsequential, and I hate myself for wasting such a cool opportunity.

Then, in an instant, the black empty void around me swirls and whirls. I still have no body nor physical presence here, but, around me, around my consciousness, the blank empty space becomes like a fully immersive television screen. Almost as if I'm in the middle of an augmented reality cube or something. I see snippets of the whole world flash before me in crazy fast speeds.

At first, people are picking up trash, just like I proposed.

Places are getting cleaner.

Then there are protests.

People chanting, "Don't tread on me!" and "You can't make me clean up someone else's trash!" and "Forced volunteerism = nazism!" and what not.

"Sheesh," I say to Queen Bean. "How long have we fast-forwarded?"

"About two days," says Queen Bean.

"Damn," I say, thinking about what I've done.

While I think, Queen Bean tells me, "Fortunately, not much time has lapsed in us realizing how bad of an idea this one was and, thankfully, nothing catastrophic has happened. We can rewind this one and try something new. But before we do that, would you care to reflect on what may have gone wrong?"

I think about it a moment and quickly come to the conclusion I'm a complete moron that should not be in the position I'm in.

"Come on," says Queen Bean. "You shouldn't be so hard on yourself. You went with your instinct, as I instructed you to do, and, yeah, maybe you went with it a bit too fast. But you have to *trust* we have chosen you for all the right reasons. Now, it wasn't the *worst* idea you could have had. Let's think it out, what went wrong?"

I appreciate Queen Bean is trying to pump my tires a bit, and, thanks to the wholehearted goodness I can feel glowing off her, her short pep talk helps. I start to really consider where this well-intentioned rule change went wrong. With that, I come to the conclusion that perhaps a rule change involving compulsion towards action may not be the right move. Like, even if the compulsion is to do something *good* for the world, there's gonna be people, especially in the US, who don't appreciate being *forced* to do *anything*. So, for my next rule, I determine to make it a behavioral one, one that's ingrained into human character. But before moving along, for another moment, my mind regresses and I'm once more downhearted at how wrong my initial instinct was. I thought I was supposed to trust my instincts and all I learned was that might be a disastrously bad thing to do. Though, to be fair to myself, my instinct *in response* to my instinct was that my first instinct was a horrible waste.

"Again," says Queen Bean, interrupting my downward thought spiral, "don't beat yourself up. For a first rule change, you could have done *a lot* worse. I'll have you know, the person in Atlantis, for his, he made it so fish were compelled to reproduce at thrice their normal rates, so there'd be an abundance of them for the Antlanteans to eat, and, well, let's just say that destroyed the balance of the oceans and a lot of time was wasted. So, with yours, not bad! And your instincts, Joelle, they will improve with experience. That's why we suggest starting with *small* rule changes. We can always adjust, so long as things don't go dire in reality, and, I suppose, as long as you adjust fast enough. You do only have fourteen changes left."

That's not exactly reassuring, but either way, I'm grateful Queen Bean is attempting to encourage me. "Okay," I say, "so, what next?"

And just like that, I'm whizzed back into my body, on the outskirts of my lawn, to the moment before I provoked the Bee to sting me. Kind of like a checkpoint in a video game. It takes me a moment to realize where I am and at once, I hear two voices talking to me:

"Joelle, sweetie, you okay?" says my mom from outside my body. In addition to her audible words and the visible aura bounding from her center, I can wholly *feel* her communicating with me. And as I focus on that feeling, other feelings start to invade this new sense.

"Joelle, you're fine. Let's get back inside," says Queen Bean from inside my head. "Oh, and those other feelings, that's your body recognizing others are talking about you elsewhere. We can work on this later, but if you focus enough, you can actually tune into those conversations and energies concentrated on you."

Oh, obviously, I think. *Of course that's it.* And despite disbelief, I try to do that, tune into whatever conversation is concentrated on me, just real quick, and to my surprise I see Queen Bean is right. I sense Darren and Colby talking about me, wondering if I'm okay and if they should hit me up or something.

Huh, pretty cool.

Queen Bean says, "Ever wonder where the woo woo belief that your ears must be ringing because someone is talking about you comes from?"

Then, realizing my mom asked me a question a few seconds ago, I say to her, "Uh, yeah Mom. I'm good."

Then I get a text from Colby in the group chat, wondering how I'm doing, which I ignore.

After telling my mom I'm good, rather than go back inside like Queen Bean suggested, I ask my mom if we can go for a walk around the neighborhood, for Maple's sake and what not. And as I'm saying this, Queen Bean directs a warning my way, "Joelle be careful now," she says. "Remember, if you die, that's it. All will be lost."

In my head, I think, *Come on, I've made it this far in life without dying randomly. I think I can safely go for a walk around my neighborhood with my mom and dog.*

But to be honest, Queen Bean's warning and apprehension changes things now. Even though I keep reminding myself this is a simulation, it feels *so* real. It feels realer than real, in a sense that for the first time, I'm actually seeing the living vibrations and energies beaming off all forms of life. The trees are *tree-ier* than I've ever known them, the grass is grassier, the bugs buggier, and what not. And all these energetic vibrations connect and interact with one another and the more I'm outside looking at it all, the more I focus on all this newness of stuff that's not new at all, of stuff I guess has *always* been around me, I'm seeing the interactions form almost concentric rings of a hexagonal nature. As if the living energies of everything on Earth overlap in a way that creates an astral beehive of life. And beneath these energies is the same 3D reality I grew up in, one that is as real as it's ever been to me, despite the fact I *know* I'm in a simulation built by

Bees. In the realness of it all, with Queen Bean's words looming in my mind, an anxiety rises in my gut and makes everything scary. Just walking around our safe and quiet neighborhood, my hands are now all clammy, my heart is racing, my armpits are leaking sweat, and every sound and movement around me spells F-E-A-R. My vision narrows and everything's bright, my face is flush, and I feel like I might faint.

"Breathe, Joelle," says Queen Bean. "Take deep *deep* breaths. In and out."

I stop in my tracks and do just that.

We make it about a hundred yards before I can't go any further. I say to my mom, "Hey, actually let's head back inside. I think I wanna sit down." And given my recent coma, she is more than happy to oblige the request.

Once we get back to the safety of our couch, my mom pulls out a book and I pull out my laptop. Maple snuggles up in between us.

In my head, I confirm with Queen Bean: *To be clear, I'm not allowed to tell anyone about what's going on? Like, I kinda want to tell my friend Sarah and ask her for advice.*

"That is correct. You *cannot* tell anyone about the simulation, about us bugs, or any of that. As we discussed, you can ask her for ideas regarding how she'd change the world for the better, but you cannot tell her specifically *why* you're asking."

Gotcha, I say inside my head. Then I ask my mom if she's cool with me having Sarah over. When she says yes, I call Sarah, but Sarah says she's going for a hike. She says she's glad I'm doing better and I'm welcome to join. I say I'd better lay low, given my coma, which she understands, so she tells me she could maybe swing by when she's done. I say Sounds good.

219

And here I am, left to my own devices, literally and figuratively. Tasked with saving the world.

Now, my mom's never been *that* much of a deep thinker, but I'm compelled to ask her all the same, "Hey mom, I got a question for you."

"What is it, sweetie?"

"If you could change something about humanity, something that would improve the world, what would you change?"

"Huh," she says, clearly taken a bit off guard, "I'm not sure, why do you ask?"

"I dunno, I guess I'm just curious. Please, humor me. Think about it. What would you change?"

Her first thought, I *see*, thanks to the energetic changes now visible to me, takes her to Dad, and I take pleasure in watching her memories of him coalesce all throughout her brainwaves. Then it hurts me to see those memories turn to pain. "Well," she says, "I suppose I'd make it so there are no drunk drivers."

"But that's already a rule, and it still happens anyway."

"Well, sure," she says. "It's a rule. But what if people just *didn't do it*? You said I could change something. That's what I'd change."

Inside my head, Queen Bean says, "That is certainly doable. But think about if you want to use one of your changes *for that*. How much better would that make the world?"

To Queen Bean's question, I obviously think of my dad. I think if it could have been implemented all those years ago, it would have made *my* world infinitely better. And then I think how many future people's lives it would make better. But still, I see her point. I'm not convinced it's *that* much of a game-changer.

After a few moments of thinking it over, I realize my mom is still waiting for me to respond. "Hey mom," I say, "I miss dad too." I shift on the couch to lean over Maple and give my mom a big hug. Some of the green goodness energy from my being penetrates hers and our two toroidal essences commingle to make us both feel loved.

Then, back to the task at hand, I realize something and think it out for Queen Bean. *Hey. If you can change behavior so people don't drink and drive, why didn't we just change behavior so people pick up trash, or better yet, so people don't litter? Why'd we have to make it some literal rule change that people would get upset about?*

In response to my two questions, Queen Bean says nothing. And in that nothingness of a response, I feel like I've been bamboozled. Why couldn't she just tell me all the rules of the game right away!? Why does she have to be so damn blasé about the fate of my species!? *Seriously*, I think, *why'd my first rule-change go down like that?*

"Because that's how *you* worded it. You said *Everyone over the age of 10* must *volunteer once a week*. If you had said, for example, *Everyone over the age of 10* volunteers *once a week*, well, then that would have been more of a behavioral change."

Okay, seriously? I didn't realize we were being so nitpicky with language here, like some sort of evil genie who is waiting for me to mess up my wish thanks to the power of semantics.

"Language is important," says Queen Bean. "It's how we communicate and get things done."

Great, I think. *Got it. Be more careful with my words.*

Man. What a waste of a rule change.

"It wasn't a waste," says Queen Bean. "At least you learned something!"

"Yeah, I learned there's still so much you haven't told me."

"I've told you the essentials, Joelle. Yes, there is a lot more I'm sure we haven't covered, but, it's like any kind of learning. If I just spill out every bit of information that pertains to what you're going through, you won't retain any of it. You have to *want* to learn the right information. Therefore, you have to specifically ask the right questions."

Honestly, at this point, I'm a little frustrated with Queen Bean. I don't care if she can tune into these thoughts.

Now I know it may be unreasonable to be frustrated with a Queen Bee who has given me access to sensing life in the sixth dimension and is apparently connected to a cohort of other Bees responsible for monitoring and protecting Earth, but still. Given all *that*, it feels like she should have been more forthright with me. Especially considering the underlying circumstances of my position.

So, given my frustration, even though she's insistent we get back to work, to fulfilling Sequence Two and deciding the fate of humanity and what not, I'm like, *You know what. I think I'm gonna chill tonight.* With that, I resign myself to spending some quality time with my mom since I've been so busy lately—pre-fifth-and-sixth-dimension-stuff—with work and everything. And even though this whole hanging out with Mom scene is existing within a simulation, it feels so real I decide it *is* real. Besides, given the chance I royally mess things up and humanity as I know it goes kaput, I'd like to spend some real quality time with the person (and dog) I love most in this world. So, my mom and I, we watch a movie and snuggle with Maple.

After the movie, Mom goes to bed and Queen Bean is in my ear insisting we get back to my duties.

To which I say, *Nah, I'm good for now. Sarah's coming over and I think what I'd like to do is get really really really high. Maybe then we can carefully brainstorm ideas to save humanity.*

Provided my conviction, I sense Queen Bean relent. "Fine," she says. "No pollen from my hive. It's just *your* batch of humanity at stake here. I'll be here long after we start with a new one."

Cool, I say, feeling like I may be finally claiming some power in this relationship, after which I wonder if that should even be something I covet. Which makes me think for a brief moment about any potential rules I'd like to create regarding the *concept* of *power*. And why and how humans generally go about coveting it.

"Yes, that is definitely something to consider, Joelle," Queen Bean says in response to my private thoughts. Then she adds, "Just remember, you can*not* tell Sarah what you know. I don't care how high you get. If you let it slip, we will be forced to cancel the simulation and, well, you know what that means."

10-4 roger that, I say inside my head. And I wait for my friend to come over.

CHAPTER 34

The Bosses had been busy Bees lately, Directly Eliminating key human actors they deemed permanently immoral. At first, they were only targeting humans responsible for ecological damage. But now their eliminations had expanded beyond that singular subset, and in doing so, had proved the Trees correct. Disregarding the Trees' concerns, The Bosses reasoned if they were to maximize their efforts with Fence Players, they should remove any human that fit within their classification of being responsible for the most collective badness.

They took out a few hundred corrupt politicians.

Decision makers in companies that dumped toxic waste into waterways.

Decision makers in companies that irresponsibly overfished or overlogged or, quite simply, overdestroyed.

Irredeemable racists and bigots.

Sexual predators and assaulters.

Those pushing the most buttons to create weaponized AI systems.

Highest-ranking media executives that consciously trafficked misinformation in order to stir up anger and perpetuate Us versus Them mentalities, all to drive clicks and ratings.

And what not.

Of course, there were many others The Bosses eliminated as well.

To carry out any of these elimination directives, typically, ants and hornets would swarm the target when they were alone.

Like one bad actor, a weapons dealer, he was taking a poop in his master bathroom when thousands of ants pushed the bathroom window up enough for a few hundred hornets to buzz in and sting him to death. They attacked when his wife and kids were out of town for one of his son's travel soccer tournaments.

As The Bosses increased the number of eliminations, it became growingly difficult to keep these disappearances inconspicuous. When they coordinated the elimination of a sex trafficker in Moldova, the young woman he was trafficking saw it all. This was a risk The Bosses willingly took, as they thought they could explain to the young woman, via the ants, what had happened. But this person who witnessed it all, this victim of human trafficking, she began telling more and more people, and legend of murderous bugs grew. Which was a legend the bugs had to pay close attention to, for if they were fully found out, then all might be lost for Batch Number 9. They couldn't risk the widespread panic it'd cause among the humans. Fortunately, the reach of this data breach was contained to a reasonable standard.

At The Bosses' daily meeting the following day, they determined they should probably be a bit more careful since Bees are not, after all, infallible.

They then moved on to other pressing matters.

Queen Bruth gave a report on her Fence Player, Jack Telda. "He's doing well. We are close to having him perform the necessary actions at Food First Service, and his wife responded better than we anticipated to our involvement."

"Quite unlike *our* Fence Player," a Boss from Paris said. "Upon further specific interactions, he said he couldn't take it anymore and jumped from a ledge off the top of Notre Dame."

At this, a few other Bosses chimed in and said their Fence Players likewise lost their minds and committed suicide.

"My Fence Player," said a Queen from Los Angeles, "saw an opportunity for personal advancement. He tried to secretly film the ants spelling out a message to then sell to a media company. Luckily, a Bee in the area detected the camera and we were able to have hornets and ants take care of the situation before anything leaked. It was a close call. We've determined he wasn't livestreaming the interaction because he wanted to sell the recording to the highest bidder, and to do that, he needed control of its dissemination. But the point remains, the humans' ability to livestream and the ridiculous number of cameras they have operating are potential weak points, if we are not diligent enough.

As more Bosses offered their experiences with Fence Players—eleven dozen spread out across the world—the news was more positive than negative thanks to the others in a similar position to Queen Bruth, whose subject was responding well to the new directions. These Bosses had Fence Players that were in positions of power or could step into a position of power that enabled them to create significant progressive change, mainly in the arenas of agriculture, politics, energy production, and public influencing.

At last, the conversation returned to the most important of all humans, Joelle Velstar.

THE BUGS

"Look," said Queen Bruth, speaking on behalf of her close friend Queen Bean, "we all knew Joelle would be slow on the uptake. It would take her time to understand her role, what she's been tasked with. We must be patient. I understand Queen Bean has not been the most efficient getting Joelle prepared, but they are at least progressing. They are now beginning to enact rule changes. Let us pray we have set the proper prerequisites and Joelle's instinct, rather than her conscious knowledge, guides her truly in the good direction. She naturally leans toward goodness, so let us hope she just gets that across in her changes."

"Yes," agreed the Queen Bosses in unison, "otherwise these humans are doomed."

CHAPTER 35

Jack Telda was not surprised to learn the ants were indeed correct. Upon his homecoming to Philadelphia and Food First Service, the acting board—a measly five-member team which was once eleven strong—showed their appreciation for Jack's return by naming him CEO. Turns out, Jack was the most senior non-board-member of the company left, and what was left of the board was in shambles trying to figure out what had happened to everyone.

There were, by the way, many news stories regarding the disappearances, none of which got to the matter at hand. It was becoming quite the mystery. And it wasn't just at FFS. Prominent members of society all over the globe were disappearing and no one had any good answers. It was a situation the NSA, CIA, FBI, homeland security, and other governmental agencies around the world were trying to get a beat on. But to no avail. The Bugs were too sophisticated, coordinated, and in control. After the small leak in Moldova with the trafficked individual, The Bugs had, for the most part, increased their attention to detail and became even more inconspicuous.

At Jack's first board meeting, the remaining board members started off with some small talk before getting to business. They asked him if he had any suspicions.

"I'm just as confused as you," he said, not necessarily lying, but playing coy all the same. "Whatever's happened, though, we still have work to do. The world's gotta eat. I say we stop needlessly speculating and get to it." He was doing his best to assert power over the board members at the onset, so he could dictate certain moves that would enable him to carry out the plan laid forth by the ants.

Throughout the first meeting, Jack assessed his hand with regards to who he was now working with. Of the eleven board members that were there before his sabbatical, six had been disappeared. Jack knew these six to be notoriously dishonest and opportunist individuals. Of the five remaining, Jack knew them to be good people, as far as his former boss, Roger, would have told him. Four of the five, at least according to the accounts he remembered from Roger, were more or less pushovers. Followers that would get in line with strong leadership. The one remaining board member who was not a pushover, Michael Peters, he'd been at FFS for decades. His reputation was that of an honest, hard-working son-of-a-bitch. He was largely responsible for FFS's becoming a monoculture powerhouse. Despite having four pushovers on the board, with Michael's presence, Jack knew if he was going to have any chance at implementing the ants' directives, he'd need a heavy say in selecting the nominations for the six new board seats the shareholders would ultimately vote on.

Now, to determine those six new members, this is how it worked: the shareholders of Food First Service would vote on nominations which were selected by the existing board. This is where Jack knew he had to assert himself.

To get on the right track, Jack dictated there would be a small committee that would select the nominations, and he subsequently placed himself as head of that committee. He justified this decision by saying FFS was experiencing unprecedented circumstances and as the new CEO, he was responsible for steering the ship, and since that's the case, he needed a say in who he'd be working with.

Skipping over the ensuing needless debates, Jack got his way and upon an emergency shareholder vote, the six new board members were, for the most part, easily influenced individuals. Fence Players that Jack could sway toward the buggy side of the fence.

From there, Jack's first order of business was to issue a press statement regarding the changes at FFS. Without running the statement by the board first, so as to get ahead of everything, this is what Jack disseminated to the press:

*Food First Service has been a global leader in food production since our founding in 1946. Since then, we have fed **billions** of people thanks to our innovative farming practices. Although this accomplishment should be heralded as a monument to modern agriculture, we must accept reality. Our innovations in increasing agriculture's yield have come at a supreme cost. Food First Service has ignored the studies—the pleas—of ecologists and others across the globe, all in a misguided effort to maximize short-term shareholder value. It is clear: Pesticides and herbicides are poisoning the land and killing off insects in unprecedented and quite frankly dangerous numbers. Massive monocultures are destroying topsoil. If we continue down this path, there will be less arable land to farm for future generations. That is why, effective immediately, Food First Service will rectify the damage we have caused by transitioning our food production model to regenerative farming practices, across all verticals of food production. It will take time to see the proverbial and literal fruit of this decision, upwards of 7-10 years, but in the span of* *humanity, that is nothing compared to what we will gain. More details will be released as they are set.*

Immediately upon releasing the statement, a pit formed in Jack's stomach. The stock market would *not* like this.

CHAPTER 36

Okay, one of my besties Sarah Lockwood is over and I'm constantly reminding myself to *not* spill the beans to her about our current reality, like the stuff about us being in a simulation and me having to save the world and what not.

When she got here, she asked me about my coma and made sure I was okay and told me what a good girl Maple was coming to get her for help.

After all that, we settled back into our old routine of just being good friends, hanging out. The only difference this time is I can see and feel and interact with her thoughts and emotions in a way I've never been able to sense before. Sitting next to me on the couch, Sarah is physically radiating good healthy loving green blue purpleness from her heart and brain centers.

But anyways, to start our hang, we go up to my room and each take a few rips from my bong, which makes me like 10X more in tune with her aura. Then we go back down to the living room to put on nature documentaries and veg out. I do my best to not think about the fact I can see and feel and consciously alter her energetic fields.

As we veg, the nature documentaries are a real trip for me. This time, unlike the countless hours of this stuff we've watched in the past, watching a naturalist explain the behavior of praying mantises, well it has a whole new meaning to me on account of my recent events involving the bugs. "I wonder who they're praying to," I say aloud, allowing Sarah or Queen Bean to answer.

"God?" says Sarah, in a way that tells me she's incredibly high without her saying she's incredibly high.

"Well us Bees, of course," says Queen Bean in my head. "They're asking for forgiveness for killing all kinds of bugs— mosquitoes, aphids, caterpillars, beetles, grasshoppers, et cetera."

Out loud, before realizing what I'm doing, I say, "And do you forgive them?"

"Joelle!" says Queen Bean, as Sarah simultaneously says, "Huh? What are you talking about?"

"Oh," I say to Sarah, "uh, sorry." I let out a fake laugh and say that since she said they're praying to God, I asked God directly if God forgives them. I conclude by saying, "I don't know. I'm *really* stoney baloney right now." Which seems to satisfy Sarah's inquiry into my sanity.

"Be careful," says Queen Bean. "You seriously cannot let her know you're talking with me. And to answer your question, of course we forgive them. We *tell* them to kill all those bugs. To protect human gardens and other beneficial plant life. As much as we Bees hate to admit it, some bugs just get outside of our control and, acting on their own nature, they can wreak some havoc."

Ahh, gotcha, I think inside my head.

A few more moments pass. I get lost in my own mind thanks to the weed and these documentaries and my new responsibilities and the fact I can now effectively communicate with Maple (she pretty much feels and says the same things I always imagined she would say). I want so bad to ask Sarah how she would go about saving the world, but in my current state, I'm afraid if we start going on about it, I won't be able to contain myself, I won't be able to keep everything a secret. So, on account of my fear of dooming humanity and what not, I say nothing of the sort. We just watch TV.

"I thought you were going to brainstorm!" says Queen Bean inside my head once it's clear I'm thinking of actively *not* doing that.

Too risky, I think.

Then, considering I'm being too big a wimp, I try to think of a way to talk about it without, you know, talking about it. The show is now featuring a forest frog and for some reason that makes me think about my dad and his favorite principle of Leave No Trace. Lots of things make me think of my dad. So, wondering if that could be a decent rule change—that humans leave no trace as they exist throughout the world—I figure it's a safe enough brainstorm question. "Huh," I say to Sarah, "if humans, and I mean *every* human, lived by the principle of leave no trace, what do you think would happen?"

Thanks to a long history of general quirkiness together, Sarah is accustomed to random and out of the blue questions from me. She thinks about it a moment, then says, "Well if you mean that *literally*, I'd guess there'd be no music or art or books or TV or, really anything, if you think about it."

"Huh," I say. "Yeah good call."

Then Sarah says, "I mean, you *could* take that a few different ways. Like, leave no trace might mean we wouldn't be able to create *any* trash, or extract *any* materials from the ground, or obviously kill *anything*, or build houses or other buildings, so, like, in that sense, I'm pretty sure that would extinct us almost immediately. We *have* to leave some sort of trace. *But,* on the other hand, like if you don't mean that literally, or like there could be a reasonable amount of trace left, or at least on a one-to-one scale or something, that could just mean everything we do has to be done with materials that can regrow or repopulate or whatever. Or if not, things that can be properly recycled to be somewhat useful again, like so there's not so much obscene wasted trash. Or maybe it just means we exist without massively polluting the planet and changing its climate or whatever." Sarah has a long-winded way of getting lost in tangents from time to time when she's high. And I love that about her. I'm the opposite when I smoke. I tend to go inward.

"Huh," I say, the weed keeping me from saying everything that's floating around in my head. "Yeah."

"She's got a point," says Queen Bean. "Ask her something else! Try something else!"

Easy, I think to Queen Bean. *Take a chill pill.* And immediately I can't believe I just said that to a powerful all-knowing Queen Bee, but whatever. Can't take back what's already been said.

"It's okay," Queen Bean says to me. "No harm done. You should know we Bees can get excited, too."

Unsure what to ask Sarah next, I augment the potential rule change of Leave No Trace to be: Leave The World Better Than You Found It, and quickly come to the conclusion that phrase is likely way too subjective. One person's better is not necessarily someone else's. I'd have to create rules detailing exactly what that means, and I just don't have that many rule-changes at my disposal. It seems like I gotta be more specific.

As the effects from the weed mellow out over the course of an hour or so, I realize I can actually bring up this heavy conversation *pretty* risk-free, as long as I stay super cognizant of not mentioning Bees and bugs or whatever. I mean, Sarah and I are best friends. We don't do small talk or medium talk or that kinda bullshit. We're always straight Big Talk. So, as we're watching a sequence on TV depict how the burning of carbon and massive droughts and extreme heat and record flooding and melting icecaps and everything are all interrelated, I say, "Man, shit." Then I pause a second before saying, "Lemme ask you this. If you were God and you could do anything you wanted, you know, within the confines of physics and what not, how would you save the world?"

Keeping my eyes on the TV, giving myself props for asking without being weird about it, I can *feel* Sarah thinking about the question next to me. Now, when people metaphorically say someone's gears are spinning when they're deep in thought, well yeah, I get that now. That's what it feels like sitting next to Sarah. Like there are gears within her clanging away as she processes my question.

"I mean," she says, "if I were God, wouldn't I be able to like *change* the laws of physics?"

"Well, I guess. But what if you couldn't. Or, better yet, let's say the old God got fired and you got hired as the new acting God of the universe. Like, you were constrained by everything the previous God had already done. But you still have *some* Godlike powers. In *that* scenario, what would you do?"

"Well, like, if I were God, at least as I envision it, I'd be able to kinda dictate how humans lived. In that sense, I dunno, I'd probably try to make some sort of utopic government." (Sarah was a poli-sci major, so it figures she'd go political to start.) Then she says, "Oh! What I'd do first is create a strict carbon tax and credit system on *every* business. Like, I'd have people way smarter than me come up with a plan to incentivize carbon sequestration and disincentivize carbon burning." (Clearly Sarah is influenced by what's on TV.) "Then," she says, "once I figure that out, I'd do the obvious stuff. Like, I'd ensure everyone on Earth has their basic human needs met. Food, housing, healthcare, electricity, internet—because, you know, that's basically a need nowadays—education, you know, stuff like that."

"So you'd implement some form of socialism," I say.

"Well, I guess? But, not like *strict* socialism. Although, since I would have Godlike powers, I suppose I'd actually be able to make socialism *work*, you know, without all the corruption and inefficiencies and stuff. I dunno. Maybe it'd be like a form of post-capitalism, kinda like a capitalistic-socialism thing or whatever."

"Huh," I say, my outward speech again hindered by how high I am. Not to mention, it's wonderful for me to sit here and observe Sarah through this new 6D lens and see her mind spin.

"Like," Sarah says, "I've been thinking about this lately. So if I'm God it'll give me a good chance to implement it. I'm thinking the system would have some rules where the highest-ranking member of a company can only make a certain amount more than the lowest ranking member, maybe on like a 20-1 or a 200-1 basis. So if an entry level employee earned 35k a year, the CEO/owner could only make 700k or 7million a year, or something like that."

"Huh," I say. "Wouldn't that, like, I don't know, disincentivize people from starting companies? Like, the allure of riches has to be a reason for all the innovation we get. Right?"

"Well," says Sarah, "think about it. First of all, 700k or, God forbid, *me* forbid in this case I guess, 7million a year is still a ridiculous amount of money, more than anyone ever needs. But to your point, yeah, you're right. It could disincentivize people from starting *businesses*. But I'm not sure it'd stifle innovation. And I mean, is that such a bad thing? Like, right now, people start all these useless companies all the time, with the main driver being they want to make money. The result is you get all these people who are just basically resellers selling all this consumable crap that doesn't need to get made. Retail arbitragers. So if you set a cap on how much money someone could make—which still allows them to live a life of means way above anything anyone could ever *need*—then you'd only get people starting companies because they think it's a company that *should* exist. Like, they gotta *really* believe in their idea. And not do it just for the money. Hence the reason I think there'd still be some innovation. Take away the money aspect and people still like building cool new shit."

"Damn," I say. "Yeah."

"And besides, if someone wants to earn let's say 20million or whatever a year, well then they'd just have to pay their lowest level employee a lot of money to make the ratio work. You'd have to figure out how to avoid loopholes so people don't create one-person companies and outsource everything else, but, you know, as God, I'm sure it could be done."

"True, true." I sit on that for a moment, think about how I could possibly put all that into a rule change. Then I ask her what else would she do, given these (to me not-so-hypothetical) Godlike powers.

Those gears in Sarah's head that were spinning are now on a roll. I can see the energy in her brain balling up to unleash a rant of wonderful proportions, but only after a quick question or two.

"Okay," she says, "as God, could I speed up the research and innovation to make lab-grown *legit* meat a thing? Like not plant-based meats. But *real* meat, just grown using stem cells. Like, I want to do away with industrial meat farming and stuff."

"Uh, sure," I say, "you can do that."

"Cool, then I'd do that. What about like safe fusion energy? Or, since I'm confined to the current laws of physics, could I make it so humanity invents light-travel or even faster-than-light-travel? Via stuff like teleportation or worm-holes or whatever?"

"Sure," I say, letting her continue that roll she's on.

"Nice. Oh! Yeah. Obviously I'd ensure equal rights and opportunities for everyone, make sure everyone treats others by means of the golden rule or whatever. And then once everyone's living peacefully, which I figure should take a day or so to get squared away, since I'm *God* and all, then I'd go ahead and clean up the oceans from all the plastic and junk, and then, since God can control the weather, I'd bring rain to drought-stricken areas in a responsible way so as to prevent flooding, and who knows, maybe God has some kind of global thermostat or something, so using that, I'd bring down the temperature of the planet, but only just a bit. Whatever the responsible amount is." (I make a mental note to check with Queen Bean to see if I can do all these things.) "What I think is," Sarah says, "by doing all this stuff, I'd reverse whatever the trending pattern of extreme weather across the globe is. And to make sure it stays well balanced and all, again, I'd implement rules to get people to sequester carbon and stop burning it more." (Clearly her focus has returned to the TV.)

In my head, I say to Queen Bean, *Please help me remember to ask you about all this stuff once I'm alone again.*

"You got it," says Queen Bean inside my mind.

Then to Sarah, I say out loud, "Damn. That's good stuff."

"Yeah," she says. "That oughta do it. Though I'm probably missing a bunch of stuff. Like how car culture sucks and cities should be designed around people and biking and shit. But I don't know, like I said, there has to be a ton of stuff I'm not thinking of right now."

"Eh, you're God," I say, "you'll figure it out."

"Oh! One last thing," Sarah says. "I think this should cover everything above. I'd make it so everyone is *happy*."

I nod to Sarah, say *hmmm* thoughtfully, then sit with that for a while.

Then, being as high as I am, figuring what's the rush, if the world's about to end pending any potential mess ups on my part, I sit back and take comfort in spending some quality time with my good friend, even if it's within this simulation the Bees built.

When Sarah leaves it's a little after 2am.

"If this is a simulation," I say to Queen Bean, "why did you make it so I get this tired? I figured it'd make sense to program it so I wouldn't be tired at all so I could work nonstop."

Queen Bean chuckles at me. She says, "You call what you've been doing tonight *work*? And you're tired because we made this simulation to be exactly as real as the real world. You know, plus all your new sixth dimension senses. Wouldn't you normally be tired after smoking weed with your friend and staying up until two am?"

"I mean, I guess. So, like, should I go to bed?"

"Your call," says Queen Bean.

I think about it, about how if I don't go to bed in the real world and get enough sleep my brain won't function as well the next day. So that's exactly what I do. After letting Maple out for her last poop and pee of the night, out of habit and not wanting to have bad breath, I brush my teeth and go through my normal nightly routine despite this whole simulation business and tuck myself into bed. Maple jumps up and lies between my feet and we try to hit the hay.

It only takes a few minutes before I realize there's no hope for me sleeping. Even though I can feel the exhaustion course through my body, my brain is too active for sleep. I think of humanity as it constitutes itself in my brain and how all of it rests in my naïve palms. How I feel wholly unprepared for this. And even though Queen Bean went to great lengths assuring me I was chosen for a reason, I still consider myself an imposter. I think someone else should have been chosen, maybe even Sarah, given how quickly she came up with all those ideas. I again think I'm not good or smart or wise enough to enact changes that will *save* and elevate humanity. I doubt myself over and over again, secretly hoping Queen Bean will jump in and reassure me. But apparently she's just letting my thoughts run wild. Or maybe she's sleeping for the night, too.

I wonder if I could refuse the position.

Like, why can't I just say no?

"Because you can't," Queen Bean says, confirming she is indeed *not* sleeping. "Simple as that, really. You just can't. Either you step up, or, well, you don't. And if you don't, well, that doesn't bode well for anyone."

Great, I think, as I fall back into the futile gesture of trying to go to sleep.

Okay, I may have gotten like 30 minutes of sleep, I don't know, but what I *do* know is I'm wide awake when the sun rises and outside light in all its undulating energetic glory enters my bedroom window.

In my pseudo delirium, my mind goes back to that day when I took a bunch of mushrooms and my ego collapsed and I made a fundamental shift in becoming a better person. Thanks to that recollection, I decide I'm going to break out the stash of mushrooms I have in my drawer. You know, to try and coax a psilocybin inspired breakthrough.

"Be careful, Joelle," says Queen Bean. "I'm not sure you need that."

But could it hurt? I think.

"Well, of course it could. You could take too much, have what you call a bad trip, and make some decision pertaining to Sequence Two that is wholly inadvisable. You could do that *without* having a bad trip. You could lose control, lose your connection to reality, and who knows, maybe you post online all you know about us bugs. You could spill the news to your friends. If you put yourself in a precarious situation, you could *die. So* many things could go wrong!"

But what could go right? I think.

"Well, I suppose there are some things that could go right, sure. *But,* does the potential good drastically outweigh the potential bad? Especially considering when the potential bad entails the temporary destruction of your species?"

I mean, Queen Bean of course has a point. So I compromise and decide to take a microdose. Enough to get it flowing in my system, but not enough to untether me from reality. Maybe make colors brighter and sounds better and connections in my brain stronger and less hampered by ego and what not. Besides, if the world is this much cooler given my new 6D lens of reality, I wonder what everything will look like with a bit of a mushroom-connection flowing through my neurons.

Since I'm showing no lingering coma signs and that I'm doing fine, Mom heads to work today. Once she's gone, I eat the mushrooms and take Maple out to go walk along the trails near us. Now I know that just yesterday, Queen Bean made me scared of even walking around the neighborhood for fear of death and what that means, but after a near sleepless night, I decide I need to move my body around, and the risk of me dying due to a walk through the woods is so preposterously low, and the benefits I get when I do walk through the woods is so unbelievably high, that it's worth it.

Within steps of breaching the forest, I have more questions for Queen Bean. Like, if I were to implement the rule change saying 100% of the world's energy is met by renewable and nuclear power, would that happen in the blink of an eye and be magically implemented? Or would it be a rule that requires the requisite amount of time to build out the infrastructure. I also ask her about all the stuff Sarah went over, about controlling weather, making people happy, how fast we could invent things like light-travel, and what not. You know, questions like that. I make sure to ask all of this one question at a time.

Queen Bean informs me that infrastructure changes, they obviously need the necessary amount of time to be carried out. However, behavioral or characteristic changes among humans, well *those* changes could be made somewhat immediately, at least as fast as it takes spiders and flies to disseminate the biological changes. But for the sake of Sequence Two, the simulation in which we're testing these ideas doesn't require the bugs to disperse the changes to humanity. The Bees can just make it so. *Then,* if the change is to be implemented, it'll take some time for the bugs to get to all the people in the *real* world. Also, apparently I can't control the weather. That's not necessarily a *rule* that can be changed.

"Got it," I say.

Now I'm walking through the woods. The aliveness of it all is making this a brand-new experience for me. I mean, I knew everything was alive before, but *now*, my God. It still boggles my mind to see everything has a pulsating aura flowing from its core, and all these auras connect hexagonally in a network of *life*. The rocks. The dirt. The trees. Ground. Everything. The hexagonal lifeforce network is all around and all-encompassing and bends and moves as I move through *it*.

Maple's trotting up ahead of me, secreting the happiest loving aura of all. The goodness she exudes warps the energies around her like some type of energetic gravity ball of joy. She stops every now and then to smell something on the trail, and when she's sniffing, I see the energy flow through her nose to her brain to create this kaleidoscopic activity of neural sensations. Meanwhile, I reflect upon what Sarah said last night. I'm basically probing my mind for things I *know* the world needs. But unsure what it needs *most*, I decide to make some sort of mental list. I conclude, at least according to my limited worldview, the world needs more:

- ❖ Love
- ❖ Compassion
- ❖ Empathy
- ❖ Equality, or, at least, equal opportunities
- ❖ People behaving like they know their actions have consequences
- ❖ Governments that work efficiently (which is laughable given their current state) and provide the basic necessities for life such as food, housing, healthcare, and all that
- ❖ More protected wildlife lands
- ❖ More carbon sequestration and less burning
- ❖ And
- ❖ I guess
- ❖ Per Sarah's suggestion
- ❖ More happiness
- ❖ Among other things

Now, given all those, what am I supposed to do? How am I supposed to encapsulate all those within the limited amount of rule changes I have left?

Since I'd like to make some changes that can happen immediately, I guess I have to focus on some of the behavioral ones on that list.

"Hey, Queen Bean," I say out loud, even though I can think it, "I have a question for you. If I make the rule change *Everyone On Earth Is Happy*, since I imagine happiness comes after all basic needs are met, does that mean, you know, everyone's basic needs are met?"

"Not exactly," says Queen Bean.

"Care to elaborate?" I ask.

"No," she responds.

"Oh," I say. "Why not?"

"Because it is not my job to make these determinations and walk you through each scenario prior to you enacting whatever rule change it may be. You must act on your instincts, play out the scenario in your head as best you can, and we will go from there."

"Gotcha," I say. So, testing the waters, growing impatient with myself, figuring I have fourteen more rule changes left, I say to her, "Queen Bean, this is my rule: Everyone on Earth is happy. Let it be done." I figure this one's gotta be a no brainer. If everyone's happy, that means no one's suffering, no one's hurting others, and all that good stuff.

Right?

CHAPTER 37

"Alright Bosses, *seriously?*"

The Queen Bee Boss from Chicago had a point.

Even though she hadn't made it yet.

"We spent more than one million years 'perfecting' our prerequisites for this round of Sequence Two all so our chosen one can go and spend the night getting high with her friend watching TV?"

"To be fair," said a Boss from Sydney, "we *did* program some of that behavior into the prerequisites. We wanted someone who spent time probing the depths of their mind, of their thoughts, sitting around asking silly questions with their friends. We can't exactly fault her for falling back on what she knows."

But the Queen from Chicago wasn't buying it. "Still, I thought some of that behavior got programmed out of her through Queen Bean's Coordinated Upgrades. I mean, for fuck's sake. She's dilly dallying!"

Some of the other Bosses were growing as frustrated with the process as Joelle had become with Queen Bean for not disclosing all she needed to know. "Yeah!" said a Boss from Istanbul. "Her first rule was an obvious disaster and waste of a change. And now, she goes with the happiness change! I mean, does she have *no* foresight? Queen Bean is doing a *horrendous* job! She has no clue how to guide a human through the fifth and sixth dimensions."

"Bosses, please," said Queen Bruth, coming to the aid of her close friend Queen Bean. "Let us trust the process. Allow her to settle into the role. Have some faith. Let us remember *none* of us Bosses have been in Queen Bean's position before. The only two Queen Bees who *have* been in her position are no longer with us, may they rest in peace. Please, go easy."

Since they're all Queen Bee Bosses and can communicate with one another as fluidly as they can feel their own feelings or think their own thoughts, the rest of the Bosses knew Queen Bruth did not have 100% conviction in her pleas. The way they saw it, a few billion years of planetary development, nine batches of humanity with varying hardware circuitries, all to have a stoner girl from the woods of western Maine waste away their best opportunity at Total Ascension. But, alas, the trigger had been pulled. Sequence Two had started. They had already used their cumulative reserves of Thoughts & Prayers. Now all they could do was wait and hope.

"I understand we played the probability," a Queen from Buenos Aires said, "and there is nothing more we can do at this moment in time. I just propose we keep record of these recent conversations top of mind, should something dire happen, and we are faced with starting Batch Number 10. I pray we were not too hasty. The Trees may have been right."

"Right or not," said another Queen Boss, "here we are, sisters. Here and now."

CHAPTER 38

Jack Telda strategically issued his press statement after the close of the markets.

While he commuted back to his freshly renovated suburban home, the after-market trading on FFS went berserk.

The next day, upon the markets opening, Food First Service's stock nosedived 60%.

Alone in his office, Jack's heart started racing and beads of sweat poured down his face. He could barely breathe. Dizzy, Jack stumbled to the door, locked it, then pinged Spencer—his assistant—to say he was unavailable for calls or anything. Inside, he longed for openness and the fresh air of being outdoors in the mountains. Here, he felt trapped. It was like the concentrated anger of tens of thousands FFS shareholders was scorching his psyche. All their fury, intensely directed towards a piece of writing *he* wrote, made its way through the air and ether, and although he could not place what it was specifically, Jack internalized this anger, and with it, he just felt *bad*.

Old habits bubbled to Jack's surface and he thought about pouring a drink. But, it being 9:35am and all, given his new(ish) state of mind, he didn't. He restrained.

Then, a trickle of ants emerged from behind his office fridge.

Jack. This is not helping. You need to be present. You cannot run FFS by feeling sorry for yourself. You have to trust us.

"But there's *no* way I'll be able to get everything done," Jack said. "I know what the numbers look like. I know the strength of our books. Why even try at this point?"

The ants rearranged themselves:

Apparently, you have forgotten the alternative to trying. You are not off our watchlist yet.

And that seemed to do the trick.

The least Jack could do was try.

Jack let Spencer know he was available again, and he was signing into his meeting with the board to face the music. He knew he was in for an earful from Michael Peters.

CHAPTER 39

Okay, I made the rule that *Everyone On Earth Is Happy*. Since I was in the woods, I found it pretty easy to get stung by a Bee so I could return to this void of the fifth dimension with Queen Bean and watch the whole simulation play out.

I mean, making everyone on Earth happy. That should be a pretty straightforward win, right? You'd think so. *I* certainly thought so. But here we are.

Again, to see this whole simulation thing get fast forwarded to test my rule change, here in a fringe of the fifth dimension built just for this, I'm basically in a fully immersive TV screen, like in the middle of an augmented reality cube. Whirls of every part of the world, all corners of human life, flash around me. And I know that sounds like it'd be a confusing mess, but trust me, *here*, it all kind of blends together nicely. Like I'm getting a pretty and organized mosaic of humanity unfold as a result of my decision. At first, my suspicions were somewhat correct. In order for everyone to be happy, everyone had their basic needs met, but then, like within a matter of seconds, that didn't work, because people no longer did the work that enabled everyone's basic needs to be met. Hundreds of millions of laborers across the world, in order to be happy, *in that moment*, simply stopped laboring. Doing that, *stopping work*, in that instant, made them happy.

Of course, once again, things quickly devolved. Yes, everyone on Earth, for that brief moment after my rule change, indeed *was* happy. But then, only a moment later, which for the sake of measurement lasted three seconds in this case, everyone returned to their normal state of being. Laborers picked up their work again. Prisoners, who at one moment *felt* free, realized the next they were still imprisoned, which re-made them unhappy. For the second time in a row, I bamboozled myself and this ridiculous rule change evaporated like a wisp of weed smoke. Everyone being happy all the time clearly is not sustainable, nor productive, nor, I guess, should it be the goal.

"Goddammit," I say to Queen Bean.

"See what ya did?"

"Yep." Well, now that I think about it. *Not really.* "Wait," I say. "What did I do?"

"Come on, Joelle. This one's easy. You have to figure this out on your own."

Well first, I realize, I didn't specify how long everyone is happy for. I just said everyone on Earth is happy. And according to that very specific wording, that can be accomplished for a fleeting glimpse of time. But I realize, even in watching those few seconds of the simulation whizz by, if I were to simply say "Everyone on Earth is happy forever," well, that's just not sustainable.

And now I'm questioning the source of happiness and what it means to be happy and if suffering of some kind is absolutely necessary in order for someone to *feel* happiness. Like a pendulum swinging, happiness is the antithetical outcome of some other sense of being, which I guess I'll just call sadness. But, that doesn't do this whole thing justice.

Ahh!

And there I go.

Getting lost in my own head again.

Since obviously my second rule change was another whopping failure, Queen Bean rewinds things a bit and places me back in my simulated body walking through the woods with Maple.

Back on the trail, I still feel the energetic kick of the microdose of mushrooms I took before heading out.

And with that kick I feel the connection to the Earth—as simulated as it is—beneath my feet. The dirt and trees and shrubs and squirrels and all life out on the trail are visibly emitting its vibrant wholesome lively force and interacting with mine, doing so in a way that irrefutably proves everything is connected. All is one. While yet, everything has *its* purpose, its being, its essence, its individuality.

Further pondering where I went wrong with the happiness thing, I search my mind for another answer. Another behavioral shift that could be made permanent, that could have a lasting change, and that could be so strong in its directive as to prohibit my self-bamboozlement.

Asking for this, my mind takes me back to a book I read in college, when I was on a modern philosophy kick thanks to my philosophy 101 class. The book, Victor Frankl's *Man's Search For Meaning*, had a profound impact on me, as I'm sure it did many others. And if only I had consulted its memory before the happiness rule, well, I wouldn't have gone with that, on account of the fact that oftentimes, one's meaning is found through one's suffering. So, now conjuring its lessons once again, my mind says, "Ding ding ding. There it is!"

And I think of course! What if I make it so every person finds meaning in their life? And, perhaps as a second or third order consequence of this, they find *fulfillment* in life.

But that alone, I quickly realize, is no good.

Harking back to Victor Frankl and what he and millions of others went through, one bad person's fulfillment could be a whole community's elimination.

Yikes.

Then I wonder, could I make the rule change saying no human is evil?

"I know I'm not supposed to help you this much," says Queen Bean in my head, interrupting my train of thought, "but I have to. Don't be so naïve. You can't just do away with an ethereal concept such as evil. The nature of the universe won't allow it, for it is the equal and opposite of another force that exists out there."

Then, before Queen Bean can go on any further, inside my head, then outward through my mouth, for the whole world to hear, I just start yelling. Screaming. As loud a primal roar as I can muster. I just want her to shut up and go away and god DAMNIT all these rules about the rules I can make!

"You know what," I say. "Fuck it. I'm done. You've built quite the simulation here. I'm just going to live out my life *here*. Fuck whatever happens out in reality. If there even *is* a reality. Who says that world and the humanity you're tasking me with saving isn't just another simulation itself? Who says I'm not in a legit non-bug-induced coma and I'm just dreaming all this up?" I start asking question after question, knowing that'll shut up Queen Bean. I ask, "Who says I'm not dead and this is what my afterlife is? Who says I *have* to do this? Who says I haven't just completely lost my mind and all this craziness is the sedative world I've concocted after the doctors knocked me out? Who says I can't call it quits and live out whatever life there is to live inside this simulation?"

After I wear myself out asking questions or thinking about other questions to ask, Queen Bean chimes in. She says, "Are you done?"

"Not even close," I say. But really, I am. I don't know where to go from here. I tell her, I say, "Hey, Queen Bean. Seriously. I'm done. I'm not playing this game anymore. Fuck this. I'm out."

But, obviously, it's not that easy.

"Ahh yes," says Queen Bean the moment I verbally commit to not partake in this mad challenge. "The critical moment of the hero's journey. Your refusal of the call to action. Quite meta of you, making me call this out. And coming quite late in the game, Joelle. Tsk tsk. This is supposed to have happened sooner. Can we please just skip a few steps and get you back on track?"

"What are you talking about," I say, unaware of what she means by the hero's journey.

"Nevermind," says Queen Bean. "Please, by all means then. Have a tantrum. Quit when things aren't super easy for you. Go ahead."

Damn reverse psychology.

I struggle to not let it get to me.

But.

Obviously.

It does.

"Argh fine," I say, putting some malice in those words.

"You can resent your fate all you want," says Queen Bean, "but that does not change your present circumstance. You are here. Now. Accept it or not, you must act."

CHAPTER 40

I am a Tree.

Though we Trees cannot do the things other living beings can do, we Trees have wisdom.

And look.

To be honest.

We understand where the bees were coming from.

This batch.

Batch Number 9.

Man, they've cut down so many of us.

And have killed so many bees and other bugs.

Extincting some, even.

And it's difficult to say whether or not the humans would have figured out solutions to their biggest problems without what the bees call Coordinated Upgrades.

And the like.

But now.

With Sequence Two in action, the bees can't exactly walk that decision back.

They're there.

Apparently they need to continue.

But we Trees are wondering:

Do they really need to continue with all their Directed Eliminations?

Seems a bit, I shall say, bloodthirsty.

And risky, too.

What started as targeting people responsible for ecological destruction has blossomed into targeting anyone they deem *bad*.

Why not let the humans *be*?

The bees believe they are supremely crafty and in control.

We Trees fear the bees overestimate their abilities.

And underestimate the humans.

Which is something—the humans have shown—is unwise to do.

CHAPTER 41

"Jack you goddam son-of-a-bitch! You've been on the job barely a month and you're *tanking* this company!" Sitting in his home office, Michael Peter's fury travelled from deep within his body, out his mouth, into his microphone, through the cloudiness of the internet, and was felt by everyone present on this board meeting, Jack Telda included. "You think you can undo eighty years of tireless work with a goddam press release? I won't allow it."

Doing his best to remain composed, Jack took a deep breath before responding. "I'm sorry you feel that way, Michael," he said. "I know how instrumental you were in building what Food First has become today. But as CEO, I have a new vision for this company that I hope you can get excited about."

"Or what?" Michael said.

"I'm not threatening you. I'm simply stating that I hope you join me in implementing this new vision for Food First."

The other board members on the call remained quiet. No one wanted to step in the path of Michael's anger.

"Now why the hell should I be excited about it?" Michael said. "We're basically printing money the way things are going. How could your hippy vision *possibly* excite me?"

As calmly and succinctly as he could, Jack did his best to reiterate the arguments the ants had prepared for him. "Michael, would you say your goal is in protecting the long-term interest of Food First?"

"Obviously," Michael scoffed.

"And by long-term—considering you've given every ounce of hard work you've had to give over your storied career—I mean that Food First continues as a global leader in agriculture, in perpetuity."

Given the compliment, Michael's ferocity subsided, but only a bit. "Of course," he said.

"Well," Jack said, "surely a man as smart as you can recognize our agricultural practices are not in the long-term interest of the land. Therefore, they could not possibly be in the long-term interest of the company."

"What the hell are you talking about?" Michael said. "Our agricultural practices are the only thing keeping Americans from starving!"

"But the land," Jack said. "Surely you can admit it is no longer as arable as it once was. And that it's trending in the wrong direction."

"Look, thanks to the farming technologies and crop modifications we've developed, we'll be able to grow corn in a field of dust for God's sake. I don't see what you're getting at."

"Clearly," Jack said. He took another moment to try and regain control of the conversation, to steer it back towards the points the ants had prepared for him. Michael was already dictating terms.

While Jack was thinking of what to say next, Michael spoke up. "This is crazy," he said, now addressing the other board members on the call. "Don't any of you have a spine? Can't you see this is madness? Switching up a winning strategy after decades of tediously carving out our space in this market? For some unproven, unproductive, unpredictable, unreliable hippy commune way of farming?"

"Well you see," said Jack. "That's where you're wrong. Regenerative farming is incredibly productive, incredibly reliable—especially given the uncertain climate we're facing—and is one of the most proven forms of growing food there is. Sure, I'll give you it's hard to predict what the yield will be, what with its requirement to grow so many different varieties, but that's part of the beauty. If there's a bad year for one thing, say corn, it could be a great year for another thing, say tomatoes, or strawberries, or kumquats, or whatever!" As Jack was saying all this, he knew these were not the kinds of arguments that would sway a man such as Michael Peters.

"*Predictability,*" Michael said. "Jack, the shareholders need to know what to expect from us. We're not operating on some first come first serve basis here. The *market* needs to know what to expect from us. Our farmers need to know what to expect for their efforts. The stores and customers need to know they'll have their perfectly shaped green bell pepper waiting for them every time they go to any grocery store they choose. Not to mention our cattle farmers need to know we have a consistent supply of corn and soy for their livestock. You're talking about uprooting the entire goddam system!"

"Maybe I am," Jack said without thinking. "I'm just trying to plan for the future here, Michael. The world is changing. We should be leading that change."

Alone in his office, Jack noticed his familiar friends making an appearance on the floor in front of him. While Michael rattled on about consistency and growth and everything, Jack read what the ants had to say:

You will not convince this man in one day. This will take time. Tell him you hear his concerns and you hope to find some way to work together.

CHAPTER 42

Okay, of course, Queen Bean is correct.

This *is* my present situation. And whether it's real, I'm in a simulation, I'm in a simulation within what's real, I'm dreaming, I'm actually dead, or whatever other options there are for explaining this whole mess, this is *my* reality, and accordingly, I must act. I tell Queen Bean I surrender, I accept, and, okay, let's do this.

Besides, I have to say, if my reality is that I'm tasked with augmenting the course of humankind to save it from destroying itself, then, well, shit, that's pretty cool. There's always been a grandiose inkling within me that I was gonna do something great with my life. Who knows—who cares—if that thought is common among countless others in my generation, on account of we've been told our whole lives we're special and what not. The fact of the matter is, well, it's now *my* true reality. I can't avoid it. The thoughts that come out of my mind these next few hours/days/weeks/et cetera will apparently determine if humanity as I know it gets to continue. So I better sit down and carefully plan those thoughts out.

Now, I typically have some good brainstorming sessions at The Joint, surrounding myself with good people. I decide to bring my computer there so I can sit down, have a beer or two, and write out all my thoughts on the matter before coming to any hasty conclusions. Not to mention, I'd love to see what it's like being there given these new sixth dimensional capabilities I'm working with. And also not to mention, it's the first Monday of the month, which means it's poker night later, and I *definitely* want to see how my new frame of mind will affect *that*.

As I think all this, in the distance, in the direction of The Joint, I can see the background energies over there vibe up a bit. Which means, apparently, I can see through space now, which is pretty cool.

"Oh yes," says Queen Bean. "Remember when I said you can tune in to the conversations going on about you elsewhere? Well, if you concentrate on that brightened background energy you just noticed, *really concentrate*, well, tell me what you see."

I do that. I concentrate even harder on that blip of vigor I saw pulse from The Joint's direction. As I focus more and more, almost like when you zoom in on your hometown from outer space on a phone, my vision is thrust to the goings on around the bar. Molly and Bob, visible to me as distinct energy beams, are opening the place up and they're talking about me. Seems as if my consciousness actively concentrating on going to visit them spurred their thoughts about me, and Molly is now saying to Bob, "Hey we haven't seen Joelle in a minute. Since before her coma. Maybe we should check up on her, make sure everything's okay." And Bob responds with, "Huh, yeah. Maybe later. I bet she'll be in soon, though. I heard she's back up and going."

All that—that is, tuning into conversations miles away that apparently happen because of my conscious thought—is yet another thing that's so far out there I can't do anything with the information besides shrug it off. I just readily accept it and move on with my plan. Which is to go and carefully think out my next rule at The Joint.

My job, I determine, does not need to be accomplished with my next thought to Queen Bean. I am not expected to, nor should I, choose the next rule change on a whim, like before. Clearly, with my first two changes, I didn't think them through enough. I went wholly with my instinct and acted on that instinct immediately, rather than let it guide me to deeper and more careful evaluation of its efficacy. Determined to be better moving forward, I decide that's what I'll do at The Burrito Joint. Really think it through. Not rush it.

When I get there, I see Molly and Bob—who are already visibly glowing in goodness and fulfillment—brighten up tenfold when I walk through the door. Upon seeing me, they put their knives down, step out from behind the bar, and both give me a big hug at the same time. The love they transfer into my skin and essence via the act of hugging feels like I'm getting injected with a drug whose side effect is the feeling your dog gets when you come home from work.

Molly and Bob say they're so glad I'm okay, they were *just* talking about me, how weird, and the coma must have been a big scare and what not.

I tell them it's no big deal, I'm all good now. Then I set myself up at a corner of the bar, tell Molly and Bob I've got a new client I'm working for, and I'm gonna hang out and fart around on my computer for the day.

"What's the project this time?" Molly asks.

Careful to not disclose any information I'm not supposed to, I stretch the truth a bit. "I've got a new client that wants me to help them define what it means to be a good human. They want me to help with this new, uh, marketing campaign they've got going on."

"Ahh, gotcha," Molly says, and I can tell by her face and the thoughts I see rippling out of her brain—her actual brainwaves—that she's like, *whatever you say JoJo.* And with that, she gets back to chopping peppers, whose energies are getting divided and subdivided with each chop.

Right then, I figure why not probe her a bit, see what she'd cook up if she were in my shoes. "Hey Molly," I say, "Before I get to it, what're your thoughts on the matter? What do you think makes a good human?"

I can see Molly really think about it for a second. "Hmm," she says. "I think I'd say kindness? And that a good person lives by the golden rule."

Bob's looking at Molly, smiling. "What about you, Bob?" I say.

"Ditto to what Molly said. And they eat a lot of burritos."

"Love it," I say. Though, it's not much to work with. Molly's idea is solid, obviously, but could it be that easy? Make one of my rule changes simply the golden rule? I sit on that for a second. How would that make a sadist act? Or a masochist? Or whatever. I quickly conclude there's too much vagueness there to work with. Settling in, I order a Yessir coffee stout and get to my brainstorm.

Before starting, I put on some headphones as the universal symbol for other folks at the bar to leave me alone.

Then, letting one thought take me to the next, I think back on my start with UMM—Upwards Momentum Marketing— and everything I was working on before this whole fifth sixth dimension Ascension stuff happened. Maybe there're some clues there.

Naturally, my mind takes me to my first client—The Burrito Joint—and here I am, putting that connection to work.

Then, I guess my mind just goes from one project to the next. I wonder: Do any of the companies I worked with have any tenets that can be broadly applied? You know, local rules global behavior complex systems 101 kind of thing.

I think of Yessir Brewing. And I guess Homegrown Clothes for that matter, too. Two companies that preached and practiced the value of local production, via newfangled technologies like indoor farming and agricultural AI and what not. On my computer before me, I make a digital Pros and Cons list of the principle: *Create food and goods using sustainable and local forms of production.*

I consider what that looks like for Maine, for other parts of the world, and for some reason, Vegas comes to mind. Then deserts in general. I think, *without rainfall, how will people in deserts grow enough food?* I think of San Diego and Los Angeles and the depletion of the Colorado River. Then my mind comes back to Maine. There's no *way* we could make everything. Like, I wouldn't be using a computer right now if *everything* had to be produced locally. Where would all the silicon and plastic and CPUs and GPUs and everything else come from?

So there goes *that* idea for complete local production.

But.

Then I go back to growing food in the desert thing. And how Yessir and Homegrown use a lot of indoor vertical farming for their production. Maybe that'd do the trick in the deserts, since that kind of farming requires less water than traditional agricultural practices.

CJ FRIEDMAN

Now look, the mind is a wild place. It ping pongs from one thought to another and before you know it, you're the good kind of lost in the woods that leads to a secret waterfall.

Work with me here: my thoughts go from my clients, to their work, to sustainable local production, to deserts, to growing food in the deserts, to indoor climate-controlled agriculture, to energy problems and constraints, to energy *abundance.* And here I am at this proverbial waterfall of an idea.

I'm contemplating making the technological rule change that humans, as fast as feasibly possible, advance *safe* nuclear technology to the point it becomes ubiquitous, since nuclear has the best power-production to space-taking-up ratio. I figure why not make it ubiquitous, you know, given any limitations with sourcing uranium and what not. And eventually, I'm thinking humanity invents safe and fool proof fusion technology. And with that, there's a ding ding ding ringing again somewhere in my consciousness. So, on my computer, before I express it to Queen Bean to make it happen, I work on a draft for my next rule change.

First, I write: *Nuclear power is as advanced as we can make it and*—just typing out stream of consciousness here—*nuclear weapons are destroyed.* Then, I stop typing. I think, *wait.* Something my consciousness remembers is fighting back. It's saying: What about the concept of mutually assured destruction? I remember reading somewhere at one point that since the nuclear bombs were dropped in Nagasaki and Hiroshima, thanks to Mutually Assured Destruction, the world has never seen such a peaceful time. *Which is crazy,* another part of my consciousness is saying, considering how much war there's been and how much fighting there still is.

268

This all leads me to spiral in thought regarding a rule change that would effectively destroy the principle of Mutually Assured Destruction. And I quickly come to the conclusion I'm too ignorant on the issue to undo it, even though some part of me is saying we should *definitely* get rid of all nuclear weapons, like fucking *duh*.

Then I think, why can't I just make the rule change: People don't kill other people, like, *at all*. Wouldn't that solve it?

But then my mind ping pongs back to my *original* point, about energy abundance.

Obviously, I've abandoned the draft and am now lost again in my own head.

The rule change was *supposed* to head in the direction that humans create fusion technology and use it to create abundant clean energy for *everyone* on Earth, at a reasonable cost, which is, you know, the cost to operate the whole network and what not. Really which is to say I want to make the rule change express something like corporations can't rip off customers. And as I'm thinking all *this*, I think about monopolies and how I should incorporate *that* into the rule and

God

Damnit.

I realize, by the time I craft a bamboozle-free rule, I'll need to create a whole freaking constitution with clauses and sub clauses and what not just to express one rule change.

Then I think about that a moment. "Hey Queen Bean," I finally say inside my mind, inside this simulation, realizing I can lean on her sometimes for answers. "Can I do that?"

"Uh," Queen Bean says, apparently taking a moment to check with whoever it is she checks with. "Yeah. So long as the

Rule change starts with *Queen Bean, this is my rule:* and then ends with *Let it be done.* Whatever you say in between those two lines will be counted as the one singular rule change, so long as whatever you say there is feasible within the confines of rule-changes."

At this point, I don't even bother getting frustrated with her for not telling me all this, an effective loophole in the 15-rule-change system. I'm more looking at it as *my fault,* you know, as in like, all this power to learn all this stuff was there for me to learn, I just had to actively seek out the knowledge and *ask the right questions.*

Now, braced with this new game-changing knowledge, I take a sip of my Yessir coffee stout and get to work, typing out my new constitution.

After three waters and two extremely slowly sipped beers, switching from stout to amber ale, after numerous additions and deletions and amendments and sub clauses, I think I have it. A rule change that will ensure abundant and affordable clean energy for the entire world, while protecting all consumers from corporations of any kind, effectively making all corporations certified B-corps on steroids, meaning they focus on a triple bottom line—People, Planet, Profits—and doing all this while ensuring countries don't destroy one another. I throw in the clause no human can kill another human, thinking that would end all wars and violence and what not, which is great, and I also throw in the stuff Sarah talked about regarding carbon sequestration and burning and its whole tax and credit system, and put the onus on figuring out the specifics of that on world leaders, who, I add as a subclause, are honest and not corrupt. For good measure, I also include the clause governments provide food, clothing, housing, healthcare, electricity, and high-speed internet as basic human rights. And I also throw in Sarah's ideas about capping the CEO or owner of a company's pay to 25X whatever the lowest level employee makes, and a quick line about how cities are designed for people, not for cars.

I re-read my 30-page document three times over before I'm confident there's nothing I missed, nothing that will sneak up on me. It takes me another beer before reading it that many times, and by the fourth read-through, Colby Winters and Andrew Stout arrive at The Joint. I nearly jump out of my seat when Andrew lifts off my noise cancelling headphones to say, "Yo JoJo what's goin on?"

Startled, I quickly slam my laptop shut for fear of them reading what I was doing. I play it off and just tell them, "You know, normal work stuff."

They ask why I didn't let them know I was getting to The Joint early, they ask about my coma, and what happened in general, and how I'm feeling. They say they're here to pregame poker.

Another dozen or so moments later, Darren Stout joins us straight from work and then Sarah arrives and now the whole crew is together.

I'm so jazzed up about my constitutional rule change I consider ditching poker night to get to it, but then I decide against that. Like any piece of work I've ever done, it won't hurt to let it sit for a while and go back to it later with fresh eyes. Besides, like I thought earlier, playing poker with my new 6D senses is going to be a real trip.

Knowing how these nights play out, I'll likely be here till closing time, so for good measure, I text my mom to let Maple out when she gets home. Now, I know this is a simulation created by Bees and that *that* Maple back home isn't really *real*, technically, but still. She whimpers and snuggles and projects pure love and is the absolute best like the real Maple, so even though she's a simulation dog, I make sure she's taken care of. I also text my mom to say, for her peace of mind, I'm feeling good and there've been no weird coma symptoms. Ok good, she texts back, that's great.

So, yeah.

Poker night.

This should be interesting, especially considering I can actually see and feel and augment (provided I focus hard enough) the energy of the people around me.

By the time we're ready to start playing, the place is packed.

To me, every interaction between everyone in The Joint is an explosion of energy right before my eyes, explosions I can *feel* in my gut. Every high five, every pat on the shoulder, every word spoken, every thought thunk in the direction of another, every interaction, it all takes the shape of bands and waves and fluctuations of *energy*. Every one of them crisscrossing one another and transferring all spectrum of colors back and forth and back and forth, bringing the room to a kaleidoscopic hexagonal equilibrium of how everyone in The Joint *feels*. And here in this room, right now, the amalgamation of everyone present feels *good*.

The more I observe and engage, the more I feel my ability to interact with these energies. I can honestly work with people's energies as easily as I can stack a chord of firewood.

Like how Andrew, the younger of the Stout brothers, is pulsing what, at least to me at first, is a legible blue-red-orange-brownness that reads he is so happy to be off work and at The

Joint drinking beers. Work for Andrew is paving roads all over the state of Maine. So me, wanting to make everyone's time better, I pat him on the shoulder and say it's good to see him, and I focus on projecting some *good* vibes his way. With them, I see his colors glow less red and orange and, in their place, get replaced by some more blues and even some green; a green which is further bolstered when he takes a gulp of beer. With his first taste for the evening, I can see the beer's coldness transfer a feeling of warmth and goodness down his throat to his belly, then back up to his brain and finally out to the rest of his body and the world beyond.

Darren, meanwhile, the older Stout brother, his insides are glowing out a legible bright green-purple-yellow-turquoiseness. Again, I say *legible* because these colors and vibrations bursting from his core are clearly showing me, as if I could actually read them, without Darren even telling me, that he had a productive day at the mountain's admin office. Apparently, according to his gut and brainwaves, everyone's expecting an awesome winter season thanks to the Farmer's Almanac predictions and now reservations and season ticket sales are going through the roof.

These colorful energetic vibrations I'm reading within each person, to reiterate, are brightest and most concentrated around two points: an individual's heart and their brain. When I see a person project two different and conflicting colors, most of the time it's due to some struggle between what the brain is thinking and the heart is feeling. And, yeah, to me, as clear and tangible as the bar I'm leaning on, I see these bright epicenters of my friends' brains and hearts pulse out in a clear path throughout their nervous systems to the tips of their toes and fingers. These pulsations then inhabit space all around their physical bodies as a kind of toroidal energy sphere circulating back to their heart and brain. These spheres, for some people, like Colby Winters, the boisterous person he is, can extend far beyond the physical body to really interact with anyone close to him. Meanwhile, people like Sarah, who's more reserved when she's in a large group, I can see her pulling her energy inward, trying to not overlap too much with all the people around us; I can see she just wants to interact with *us*. Oh yeah, Sarah, by the way, is giving off this yellow-greenness that is typical of her, showing me she's calm and content and present.

Okay, we're now a few rounds into poker and let me start by saying: I could have won everyone's money the first hand if I wanted to. Thanks to their energetic outpourings, I can effectively tell exactly what cards they have, and then, based on how I'm projecting feelings towards my cards and theirs, I can alter their decision making trees to make them bet more and more and more, even if they have bad cards, or, to have them bet and bet and bet, and then fold if I were to make a significant bet myself. It's really weird. I can *literally* control things here, which is a strangely powerful tool *I do not want to use*. I can see how this could be potentially disastrous if *everyone* had this ability. Makes me think I should keep this top of mind when going back to my new constitutional rule change.

Not wanting to abuse my powers, I play legit to keep the game more fun. And rather, I really just concentrate on the rest of the room, how The Joint is flowing, and how everything is working, you know, given the new 6D lenses I'm looking through.

Like with Andrew, who must be on his sixth or seventh beer. I remember when he was sipping from his first round, how the cold beer propagated a green warmth of goodness throughout his body. But now, with each sip, a red-brown murkiness seeps into his system, and it's *not* good. The goodness I could see he received from beer stopped sometime near the end of his second round.

Anyways, while Colby's shuffling, Darren's phone starts ringing on the table, and with it, only visible to me, a dark red glow is forming. Darren picks it up, "Hello?" he says.

The others at the table can't hear what's being said through the phone, but I can see the words are: *Darren, this is Doctor Jones over at Franklin Memorial Hospital. Your mother had a heart attack and she is now in surgery. You were the first family member I could notify. I recommend you let the rest of your family know and you get to the hospital as fast as you can.*

This is a moment in which a metaphorical colloquialism is actually pretty damn spot on. The moment Dr. Jones says all that and the informational energy transfers through Darren's ears and into his head, I can see a literal dark pit of despair form right around his stomach area. Hearing his mom's life is in jeopardy, Darren formed an actual pit in his stomach.

Darren asks the doctor a few more questions. Everyone at the table quiets down.

Listening to his brother on the phone, seeing his face, Andrew starts to project a fearful energy.

After hearing things weren't looking good and he should really get to the hospital as fast as possible, Darren hangs up.

He lets Andrew know, who isn't developing a pit, per se. But Andrew's energy is definitely *scared*.

The power of the fear and confusion coming from Darren and Andrew completely change the energy sphere encircling the table. Luckily, Darren was sober driver tonight, so he's only had one beer. They tell us they have to go. We all say Yeah, of course, we understand. I want to tell him not to worry, this is just a simulation and it's not real and that everything is going to be fine, but obviously I can't do that. I let them leave.

And now it's only me, Sarah, and Colby, with a pile of chips and cards on the table.

Again, I know this is a simulation and everything, but *damn.* Their pain and fear was so *visceral.*

Simulation be damned, I hope their mom is okay.

"Don't worry," Queen Bean says inside my head, "this simulation is just built on probable statistics. Back in reality, well first of all not this much time has passed, and secondly, Mrs. Stout is doing just fine."

Still though. My friends' pain, even if only simulated, pained me.

Colby, Sarah, and I divide the money, call it quits for the game, and decide to hang out. We're all too affected by Darren and Andrew's burden to continue.

By closing time, I'm a little sauced up, and Molly and Bob offer to drive me home. Now, a few beers deep, the alcohol is blurring the visible auras of everything around me, melding it into a *less* comprehensible mess.

It's 11ish pm when I get home.

Upon arrival, I let Maple out again, and, feeling so good about all the work I did during the day, I open up my computer to read through my 30-page rule change.

And you know what, even though the words are *slightly* doubled as I go through it, I'm happy with what I've written.

Before I know what I'm doing, having only re-read 4 pages or so, I say, "Queen Bean, this is my rule—"

"Hold on," says Queen Bean, "are you sure you don't want to wait till morning, when you are sober, and you can read it again after sleeping on it?"

But I can be quite stubborn, especially when I've been drinking. After taking all of two seconds thinking it out, I say, "No, I'm going with my instinct. Queen Bean, this is my rule:" I read the 30-page constitutional document out loud, and conclude by saying, "Let it be done."

CHAPTER 43

Okay, I read my ridiculously long rule change out loud, confident I didn't miss anything, thinking that if I spent any more time on it, I might actually overthink everything and I could potentially undo some good shit that's in there, and so yeah, I went with it. My third of fifteen rule changes. It's a doozy.

Then, since Mom's in bed, I go out to the back yard and agitate the hive of Bees that's just on the outskirts of my lawn. I get stung and sent to the fifth-dimension simulation viewing room, and here we are. So far in the simulation, things are going *way* better than the first two, both of which ended almost immediately. This one, we're already sped up like fifty years or something. All energy across the world is powered by strategically located solar, wind, hydro, nuclear, and yes, now even fusion technologies. Pollution is *way* down, and things on that front are looking good. Carbon sequestration incentives seem to be working and the world is actually carbon negative now, and trending in the right direction. And there's drastically less income inequality due to my salary ratio rule.

But, there's still war.

Like, *lots* of it.

Fighting over what's left of rare Earth materials. Also some religious and territorial and other political stuff, too.

Queen Bean and I are watching as a not-to-be-named-country is developing a fusion bomb that really, would just mean the end of everyone and everything, which, in other words, would trigger what Queen Bean and the Bees call the Final Alarm, where they exterminate us humans and start all over again.

At one point I think, *Wait, I thought I made the rule change humans couldn't kill one another.*

Then, as quickly as I think that thought, it hits me. I've bamboozled myself again.

When a war is fought primarily with drones and rockets and even guns for that matter, it's not a human doing the killing. It's literally a bullet or bomb or something of the sort. The human may be making the decision, may be pulling the trigger, but they're not the final cause of death.

Figures. I screwed that one up.

But, based on how everything else seems to be going, the rule change, overall, seems to be a decent one. I ask Queen Bean if we can rewind things, so I can add the sub-sub-clause in: Humans cannot kill one another, nor can they make decisions that directly result in some *other* object killing someone. Or something like that. I'm tempted to write, *People are cool to one another,* but I know better than to leave that type of vagueness within a world-altering rule change. I also determine to add in a clause about universal religious freedom, toleration, and what not, and for good measure, something about how whatever compels people towards racism or sexism or other types of *isms* is thusly eliminated. (I of course check with Queen Bean to see if that's doable, and I guess it is, which makes me feel like a bad person for not including it in the first constitutional rule change.)

Queen Bean says yes, we are allowed to rewind and add in all those sub-clauses and everything. "By the way," she adds, "just a reminder, due to how the relation of time works here in this simulation vs back in reality, a good portion of time has passed back in the real world."

Oh, fuck. I forgot about that. "How much time?" I ask.

"A little more than a year."

"Shit." Then, remembering I can check in on my physical body, I ask Queen Bean for a quick peek. And there I am, still in the hospital, and Mom is right there next to me, looking a bit worse for wear. Maple is still there too. "Shit," I say again. "What happens if this new amendment is so good and time fast forwards even more?" I ask this knowing the answer.

"I think you know," says Queen Bean. "Still, we must continue."

"Well, how can I make it so I get back to reality before too much time passes?"

"The only way to do that is to create the perfect conditions under which The Bosses deem humanity is safe to Ascend. Other than that, we are here for the long haul."

Thinking I shouldn't waste any more time, I decide to stop worrying, go back, add a clause that really firms up the no killing one another thing and the bit about how humans are cool to one another (but with more specificity). As I'm thinking that, I figure why not do away with all guns anyways, since, contrary to what some people might say about the only way to stop a bad guy with a gun is a good guy with a gun, I'd say what stops a bad guy with a gun is the bad guy *not* having a gun in the first place. Back in the simulation, I add all these clauses, and now that I'm sober, for good measure, I give the whole thing another once-over.

As I read, I decide I'm on to a good kind of strategy here. That if a rule change is not absolutely *perfect*, I can always come back and add on clauses and what not to make it more perfect. Twelve more tries ought to be enough, I hope.

"Indeed," says Queen Bean, "I agree. You're on to something here." And for the first time since we met, I can feel some semblance of confidence in the way she's speaking to me.

Once I'm happy with the new document, I read it out loud, say so be it, go ahead and get myself stung, and hot damn, this new simulation is going *good*. So good, in fact, I'm getting worried again about how much time is passing.

We're already like two hundred years into the future and as I predicted, there's no more war and people aren't killing one another and there's abundant clean affordable energy which is powering whole new innovations that are pretty kick ass. Like new ways of flying and personal transportation. It's likewise doing wonders for space travel and exploration. And in addition to clearing up pollution by eliminating fossil fuel consumption, it's also enabled abundant water desalination plants across the world. Which means massive droughts are no longer such dire events, since some of the other innovations that've sprung up use this new energy and source of freshwater to refill water tables and virtually eliminate the effects of drought, which, it turns out, more or less eliminates what I thought would be a need for indoor agriculture.

I mean, I start thinking to myself, *Damn, I'm not sure I could have done any better.*

I mean, also, yeah, it sucked when I saw all my friends and my family and Maple die during the fast forwarding, but that also happened in the last rule change, when it went forward fifty years or so. I'm able to rid myself of any hurt by reassuring myself it's all a simulation that can be rewound and those deaths weren't real. My only fear is that too much time is now passing in real reality.

Then, after fast forwarding about three hundred years, as if in response to my internal dialogue, Queen Bean says, "Hey Joelle, I thought you should know, given how much time we've simulated between this change and the previous, about seven years have now passed in *real* reality. Your mom, I've just got word, your *real* mom, she's sick."

That pit of despair I saw form in Darren's stomach during our simulated poker night, yeah, I can now feel it despite not having a body in this fringe part of the fifth dimension.

It's honestly crazy what time is like here. I've watched 300 years fast forward in what feels like a normal movie timeframe, and another 50 years from the last simulation in what felt like a song, and meanwhile, *seven* years have really passed.

Fuck.

My mind starts to cripple itself with worry. What was Mom doing these past years? Did she ever leave my side? Have I been in the hospital *that* long? How the hell was she able to afford that? Why didn't she give up on me and have them pull the plug?

"Hey Joelle," says Queen Bean, "I know you weren't asking me directly, so even though you just asked a whole lot of questions, I'd like you to know, as I said when we first went over this, we Bees were able to pull some strings to allow you to continue living in that state; your friends set up an online fundraiser and we instructed an individual to donate several million dollars to the fund, which effectively took care of your bills and your mother's financial worries for that matter. Your mother has been visiting with you pretty much every day. The doctors, according to their knowledge, have told her they have no idea what's going on and you could wake up any moment, hence the reason she hasn't pulled the plug, as you say. They're baffled as to how your body has maintained its muscle, unaware of course that it's been us Bugs, as I've already told you. They told your mom the fact you are still so healthy in every other respect besides your consciousness bodes well. But now, as I said, I'm sorry to report your mom is sick."

This all tosses a ten-pound axe in my gut. I feel *so bad* for my mom. My *real* mom. Like, she doesn't deserve this. Then, while thinking about my mom and the passage of time, it hits me. "Wait," I say. "What about Maple?" Seven years later, that'd make her a little over twelve.

"Maple is still alive," says Queen Bean, instantly reassuring me. "But she's an old pup now, Joelle."

In an instance of positivity, I think: well at least my mom had Maple all these years and Maple had her. They did both love each other.

Though after those few good thoughts, everything Queen Bean has said finally starts to settle, and I ask her all about what's going on with my mom. She tells me my mom has pancreatic cancer and there's a small chance of getting it cured.

I honestly don't know how to respond to that. My mom's mortality hasn't been something I've seriously pondered before. This sudden news has blindsided me.

Bringing it back to where we are and what we're doing, I wonder, I ask, "Wait, about this simulation that's being fast forwarded... If we keep fast forwarding to see how it goes... will I ever be able to go back to Earth, to reality, and see my mom and

Maple again? Like, maybe we can pause Sequence Two or something."

Queen Bean once again reminds me of the rules. That they cannot stop *real* time. And to carry out Sequence Two, although a lot can happen over the span of real earthly time, like the witnessing of 300+ years of simulation being played out, they cannot do anything about reality. And if I want to get back to reality, I have to solve this problem and get The Bosses to approve Total Ascension for humanity and what not. Only *then* will they be able to place my full consciousness back into my real body, which will precede them giving all of humanity access to these sixth-dimensional capabilities I've been experiencing.

I think about it a second before saying, "So, like, should we keep going with this fast forwarding? I forget what we're looking for."

"Well," says Queen Bean, "We're looking for the qualifiers to be indicated that the proposed rule change can trigger Total Ascension. You're off to, I guess, a decent start here. To be honest, we've never triggered Total Ascension for humans before, so we're not 100% sure what's supposed to happen. It's kind of like the definition for porn you humans came up with: we'll know it when we see it."

"Great," I say. "Just great. So three hundred plus years isn't good enough?"

"Apparently not. But, look on the bright side! At least it hasn't proven to be a total failure yet, right?"

"Yeah, right."

I stew on this for some time. I know I'd get to see Maple and my mom in this simulation, if we were to rewind again, and all that *feels* real and everything, but I start to bug out. I want to pet

Maple and hug my mom *for real*. I start wondering how I can speed things up without, you know, speeding things up. I want to unlock the key to whatever Total Ascension is and I want to do it *now*. Then I think, wait, holy shit, do I even get to see Maple and my mom in *this* simulation anymore? Addressing Queen Bean with my thoughts, I ask, "Can we rewind this thing and start with a new rule change?"

"You can do that," says Queen Bean. "Or, you can add rule changes onto where we currently stand, to see how they affect the society that has formed as a result of the change they're living under now. Just remember, if you are to rewind, and we have to fast forward this much again, that'd be another seven years or so in reality just to get where we are. Based on our experience with the man in Atlantis, it's best to add on to existing rule changes to see how it alters the structure of society you've affected thus far."

A real Sophie's Choice I got here.

I wonder what result would get me back to my real family fastest.

Then I realize, if things are going as good as I hope in the simulation that's running now, maybe I just need a *few* tweaks to get it going perfectly to trigger whatever needs to be triggered. Accordingly, I start wracking my brain for new clauses to add, ones that'll perfect human society.

A small and easy task, I know.

Creating the platonic ideal of humanity.

Or whatever.

But that's just what I set out to do.

I wanna hug my real mom and snuggle my real Maple girl again.

PART THREE

CHAPTER 44

Antonia, an ant, in perfect lockstep and beat with her four million immediate kin around her, chanted:

"CHARGE!

CHARGE!

CHARGE!

WE WILL CHARGE!

CHARGE!

CHARGE!

TOGETHER WE ARE LARGE!"

Millions of ants, all chanting the same chant, all marching with one directive.

Meanwhile, Horatio, a hornet, chanted—well, buzzed—with his kin as they flew ahead of the marching ants:

"YEAH!

FUCK YOU!

WE'RE HORNETS!"

Over and over again:

"YEAH!

FUCK YOU!

WE'RE HORNETS!"

Their collective target: Michael Peters. The board member at Food First Service who has been a real stinger in Jack Telda's side ever since Jack took over as CEO, seven years ago.

Over the past seven years, by the way, the bugs had taken out more than a few negative influencers who have presented strong oppositional voices to the plans Jack was directed to carry out, provided, of course, they were bad people that showcased no inclination towards changing for the better. They hadn't taken Michael out yet because although he provided an oppositional voice, he wasn't really *bad*. He was an honest man that behaved in accordance with his own self-perceived virtues.

Only recently did Michael consider taking to dishonest means.

For the past seven years, Michael had been growing angrier with Jack as he wrangled FFS away from industrial monoculture farming, something Michael believed to be a cornerstone of feeding billions of people across the globe, and something he had personally oversaw the development of during his thirty-five-year tenure at the company. Michael finally reached his limits after Jack orchestrated the sale of the last of FFS land in Brazil to a local conservation organization for pennies on the dollar.

To get Jack ousted from his CEO position, Michael started concocting a scheme that would result in Jack getting falsely accused of some type of abuse. What that type of abuse was, Michael had yet to decide. The plan only got so far as him broaching the topic with his pet snake.

Michael, a forever bachelor, vented to his snake every time it circled and consumed its live mousey meals. Of course, these conversations were monitored by various kinds of flies in Michael's house, so, when he talked of plans to get Jack in trouble, the news was immediately reported to the Bees. About how he was going to get someone to say Jack engaged in improper conduct, like sexual assault or something. The Bosses, hearing this, wanting to make Jack's mission of turning FFS into a *true* agricultural friend of the environment as frictionless as possible, decided this type of dishonesty was enough to take action.

Now, as Michael sat on his porch smoking a cigar at sunset, the ants and hornets marched and flew.

What's that? Michael thought, seeing the approaching horde of ants on his lawn before him. He stood up from his Adirondack chair to get a better angle.

By the time he could hypothesize the moving mass crawling across his lawn was millions of ants, the fastest hornets were already upon him. Ten, thirty, a hundred hornets now, swarming and stinging his face.

Michael slapped and slapped at the hornets, tossed his cigar, then instinctively sprinted for the inside.

Six hornets made it in with Michael by the time he slammed the door closed.

Inside his house now, the six hornets attacked and attacked, but Michael, after first choosing flight by coming inside, now chose fight. He slapped and grabbed at the hornets as they flew about his head. He snagged one in his hand to squeeze it, did so, but not before the hornet stung his palm. At this point, though, the pain didn't even register. Michael's adrenaline was pumping like it never had before and he fought like that was the case, swinging wildly and viciously at the hornets buzzing about him.

By the time he killed all six hornets in his house, Michael's face was a puffy mess from the twenty or so stings the hornets were able to get on him from the onset.

Though the house was temporarily clear, there was no time to calm down and reflect upon the madness because the moment he paused to confirm there were no more hornets buzzing about, fifty steady streams of ants were now crawling in from various points in his house. All converging directly on him.

Michael's first thought, pulled from his subconscious, went to all those years ago, when one of the junior VPs at FFS disappeared and his wife claimed it was hornets and ants that did it, and how she was involuntarily committed as a result.

Thinking quick, moving faster than the ants, Michael sprinted for the secret safe room located in his basement.

As a person others might describe as paranoid, Michael had installed a safe room when his house was built in case of a gas attack, nuclear fallout, freak weather event, something like The Purge broke out, or whatever. It was a solidly built air-tight room which was impenetrable from the outside – essentially a steel box the size of a tiny studio apartment within a concrete housing, with enough dry food and water to last at least twenty-four months. In it was a self-contained toilet system which had no connection to the outside; it just released the human waste into a compost mechanism somewhat beneath the safe room, though still sealed airtight. For fresh air and oxygen, there was an oxygen and CO^2 filtration system with enough supply for three years (given one inhabitant). Michael's home security system within the safe room allowed him full view of the goings on around his house while he waited out whatever catastrophe prompted him to enter, provided there was still power to the house, which, there should be, on account of his redundancies of rooftop solar with an accompanying battery system that shielded him from grid outages. In this case, with his heart still pounding from his sprint down to the safe room, Michael watched an incoming flood of millions of ants now congregating just outside his safe room door, apparently waiting for him to exit. The ant horde was knee-high and growing by the second. Shifting focus from the ants, he checked the camera positioned on Sylvie, his snake, to make sure they did not harm her. In all this madness, it was a relief to see they had left her be.

Oh. Yeah. Also in Michael's safe room was a full communications station that allowed connection with the outside world via Wi-Fi (if it were still available depending on the catastrophe), radio, ham radio, satellite phone, and a landline.

Queen Bruth was *not* liking what she was seeing. "What the hell!?" she transmitted to her drones in the field. "I don't pay attention to 100% of every single detail and *this* is what happens!? How did we not know about this safe room!?" Over the past seven years, Queen Bruth had become increasingly focused on what Joelle was doing in the simulation with Queen Bean, and as such, had relinquished some crucial control of certain operations to her worker and drone Bees in the field.

"Queen, I'm sorry," said a drone. "We knew of the safe room but determined it would be a nonissue provided we got to him fast enough."

"Well for fuck's sake, honey! It appears to be a pretty big goddam issue!" Queen Bruth did a quick download of all the information any fly had ever collected regarding Michael Peters. She realized he had a full comms site in his safe room, and the safe room was inaccessible to any kind of bug. She knew whether or not they cut power to the house or the phone landlines or even the local cell towers didn't matter, thanks to all the redundancies Michael had set up. "Okay, scatter the ants and hornets in the neighborhood ASAP, but you know, do so in a way that looks like it was less a controlled sentient mob, and more just a random albeit abnormal invasion of pests."

"On it," said one of Queen Bruth's drones. "Is there anything else we can do, Queen?"

Queen Bruth thought about it a second, considered the options they had at their disposal. Finally, simply, somberly, she said, "Pray he doesn't share any of the video he got. And, also, just in case, prepare a message for Jack Telda."

Safe inside the room he built so he would be just that, Michael Peters watched his security cameras as the ants dispersed in a disorderly fashion.

He certainly did not *feel* safe.

He had no clue what to do next.

He wondered if he should call the cops, send them whatever home video he got of the ants and hornets attacking him, if he should share the video on the internet.

He quickly came to the conclusion that if ants and hornets or whatever bug out there wanted to kill him and they all acted in conjunction, short of living in this safe room for the rest of his life, there was nothing he could do to stop them. There was no police department, no army, no pest control company that could help.

Still though, human nature being what it is, Michael tried to think of any means possible of survival.

How could he broadcast the danger he was in and seek *any* form of help, without sounding insane and therefore destroying whatever reputation and position in life he clung to?

How could he rat out The Bugs?

CHAPTER 45

"We may have a problem here," Queen Bruth said to the other Bosses, knowing full well her alarm signal had already sounded.

"Yes," said a Queen Bee Boss from Tianjin. "This is a reminder to us all we are not, as we potentially *could* be, unerring. We must be ever more vigilant, now that we have made it this far."

"And in the meantime," said a Queen from Kolkata, "in the event Queen Bruth's blunder leads to its most unfortunate result and our cover is blown, let us begin preparations to ring the Final Alarm."

"Indeed," said Queen Bruth. "My apologies, sisters. I did not employ the attentiveness required of my position." Queen Bees, by the way, were always quick to apologize and admit whenever they made a mistake, however rare they were. Likewise, they were quick to forgive, which the other Queen Bee Bosses did immediately upon Queen Bruth's apology.

Queen Bruth continued, "We suspected there existed bunkers and safe rooms that could prevent us Bugs from carrying out the Final Alarm, but now is the first time one has been put to the test. Regrettably, they are indeed impenetrable. Worst case scenario, I surmise, is word leaks, the humans panic, and enough of them manage to get into bunkers built for apocalyptic situations, in which case we may have to wait dozens of years before those who make it to those bunkers either run out of resources, or until they think the coast is clear and they come back to the surface."

"Not to mention," said a Queen from Madrid, "there is the risk of humans panicking once they know what we bugs can do. Maybe some humans see Michael Peter's footage and they begin to act irrationally."

Another Queen from Tokyo continued the thought for her sister, "And maybe they adopt the attitude that if us bugs are after people, then they're doomed, and they begin thinking *If I go out, everyone's going to go with me,* and maybe weapons of mass destruction get launched."

"Maybe there's total fallout from the panic."

"In which case, of course, we need to act, *now.*"

"This is what the Final Alarm is for," agreed Queen Bruth. "Queens, I've said it once, you've all energetically forgiven me, but, let me say again, I am sorry my blunder has led us to this position. We are contacting my Fence Player now. He knows this Michael Peters. We will see if he can lure Michael out so the situation can be remedied. Once more, I am sorry."

"Well," said a Queen from New York, "there is no changing what has happened. We can only control how we respond to what has happened. And it seems, it will all come down to what does or does not get broadcasted from Michael Peters' house."

CHAPTER 46

Okay, look, I know it's selfish. Wanting to rush the process of me saving humanity or whatever all so I can see my mom and my dog again.

I mean, I *think* I know that stuff should be put out of my mind. Like, weighing the fate of humankind, which is what, almost eight billion people alive right now and potentially infinite billions more in the future, against the weight of *my personal wants*. And to be fair, I of course *also* want humanity to continue going on and elevate to whatever natural step is next for us, but I guess it's just my personal wants in this regard have to deal with doing all that *and* getting to see my loved ones again. I don't know. It seems obvious I should try to put my mom and Maple out of my head as much as possible and give my task as much dedication and attention as it deserves, regardless of the time it takes.

But, still.

You know?

Consider something like the trolley problem.

The train is going down the track and it's heading *straight* for your mom and your dog. You could pull the lever and divert the train from killing your mom and dog, but, if you do, it changes track and instead heads right for eight billion people and brings about the end of humanity as it's currently constituted. Keep in mind, the trolley already killed your dad miles and miles ago, so you're even more scared of losing your mom and dog.

However, the thing is, there's a twist to this trolley problem, *my* trolley problem. If I pull the lever to save my mom and dog, there's *still* a chance the train might veer off on a *third* rail, in the however uncertain likelihood I make the right decisions in the right amount of time, and it avoids killing all eight billion people as well.

The problem with this, though, is I don't know what those odds are.

Not knowing the odds, it makes it all the more difficult for me to calculate my position. It's like a ridiculously high stakes game of existential cosmic poker.

"Joelle," says Queen Bean, interrupting my train of thought, "I hate to bother you while you're on a decision-making roll here, but I just received word there is a situation happening."

I resent the way she says that with underlying sarcasm about my decision-making process and the way in which she tells me there's important information I need to know without *telling me the important information.*

"Okay," I say, "what's going on?"

"Using a turn of phrase from your people, *long story short*: A gentleman is holed up in a safe room and is threatening to leak footage of us Bugs which would trigger us to enact the Final Alarm. So, yeah, we kinda need you to hurry here."

CHAPTER 47

"Jack," said Michael Peters from the safety of his safe room, "I know, I must sound insane."

"Michael, it's okay," said Jack. "It's fine, really." Then, attempting to imbue the call with some of the good humor he's added to the company culture at FFS, he said, "I only think you're *a little* crazy." Jack let out a good-natured laugh, and, in an effort to appease his own conscience, confirmed he wasn't lying by bringing to mind images of Michael feeding his pet snake. "But you say the ants are no longer there? They just... dispersed?"

"I know," said Michael, "it sounds *crazy*. But here, see for yourself." Michael sent Jack video of the whole incident.

Jack was sitting on his back patio. He was positioned next to a spider's web, flies were buzzing all about him, and ants were hurriedly forming responses for him in real time. "Holy shit," he said, ad-libbing the colloquialism before saying what the ants had spelled out. "And you haven't shared this anywhere else?"

"No," said Michael. "This is *crazy*. I'm telling you because, well, you remember Mitch David, right? What his wife said. It's insane but maybe she was right all along. I don't know. I feel like I'm losing it over here, Jack. This can't be real."

Jack waited a moment before responding, less out of customary and polite engagement rules, more out of necessity to allow the ants time to rearrange themselves to show what he was supposed to say next. "Michael," he said, pausing, allowing the ants to finalize the last bit of the message, "seriously, it's okay. I'm glad you called. Why don't I come over there and we figure this out? *Together*."

The conversation required a few more back-and-forths. First Michael expressed fears for his own life. Then he refused because he thought Jack was going to have him committed. Eventually, Jack was able to convince Michael none of that was true and that he just wanted to come over and help.

"Alright alright," Michael said, the remnants of his sanity dangling by something as strong as a spider thread. "The key to get in my house is 686688. I'll let you in the safe room when you're outside the door and there are confirmed *no bugs*."

"Okay, it looks like a 35-minute drive. I'll be there as fast as I can."

Before leaving, though, Jack took a moment to check with the ants. Somewhere inside of himself he already knew the answer, but he asked anyway. "So, why exactly am I going over there?"

As he asked this, there was a Bee hovering two feet in front of his face, the way Bees do that before flying off. It was analyzing his facial muscles and energetic vibrations. As a result, the Bees knew what he was thinking, how he was feeling. The torment on his face was painfully evident. They could see how he was processing the facts of his situation.

For Jack, knowing people were being killed by The Bugs was one thing. But actively participating in the killing of another human being, *helping* The Bugs get to their target, obviously this was a whole other thing.

301

Given the gravity of, well, everything, it took some time for the ants to prepare Queen Bruth's message:

Jack, Michael is a threat. We need to eliminate him. Until now, you've acted out of self-preservation, out of fear of us killing you. Now you must consider others out there. If Michael shows proof to the world what we Bugs are capable of, that will trigger us to not only take out you, we will be forced to take out all of humanity. Please, we do not have time to get into all this right now, but you know, in your heart, if we bugs wanted to eliminate all humans, we could do it within the hour. For fuck's sake, there are just about ONE QUADRILLION ANTS OUT THERE. That's 10,000 trillion ants. One million billion. And that's just ants! Think of all us bugs out there. There is no time for you to ask why we will be forced to kill everyone. There is no time for anything at all for that matter. You simply have to trust us, as you have wisely done so far. We need to get to Michael Peters before he forces our hand. You must help us.

CHAPTER 48

Hello again.

It's me, a Tree.

Look, we've been right all along

I mean, we're *Trees*.

Now, though.

We don't know.

We are teetering on the precipice of two vastly distinct outcomes.

Both of which have us Trees in the future.

But only one of which carries us to higher and deeper levels of existence.

So.

In that case.

Let's go Jo!

Let's go Jo!

We believe in you!

(Insofar as we believe in *life*.)

CHAPTER 49

Jack, this is it. Get in your fucking car right now and go get Michael Peters out of his safe room.

Queen Bruth had exhausted her bargaining skills with Jack Telda. She hoped the use of profanity would add a necessary sense of urgency to her message.

"I'm not going," said Jack. "You can't make me."

You're right. We can't make you. But we can kill you.

With her last bargaining chip, Queen Bruth resorted to Jack's foreboding doom.

"So be it," said Jack, exuding a sense of calm he had not exhibited perhaps in all his life.

Jack, all of humanity will be killed if Michael leaks the footage he has.

"Yeah, but we don't know for sure he's going to do that. The way I see it, if he hasn't leaked it yet, he may not leak it at all. On the other hand, if I go over there and get him out, there is a 100% certainty you will kill him."

Jack, for fuck's sake. We were going to kill him anyway! That's why he's in his safe room! Do you know how many people we've killed on your behalf? How many people we have eliminated so you and Food First Service could start the thousands of regenerative farms you've started? Do you know how much good you've been able to create in this world, on account of us eliminating the people standing in your way? Stop being so goddamn naïve and go over there right now!

"See," said Jack. "All those people, I didn't ask you to kill them. And if you asked me, I would have said let's try a different way. With them, I didn't actively participate in their death. This is different. You're asking me to be an active participant in killing Michael."

Jack, you do understand you may be dooming all of humanity, right?

"Yes," said Jack. "I *may* be. But like I said, on the other hand, if I go, I am *definitely* dooming Michael. You said I needed to reconsider my ways. You said I needed to change. Well, my whole career, I never thought of the lives at the end of my decisions. I never thought of the plants and animals and *people* that were affected by the decisions I made. Well, now, it couldn't be clearer. There is a real live person right at the end of this decision. And I *won't* kill him."

Jack, think of Jack Jr. Think of Amy. Think of the new relationship and life you have built for your family thanks to us. You are dooming yourself. Your family. If you do not get in your car and go to Michael Peters in the next thirty seconds, we will kill you. All to protect some guy who was going to frame you.

With a sense of calm and peace reverberating throughout his being, Jack Telda said, "So be it."

CHAPTER 50

Okay, this is it.

Do or die.

Literally.

"Alright," I say to Queen Bean, "So how much time do I have?"

"Honestly, I'm not sure. The situation is currently unfolding negatively. We hoped to get an intervention but the human we were hoping would intervene has decided not to help us. We don't know what the man with the footage is going to do. He could trigger the Final Alarm any second now; he may never trigger it at all."

"Gotcha," I say.

I start to wonder, what with eleven rule changes left at my disposal, if it would be worth it, given this new time crunch, to start throwing some random ideas at the wall, hoping at least one of them has some magical sticking power. The simulation we're watching, as it's currently fast-forwarding, is still going good, I guess. I mean, it's going good in the sense that humanity seems to be thriving, not destroying itself or the planet, and there are no signs of it doing so any time soon. And in fact, the planet seems to be healing itself from the destructiveness of the past, which is great. So I'm left wondering, why wasn't this good enough?

At this, Queen Bean interrupts my train of thought. "Simply progressing is not the end goal here, Joelle," she says. "As life currently exists on Earth, us Bugs at one level, humans below us waiting for the opportunity for Ascension, and then whoever or whatever God is above *us* Bugs, we are waiting for humans to bring us *all* to the next level beyond wherever we currently are. To do that, we need humanity to Ascend to this level, which involves a fundamental shift in the essence of humanity. All that is to say, maintaining whatever the status quo is won't do. It appears these rule changes you've enacted that have allowed for the progress we've seen so far are clearly not enough. They are not allowing humans new modes of *being* that progresses whatever is necessary for elevation."

"Okay," I say. "So, like, do you have any suggestions for me?"

"That is not what I am here to do," says Queen Bean. "*You* are the one with the instincts we have entrusted. *You* need to tap into those instincts and bring forth whatever it is that is necessary."

Great, I think.

And then I think some more.

About what, I don't really know.

Now, I gotta say, meditation is a bit easier here in this particular void of the fifth dimension. The emptiness all around makes it easier to clear my mind. So I decide to use that. I close my consciousness to the fast-forwarding of the simulation around me and I say to Queen Bean, "Alright. Give me a moment or two. Let me ponder."

"Okay," says Queen Bean, "but, you know. Please, *hurry*."

Ignoring the time crunch while simultaneously letting it seep into my unconscious thought, despite the fact I have no body here in this empty space where Queen Bean has brought me, I focus on what *would* be my breathing. With my non-existent eyes closed to the simulation before me, I concentrate on an imaginary point of light that would exist somewhere between my eyes, a few centimeters in from my skull, in that spot of the front part of my brain. The front part of my mind. I focus on that point of imaginary light until it grows bright enough to illuminate what I imagine to be my whole neocortex, pulsating with the memories and experiences and emotions and intuitions and everything my mind and brain has ever witnessed.

Letting instinct take my thoughts where they may go.

Moving to Carrabassett Valley.

Getting ruthlessly bullied for an entire month at that summer camp.

Getting into all sorts of trouble with my friends.

Being with my dad. On top of Bigelow Mountain. Or at home. Or wherever. Riding high on his shoulders grabbing at the leaves.

Recounting all the stories Mom has told me of Dad.

Recalling my instinct about perhaps enacting the rule change saying people should Leave No Trace.

Then recalling my conversation with Sarah, albeit in the simulation, and how she's right. It's impossible for humanity to Leave No Trace, without, you know, humanity ceasing to exist and what not.

And then, at this recollection, it hits me.

"Hey Queen Bean," I say, thinking of something we had not yet addressed. "In these rule changes, what kind of power can I give to the Bees? Like, am I allowed to give them the authority to set the parameters or definitions for something?"

In the moment or two Queen Bean says nothing, I again realize I just asked two direct questions, and that in response to more than one question at a time, I cannot and will not get an answer. I recalibrate. "In enacting any change," I say, "can I rely on the Bees' judgment and have them define certain terms?"

"Why yes," says Queen Bean, "that is always an option."

"Great!" I say. "Alright. I think I'm ready. Let's head back to the simulation. I know what change I want to enact."

Just like that, I'm beamed back into the simulation.

As the fast-forwarding has occurred, I'm thrust into the year 2546. I'm back in Carrabassett Valley, and everything here, at least, is remarkably similar to the way it was hundreds of years ago. There are still trees everywhere. Though, to be fair, the modes of transportation have changed quite a bit. People seem to have their own personal drones flying them wherever they need to be, that is, when they're not mountain biking, which is still a thing.

Granted, things elsewhere in the world are *quite* different, from what I've recalled of the fast-forwarding. You know, places like New York and Cairo and wherever. All the big cities are a lot more *green* now and less car-focused. But whatever. That all is beside the point. I came back because I have a rule change I want to enact and I apparently have to enact it as soon as possible because back in reality, an (understandable) madman is holed up somewhere threatening to leak footage of bugs trying to murder him, which, I'm told, will trigger the bugs to wipe out humanity. So yeah, time crunch.

Heeding my previous thoughts about the Bees playing some part in the rule change game and what not, I say to Queen Bean, "Alright, Queen Bean, this is my rule: In addition to the rule already constituted, I add the following amendment: First, I place within the Bees' discretion this: The Bees are responsible for defining the word *Good* and what *Goodness* is. They are also responsible for defining *love* and *loving*. In every sense of the words. Once defined, apply it here: Humans—wherever they go, however they behave, whatever they do—leave a *good* and *loving* trace. Let it be done."

EPILOGUE

I am a water molecule.

The trees think they're so special, huh?

Tell them to try and live without me and my kind.

Epilogue[2]

I am a carbon atom.

Epilogue[3]

I am the solar system in which Earth orbits, on which humans and bugs and trees and water and carbon live.

I am the carbon atom kind of solar system in the Universe.

Epilogue[4]

I am.

ABOUT THE AUTHOR

CJ Friedman is a former food truck owner, solar salesman, and digital marketer. When he was 25, CJ lived within a Stephen King novel and was the caretaker of an off-the-grid eco-lodge in the woods of western Maine. During a two week stretch in which he saw no other people, CJ dreamt of a world that was controlled by bees and other insects. Then, while living in Philadelphia, he wrote The Bugs. CJ now lives in New Hampshire with his wife, toddler, and two senior pups.

ABOUT THE PRESS

Unsolicited Press is based out of Portland, Oregon and focuses on the works of the unsung and underrepresented. As a womxn-owned, all-volunteer small publisher that doesn't worry about profits as much as championing exceptional literature, we have the privilege of partnering with authors skirting the fringes of the lit world. We've worked with emerging and award-winning authors such as Shann Ray, Amy Shimshon-Santo, Brook Bhagat, Kris Amos, and John W. Bateman.

Learn more at unsolicitedpress.com. Find us on twitter and instagram.

Printed in the USA
CPSIA information can be obtained
at www.ICGtesting.com
CBHW032153211024
16214CB00032B/410